CATCH YOU

A REBEL INK NOVEL

TRACY LORRAINE

You will Survive and you will find purpose in the chaos.
Moving on doesn'tmean letting go
- Mary Vanhaute

WOULD YOU LIKE A FREE BOOK?

Get your free copy of All In On You, the prequel to my steamy contemporary romance series, Rebel Ink Subscribe to my newsletter for your free copy!

ABOUT CATCH YOU

Some might say I'm running. I say I'm chasing the life I've always dreamed of.

Because it's all I have left. LA is everything I hoped for: chaos, clarity, and just enough space to outrun the wreckage I left behind. A blank slate. A breath. A chance to remember who I am.

But before I can, I meet *her*.

Harlow Winters crashes into my world like a spark to gasoline—and suddenly, nothing makes sense except her. The artist in me recognizes her beauty. The broken man sees the darkness.

I'm trying to escape my past ... but she refuses to let hers go. With our scars inked onto our skin, can we salvage a future under the weight of our memories—or will they crush us both?

1

———————

HARLOW

"What the hell do you think you're doing?" Brooke, my best friend and roommate, asks when she discovers me sitting on the couch with a blanket over my lap, a tub of ice cream in hand, and a rum and Coke on the coffee table.

"Err ... Friday night in?" I say, my brows drawing together, trying to figure out if I've forgotten something. The look on her face and the way she's standing impatiently with her hands on her hips sure points to that.

She's had a long week at work, so I was expecting her to take up residence on the other couch with a glass of wine while we caught up with her favorite trashy reality show.

"It's Milo's birthday," she says with a roll of her eyes.

"Right ..."

"We're going out. We're meeting everyone at Club 52 in"—she pulls her cell from her back pocket and looks at the time—"in like ... an hour. So we need to get our shit together."

Before I have a chance to argue, she's standing before me and pulling the ice cream from my hand.

"Come on, H. Move that sexy ass and go and find a hot little dress to wear."

After depositing the tub on the coffee table, she rips the blanket from my lap and attempts to pull me from my hibernation spot on the couch.

"Really?" I sulk. "Milo won't care if I'm there or not. I barely know the guy." We might work for the same organization, but it's not like we spend any actual time together, other than the odd charity event.

"I told him you'll be there," she says, wiggling her brows, clearly excited that she's going to get to hang out with the team tonight.

"But you didn't think to tell me," I mutter before eventually going easy on her and standing.

"I could have sworn I'd mentioned it."

"When could you? You've hardly been home this week."

She shrugs. "Well, you know now. It's going to be a great night."

She ushers me out of the living room—thankfully after I rescue my drink. I have a feeling I'm going to need it.

When we get to my room, she at least affords me the decency to get ready alone, which is a relief. The last thing I need tonight is a Brooke makeover.

THIRTY MINUTES LATER, after smoothing down my silk top, I add a layer of gloss to my lips and slip my feet into my court shoes.

Brooke's still sitting in front of her mirror when I join her in her room.

"How are you ready al—no, no, no. You can't wear that,"

she says, looking at me in the mirror. I glance down at my skinny jeans and black blouse.

"Why not? It's perfectly fine."

"Yeah, for an afternoon with your aunt."

Minus the height of my heels, I can't argue with her.

She spins on her chair, and I get a look at her dress—if it can even be described as such. It's fire-engine red; I swear I've got underwear that covers more skin.

I run my eyes over her, suspicion stirring in my stomach. "This isn't just a night out for Milo's birthday, is it?"

"His cousin's coming."

And now, it all starts to make sense.

"The British one?"

"Yes! I can't wait to hear him say my name." She swoons, getting this far-off look in her eyes.

I shouldn't be surprised—she's been telling me about him for quite a few weeks now and trying to convince Milo to introduce them.

"You mean moan your name," I mutter.

"Harlow, I'm not some easy piece of ass, you know."

"Really?" I ask, my brows lifting, my lips curling in amusement.

"Okay, so maybe I am, but only for the right guy."

"Riiight."

She gets up from her seat and walks toward her wardrobe, thankfully pulling her ridiculously short dress down in the process so I don't have a front-row seat to her easy ass.

"Now, let's see what I've got."

"Oh no, B. You're not getting me in one of your dresses. They barely fit you; they'll never cover my ass and tits."

"Have faith, girl. Have faith."

Sadly, I have little. I love Brooke, but she has

questionable taste at times. Our styles are opposite in every way—not just with how much skin we deem acceptable to expose.

"Yessss!" she squeals, and my stomach drops into my heels. "This will look killer on you."

She pulls out a scrap of navy fabric and holds it up in front of me with a wide smile on her face.

"You won't catch me dead wearing that."

"Just try it on. It's a little big for me." I don't see how that's possible, considering it looks like it's a size zero from this distance, but I keep my mouth shut. "It'll be perfect. And," she adds, an idea hitting her, "it might help with your little … *situation*."

"I'm not in the middle of anything," I protest. "And like you just said, we're going out with the team." I swipe the hanger from her because I already know that fighting her on this is pointless. I may as well just try it on, prove it doesn't fit, and then hope she'll allow me to revisit my wardrobe for a dress that might actually cover what God gave me.

"There will be other guys there, too. It's been what? A year since a guy so much as touched you?"

It's been almost a year and a half since my last failed attempt at a date, but I refrain from correcting her.

I shimmy my jeans down my legs and carefully pull my blouse off before laying them out over Brooke's bed. "What?" I ask when she shakes her head at me.

"You know it is okay to sometimes leave clothes in a pile on the floor, right?"

I roll my eyes, and she hands me the dress once I'm in only my underwear.

Deciding that pulling it up might be the easiest option, I step into the fabric and attempt to drag it over my hips. The material has more stretch than I gave it credit for, because it skims happily over my curves. I pull the straps up my arms and put them into place over my shoulders before looking down.

"Okay, you are *so* wearing that. Have you seen your ass?"

"Weirdly, no," I sass, looking over my shoulder at the mirror behind me. I can't deny that the fabric hugs it pretty nicely.

"You gotta lose the bra, though."

"Nope. Not happening."

Brooke's hip juts out and she rests her hand on it as she stares at me in a 'go on, try and argue' way. "There's enough support in the dress."

"I'm sure it'll hold them up just fine. I'm more worried about flashing someone."

"Making your mission a sure success."

"I'm not on a mission. I'm perfectly happy as—"

"Nope. You need a man-induced orgasm. End of."

I know I've been a little uptight recently, but it's not my lack of male attention that's causing it, and I doubt a night with one will solve the issue.

Brooke must see my shoulders drop, because she takes my hands in hers. "I know you're worried about her. I am too. But sitting around the house feeling guilty about not being able to do more isn't going to help. No matter the results, you still have a life. You may as well at least attempt to enjoy yourself."

"I guess." I don't feel all that enthused, but I know she's right.

"Now, drink this," she says, handing my glass back to me. "Then let the girls free, and we're out of here."

I tip my glass to my lips and swallow what's left before doing as I'm told. I'm soon following Brooke out of the house to the waiting car. Despite my earlier disinterest, tingles of excitement start to ignite in my belly.

I can't deny that I look good tonight. I also can't deny that I'm currently showing more boob than I have to anyone outside the bedroom in too many years to count.

I shake the memories from my head and climb into the car as Brooke begins flirting with the driver. Just because I'm dressed up and showing a little skin, it doesn't mean I'm going back to a time in my life I'd rather forget. I'm just going out for a night of drinking and dancing with my best friend. It's exactly what I should be doing. I'm young with no ties; a Friday night out for a colleague's birthday should be a normal thing to do.

Brooke flashes me a wide smile, and I try to relax.

"Tonight's going to be great. Reese and Fletch managed to secure the VIP section for us," she says, wiggling her eyebrows.

I groan just like I do every time she mentions Fletch.

"Please don't tell me you're still scared of being in the same room as him?"

"I'm not scared," I argue, although I'm not entirely sure that's true. "I just always make myself look like an idiot any time I'm near him. I turn into a fumbling teenager." My cheeks heat. I don't need to tell Brooke this—she's witnessed my mortifying behavior time and time again when it comes to him. Fletcher Ferguson. My teenage heartthrob, incredible hockey player, and all-around nice guy.

It should be illegal to be that good looking, kind, and generous.

I was obsessed with him in my former years, thanks to discovering a trashy magazine on the coffee table after school one day with him on the cover. No matter how much time has passed, it seems the second I'm in his vicinity, I return to that point in my life when I had no idea how to control my raging hormones.

Or to keep a leash on my mouth.

"Oh, I know. Why do you think I demanded you come? You're tonight's entertainment," she says with a laugh.

"B," I squeal, swatting her shoulder playfully as she teases me. "I have no idea what's wrong with me."

"I get it. He's ... captivating." Her eyes darken as she relives the one moment of her past that she'll never let me forget. "And the way he kisses," she says on a sigh.

"Oh, get over yourself." I chuckle. "You know full well that he's forgotten all about that. No woman other than Reese exists for him now."

"I know. And I still stand by the fact that I rocked his world so much that night that he lost his mind a little after. I mean, why wouldn't he want more of this?" She gestures to herself with a pout.

"No idea, B. No idea."

"Well, I'm over it." Based on how often she brings it up, I beg to differ. "I've got my sights set on a British banger tonight."

I bark out a laugh. "Do you even know what this guy looks like?"

"Only in my imagination."

"So he could be an old cockney with a beer belly and a bald head?"

"Yes and no. He's still in his twenties, so I'd like to think he's at least not bald. Although you never know these days."

"Still leaves a lot to go wrong, don't you think?"

"Nah, it's all good. I can feel it in my blood."

"I'm pretty sure that's the wine."

"Meh, tonight is my night, H. Just you wait and see. I'm

gonna snag me a Brit, and I'm not letting this one out of my sight."

"If you say so." The neon lights of the club come into view.

After saying the right words in the bouncer's ear, he stands aside and allows both Brooke and me to enter the club, although not before he gets his fill of her scantily clad body.

"You offering up sexual favors again?"

"Not necessary this time. Come on—stop dawdling. The bar and the Brit are calling."

She grabs my hand, and together we make our way through the crowd and toward the roped-off stairs that lead to the VIP section.

As we move, the loud bass from the music vibrates through me, and even though being here tonight was the last thing I wanted to do after a long week, I can't help a little excitement creeping in. It's been a long time since I've let go and forgotten about the world for a few hours.

After sweet-talking the second bouncer in as many minutes, we're climbing the stairs away from the masses of people.

We're only three-quarters of the way up when I first see him. My nerves hit me like a sledge hammer, and my body starts to tremble. It doesn't matter how many times I see and talk to him. It doesn't matter that I hear stories from Reese about what a 'normal' guy he is. To me, he's still the man I had pinned to my bedroom walls and said goodnight to before falling asleep.

I focus on my shoes as I climb the stairs, the gems on the front glinting from the spotlights above and providing a distraction from the man I'm walking toward.

I've got one more step to climb. Thinking I'm safe, I look

up, but the second I meet his piercing blue eyes, my feet falter. The platform of my shoe connects with the step, and I go tumbling forward.

I reach my hand out in the hope that it connects with something to break my inevitably painful collision with the tiled floor, but thankfully, the pain never comes. Instead, my hand hits something warm and soft.

The second I see what I used to stop my fall, I gasp in horror and stumble backward into someone else. Large hands grip onto my waist to steady me as I keep my eyes locked on the floor. My cheeks flame so hot I swear they're going to catch fire any moment.

"Jesus, Harlow, that was some entrance," Fletch says with a laugh as I continue to die a thousand deaths.

"Are you okay?" A deep, smooth voice washes over me from behind, making me wish the ground would just swallow me up. I nod, but not before I hear the laughter of my best friend behind me.

"I'm fine. I'm fine," I mutter, looking up—but only so I can see which way the bar is so I can wipe this disaster from my memory. "T-thank you," I whisper to the man behind me who's still holding me upright, probably thinking my legs don't work correctly.

"Anytime." I push to move away, but his voice makes me pause. It's deep, rough, and his accent is ... I don't have time to try to figure it out. I just need to get away from Fletch's blue eyes that turn me into a fumbling moron.

His wife is literally my boss. I need to get a grip on myself.

"Oh my God, Harlow. That was classic," Brooke howls beside me as I wait for the bartender to notice me. "I mean, Fletch is used to women falling at his feet, but using his cock to save yourself from breaking your nose? That was fucking—"

"Enough," I bark. "This is all your fault." Turning to her, I narrow my eyes in the hope it'll shut her up.

"Me?" she asks, innocently pointing to herself.

"Yes. I should be on the sofa right now with my second tub of ice cream, watching others falling in love on some shitty reality TV show."

"Oh yeah, that sounds like a winning way to spend your Friday night, H. I'll call you a cab right now."

"Really?" I ask hopefully.

"No. Harlow. No. You embarrassed yourself. So what? Fletch doesn't care, so neither should you." She waves and the bartender comes right over—of course he fucking does. One look at her and he's like putty in her hand. I roll my eyes as Brooke orders us four shots of—

"Tequila?" My lip curls in disgust.

"Yes, hopefully it'll give your confidence a boost and loosen you up a little."

"Here's hoping," I mutter, more to myself than her as I pick up the first one and knock it back before immediately going for the second. The alcohol burns my throat, but it's only seconds before it starts warming my belly. Maybe it will have the effect Brooke intended.

"Oh, the birthday boy's here. Let's go and wish him a happy birthday." I look over to where Brooke's focus is and see both Reese and Fletch standing before Milo and a number of other team members.

"It's okay, you go. I'll order some more drinks."

"He's just a guy, H. You can talk to him like any other."

"I know. And I will talk to him ... them. I just ... I can only embarrass myself so much every hour."

Shaking her head at me, she takes off across the room, her heels clicking against the black polished tiles and her mile-long, tanned legs eating up the space. I don't need to look around to know she's got the attention of at least a handful of men as she moves. It doesn't matter that she's off-limits to the guys. Brooke has this aura surrounding her, one that turns all attention on her. Something that I most definitely don't possess.

I'm just the best friend who makes an idiot of herself as often as possible and only helps to make Brooke look so much more desirable.

Blowing out a long breath, I turn back to the bar, only to find that the bartender has once again vanished to serve someone else. Fantastic.

Thinking that I'll just order a cab home, I turn to slide from the stool but come to a stop when I find a guy standing before me. One side of his mouth curls up in an unsure smile.

"Hey, how are you doing?"

His deep voice is immediately recognizable, and I feel the warmth of his hands against my waist from not so long ago.

"Oh yeah. I'm sorry about that. I'm a bit of an id ..." My eyes run up exposed forearms that are covered in ink, the fabric of his shirt straining over muscular biceps. It's open one button too many at the neck, showing even more art, but it's when I find his light blue eyes that it feels like my world tilts slightly.

His lopsided grin turns into a megawatt smile, exposing perfectly straight white teeth beneath, and my entire body sighs.

"Can I buy you a drink?"

It takes me a few moments to register that he's said

anything, but once I do, I tilt my head to the side and look at him once more.

"Y-you're the Brit?"

That lopsided smile returns, but this time a dimple pops up in his cheek.

"What gave me away?" I bite down on my bottom lip, and his eyes drop to focus on it. "It's Corey. And you are?"

"H-Harlow."

"Well, it's a pleasure to meet you, Harlow. Shall we?" he asks, gesturing toward the bar before lifting his hand to signal the bartender.

Ignoring the vacant stool beside me, he chooses instead to stand next to me, just close enough that his warmth heats my side and his scent fills my nose. This guy knows what he's doing. It should be a turn-off, but I can't help but fall for his charm.

Maybe Brooke was right.

I bite down on my bottom lip as I attempt to remember what it feels like to be touched by a man.

Brooke's going to kill you for talking to him first, I think as I look up at him once more, my cheeks burning. When I glance over my shoulder, I see she's still preoccupied with Milo and a few other LA Vipers staff along with Reese and Fletch. That's enough to tell me that I'm not heading over there anytime soon.

2

COREY

Tonight is my first night out—night off, actually—since setting up the studio over here. But Milo gave me little choice about it. He first mentioned it a few weeks ago and I pushed it aside, assuming he'd forget about it—or at least forget about me. But when he called again at the beginning of the week and told me I had to be here, I didn't stand a chance. Part of my moving here was so I could spend time with this side of my family, a fact he was all too happy to use against me. Turns out, he didn't need to try quite so hard; all he had to do was mention the quality of the women, and I'd have followed orders in a heartbeat.

I've been so busy since I arrived in LA that women haven't been on my radar all that much. I mean, I've spent my fair share of time inking them, but that's about as close as I've got. And my lack of action hasn't been more obvious to me than those few seconds I found myself following a curvy redhead up the stairs to the VIP area, her arse swaying before me.

"So, you know Fletch?" I ask once we've given the

bartender our orders. A pint for me and a rum and Coke for her. I must admit, I was surprised. I was expecting her to order a glass of bubbles like I've seen the other women drinking, or at least a glass of wine, but it seems this woman has been sent to surprise me tonight. First, her fine arse, swiftly followed by her damn near falling into my arms not long after, and now this.

"Thank you. I need this," she says, swallowing a generous mouthful before turning to look at me. "Reese is my boss."

"You work for the Vipers?"

"Assistant foundation coordinator," she says before taking another sip of her drink.

"Sounds like fun."

"I love it," she says, her eyes lighting up, evidence of her passion.

I nod at her, finding myself lost in her chestnut eyes as she stares back at me.

She coughs, clearing her throat and breaking the tension between us after a few seconds, and I'm forced to look away.

"So, what is it you do?"

"Harlow, there you are! I thought you were coming to talk to the birthday boy," a high-pitched voice says from behind me before a blonde wrapped in the smallest dress I've ever seen stands so close to me that I have to take a step back.

"Yeah ... I ... uh ..."

"Oh, are you still embarrassed about that? I'm sure Fletch has already forgotten." She waves her friend off with a swish of her hand, and my eyes widen in shock. "Who's your new friend?" She turns to me, her eyes running over my face as what I guess is supposed to be a sexy pout appears on her lips.

"Corey," I say politely, holding my hand out for her.

"Oh, my Brit." *My Brit?* My eyebrows rise. "Milo didn't say you were here yet." Ignoring my hand, she steps right into my body, pressing her breasts into my chest and stretching to drop a kiss to my cheek. "I've been so looking forward to meeting you."

"Oh really?" I ask, placing my hands on her shoulders, trying to remove her from me. "I'm not sure Milo's ever mentioned you."

Harlow snorts a laugh, and when I look up, I find the most breathtaking smile lighting up her face.

"Oh, that can't be true. I'm sure you've just forgotten. I can only imagine that you've met so many new people since you arrived. I'm Brooke—I work with your cousin. He's told me all about you."

"Is that right?"

"Sure is. So, tell me about yourself. I can't wait to get to know you better."

"Well, actually, I was in the middle of a conversation with your friend here."

Brooke stands back and looks over her shoulder. "Oh, okay, well ..." She sounds dejected, making me wonder how many guys turn her down. Not a lot, I'm guessing.

"Would you like a drink, B?"

"I'd love one, thanks." I watch as Harlow orders Brooke a sauvignon blanc. They're both stunning, Brooke more so now I don't have everything thrust in my face, but to me, Harlow stands out by a mile. Her red hair, her large, dark eyes that just ooze innocence ... I bite my lip as I study her while she talks to her friend. She must sense my stare, because her eyes flick to mine, and she startles when she finds me looking back. Colour hits her cheeks, and it only makes her more alluring.

It looks like coming here tonight was more than worth it.

My cock stirs behind the fabric of my jeans, desperate to end the evening with my first bit of action in a while.

Brooke lifts her drink from the bar and takes a sip while looking between the two of us suspiciously.

"So ... I'm just going to go ..." She trails off before disappearing off into the crowd.

"Good friend of yours?" I ask once I'm confident she's out of earshot. I take a step closer, her perfume filling my nose and making my mouth water.

Harlow laughs, and excitement shoots through me. She's exactly what I need tonight.

"Yeah, actually. My best friend."

"Really? You seem so ..."

"Different?"

"Yeah," I say, relieved that I'm not the only one who sees it.

"Don't let her front fool you. She's a great person. She just comes across a little—"

"Desperate?"

She laughs again. "I was going to say full-on. Everyone around us seems to be coupling up," she says, flicking a look over to where they're standing with their girls. "She's just feeling a little ... left behind."

"And she thought I might get her up to speed?"

I watch her lips, enthralled as she purses them to take a sip of her drink. "You have no idea. She's been going on and on about meeting you since Milo told her you'd first moved here."

"Why? I could be a right arsehole." A smile curls at her lips.

"The accent," she says, like it should be obvious. "She was hoping you'd talk all sexy to her." Harlow rolls her eyes at her friend's insanity. "So, are you?"

"Am I what? Going to talk all sexy to her?" I drop the tone of my voice and delight when the roughness of it makes her pupils dilate. My brows pull together as I cast my mind back over our conversation, trying to figure out what she's asking me.

"No. An *arsehole*," she says, adorably trying to mimic my accent.

"Some would probably say I am. Others not so much."

"Cryptic."

Closing more of the space between us, I reach out and tuck a lock of her hair behind her ear. "Maybe you'll just have to find out for yourself."

Her lips part but no words come out as my fingertip brushes the shell of her ear. "I ... um ..."

I search her eyes, trying to read her. She seems reluctant, yet there's something there. Something wild that I know is screaming to get out.

Our connection holds before she sucks her bottom lip into her mouth and my gaze drops to watch.

"Harlow," that familiar voice calls from somewhere. "We're going to dance. You coming?"

My eyes jump back up to hers. I want to ask her to stay here with me, but I've just met her; I've got no right to even suggest keeping her away from her friends and colleagues.

After another second, she rips her eyes from mine and looks at Brooke, who holds her hand out.

I stand back, allowing her some space. She downs her drink before giving me a small smile and walking towards her friend.

Her arse sways as she makes her way over, and my trousers suddenly seem a little too tight as I imagine what, if any, underwear she's got on beneath. When I look up, I find Brooke watching me.

Her eyes are narrowed, and I'm not sure if it's jealousy or a warning.

3

———

HARLOW

"Have you just stolen my Brit?" Brooke asks after pulling me into the middle of the packed dance floor. Along with a group of other Vipers employees, we left the VIP section in favor of bumping and grinding with the rest of the club.

"We were just talking," I say innocently, trying to forget the tingles that erupted within me every time he looked at me, or the way my temperature spiked at his touch.

"Oh yeah, just talking," she mocks. "You didn't see the way he watched your ass as we walked away from him. I told you that dress was pure gold."

"I'm not interested, B. You know I don't need a man."

"Who said anything about needing one? No one *needs* a man; we're all perfectly capable without one. But that doesn't mean we couldn't do with one to help us let our hair down every so often ... before he pulls on it as we scream his name."

"I don't want that, either," I argue, hoping it's dark enough down here that she doesn't see the color staining my cheeks as the image she's just conjured up takes over my thoughts. His strong, tattooed arms, his fingers threaded in my hair as I climb toward...

Nope, don't go there.

"You're only lying to yourself, and you know it. Give yourself a night off. Let go of the tension. Trust me; you'll thank me for it in the morning," she sings.

"What about you?" I ask, hoping to get the heat off me.

"What about me? I wanted him, yeah. Especially now I know just how hot he is. But I don't think he's all that interested in me."

"I'm sure he is. You bulldozed your way into our conversation. He was just a little shocked, is all."

"Yeah, you keep telling yourself that." Her eyes focus on something over my shoulder, but, assuming it's just a guy who's caught her attention, I block her out in favor of losing myself to the music.

Brooke is right about one thing: I do need to let my hair down.

As the beat of the music flows through me, I immediately feel lighter. I allow the stress of work and the pressure I put on myself to do a good job to fall away before attempting to forget about everything else, if only for a few minutes.

With the alcohol flowing through my veins, I forget that I'm surrounded by hundreds of people who are potentially watching me and lose myself in the movements of my body.

My eyes close and my head falls back as I raise my hands above my head and move my hips. It's the freest I've felt in a long time.

I still the second hands land on my hips. I drop my arms immediately, ready to push away whoever it is who thinks they've got the right to touch me, when a familiar voice rumbles in my ear.

"Do you have any idea how sexy you look right now?" His familiar deep voice drags me from my own little world, and I immediately relax back, allowing the tingles his touch creates to flow around my body. "Dance with me?"

I don't bother replying. Instead, I just move with him when he presses the length of his body against my back. His touch burns as he pins me against him.

"I was watching you." A groan rumbles up my throat. "The way you move. It's intoxicating." His fingers clench against my skin, and I welcome the slight bite of pain as my body takes on a life of its own. "I don't dance, but I couldn't bear to watch someone else take my place."

Oh God.

My head spins, and I'm not sure if it's the alcohol or just the effect he has on me.

Our hips move in time with the music, and I shut off everything but the beat and the heat of him surrounding me. With my eyes closed, I rest my head back against his chest and just ... *feel.*

I have no idea how much time or how many songs pass, but eventually just dancing must get too much for him. I've been able to feel his length against my ass almost since we first connected, and I can't deny that it hasn't sent a little thrill or two through me.

Releasing one of my hips, he lifts his fingers so he can sweep my hair from my neck before placing his lips to the sensitive skin below my ear. My body shudders with the contact, and his lips curl into a smile.

"You're driving me crazy, baby." I melt in his arms and give in to temptation.

Spinning so we're facing once again, I look up into his eyes. The blue is significantly darker compared to when I first looked into them earlier this evening.

His tongue runs along his bottom lip, and I can't help but watch its journey. His eyes bounce between mine before he lowers his head.

Time seems to stop as I wait for us to connect, but the second his lips brush mine it's like someone hits fast forward on my life.

He kisses me softly, just an innocent brush of lips, before his hands slip up to my waist and his tongue teases my lips. I press myself into his body, and my lips part, eager to accept what he has to offer.

The second our tongues collide, something explodes between us. My fingers grip the fabric of his shirt, and I cling onto him for fear that my knees are going to buckle as our tongues explore and our teeth clash. It's been a long time since I've been kissed, but fuck, I don't remember it ever being like this.

One song blurs into the next, but eventually we part in favor of dragging some air into our lungs. Although, Corey doesn't go all that far as he runs kisses along my jaw and down my neck.

"You're driving me fucking crazy," he murmurs into my ear when he gets there, making me shiver with delight.

"I ... uh ..." I stutter, now feeling a little awkward, seeing as we're standing in the middle of a massive crowd, having just made out like teenagers in front of them all.

In front of my colleagues and an entire hockey team.

Both our chests heave, and when I look into his eyes, I find them almost black with desire. Lust hits me right in the core, knowing that I can cause that kind of reaction in a man like him. It's usually Brooke who does this kind of thing. I wonder for a moment what's come over me. It's been years since I've pushed everything aside in favor of the type of pleasure only a man can offer. I tell myself that it's either the tequila or the dress—possibly a mix of both—giving me a bit of the confidence I used to have in my younger years.

Blowing out a breath, knowing that I need to put some space between us before this goes too far, I stand back.

I don't look up at him again for fear of what I might find on his face.

"I ... uh ... need to use the bathroom." I step around him and squeeze between the bodies dancing beside us. I'm almost at the edge of the crowd when his arm slips around my waist.

"You don't need to run. Let me walk you."

I want to tell him no, that he should go back to the party and leave me to do my thing, but as I open my lips to say the words, they die on my tongue. Having him beside me feels too good to ignore, so instead, I allow him to walk me to the bathroom.

"Thanks," I mutter, feeling embarrassed all of a sudden, which is crazy seeing as I was basically dry humping him out on the dance floor not all that long ago. "You should go back up to the party. Milo might be looking for you."

"Why do I get the impression you're trying to get rid of me?"

My eyes go wide—I don't want him to think that. "No, not at all. I just didn't think you'd want to hang around the bathrooms like a loser."

"You think I'm a loser?" One side of his lips curls into a smile.

My cheeks heat and my breath catches. "No, that's not what—"

"I was joking." He lifts his hand to my cheek, his thumb brushing over my bottom lip. "Don't look so worried."

I nod, unable to say anything with the way he's looking into my eyes.

Thankfully, someone jostling him from behind breaks our connection.

"I'm just going to ..." I trail off, gesturing behind me.

"I'll be upstairs." He winks before turning and leaving me with the space I need to breathe.

After standing in line for what feels like hours, I eventually manage to get to a stall to do my thing.

I'm standing at the sink, reapplying my lip gloss, when a familiar flash of blonde appears over my shoulder.

"Sooo ... is he as good a kisser as I predicted?"

"I don't know what you're—"

"Oh, no, no, no. I watched you two going at it on the dance floor, so don't even think about lying to me. You don't get to steal my man and then kiss and not tell."

"I didn't steal—"

She waves her hand in front of me, brushing aside my argument. "Was he good?"

I sigh, wondering how to describe him.

"Forget it. That sigh and the goofy eyes say it all."

"It says nothing, B. He was a good kisser. It was fun. But that's all this is."

"Why?"

"Because in case you'd forgotten, I have no interest in dipping my toe into the dating world. I've got too much other stuff to worry about. I don't need the whole 'does he like me, doesn't he? Is he going to call?' thing adding to my stress."

"But he could be the perfect stress relief."

"Men always come with drama."

"Only if you allow them to. Think about it ... one hot night. Let him banish the tension that's been pulling your muscles tight and then allow him to walk out the door, knowing you both got what you needed. Bam. He's happy. You're happy. You can continue with your life. End of."

I sigh once more, but this time it's not with memories of how his kiss felt. It's heavy with the regret of my past. I know what Brooke is saying is right, but I've been there and done that. I know that one night of passion, of pushing my problems aside, isn't going to help in the long run. Hell knows I've tried.

I know she's just trying to encourage me to enjoy myself, but she has no idea what it's like for me. She might have been there with me through most of it, but still, it's not the same. I'm always terrified of falling back into old habits and returning to a side of me that I never want to visit again.

"Thanks, B. But I know what I'm doing."

She gives me a sad smile as I walk away from the mirror. I'm half expecting him to still be waiting for me when I step from the bathroom, but I'm pleasantly surprised when I don't find him.

Making my way through the crowd, I head up the stairs in the hope of a new drink before I wish Milo a happy birthday and sneak out while no one's paying attention.

I only realize my mistake when I come to a stop beside the small gathering in front of the bar.

"Harlow, there you are. Brooke said she'd dragged you here, but I was beginning to think she was lying," Milo says, Linc and Calvin standing beside him.

"Oh, she made quite the entrance. I'm surprised you missed it," Fletch announces, much to everyone's amusement.

"Yeah, I'm ... uh ... sorry about that," I mutter, unable to look into his eyes.

"It's fine. I'm used to it."

"Stop bragging," Milo says with a laugh. "Not all of us

have women falling at our feet on a daily basis." He's clearly been filled in with all the mortifying details.

"Think that says more about you that anything else," Linc deadpans.

As a starting defenseman of the LA Vipers, we all know that Milo gets more than his fair share of offers.

Milo shrugs, not in the least bothered by their banter, while Corey assesses me with an amused smile on his face.

"Corey, have you met Harlow?"

"Yeah, you could say we've met." He winks at me. Both Milo and Fletch turn their attention from him to me, and I pray that the floor will swallow me up.

"Is that right?" Milo says, looking a little too intrigued.

"He just bought me a drink earlier." I drop my eyes to the floor. Anyone who knows me even slightly would be able to tell I'm lying from a mile away, but I'm hardly going to announce that I let him dry hump me on the dance floor —it's bad enough they could have seen it.

Thankfully, Reese joins us, wrapping her arm around Fletch's waist and looking up at him like he's a god—which, to be fair, he kind of is.

A bolt of jealousy threatens to double me over. It's not because she has him or anything—I know my previous infatuation with him was just that—but it's the love that passes between them. It's so pure, so honest. It reminds me of how my parents used to look at each other, and that thought alone is enough to have a ball of emotion growing in my throat.

"Sorry to be a party pooper, but we need to head off," Reese says sadly.

"Not at all. I'm so glad you could come." I stand aside as Milo says his goodbyes and then mutter my own, managing to keep my hands to myself this time.

A weird tension settles between Corey and me as we watch the couple depart. When he turns back, he looks between Milo and me with his brows pulled tight.

"Drink?" Milo offers.

"Nah, man. It's your night; I should be buying you the drinks."

"I'm not going to argue with that."

"Harlow?" he asks, his deep, rumbling voice vibrating through me. The effect it has on my body is enough to finalize the decision I'd already made while I was in the bathroom.

"No, thank you. I actually need to get going."

Corey's mouth opens like he wants to say something, to argue, but Milo's name being called distracts us all.

"Hey, how's it going?" Milo asks, taking a step away from us to greet whoever it is.

"I'll bring your drink over," Corey says as he leaves us.

He turns his dark eyes on me. The sight pulls at my insides, but leaving is the right thing to do. If I stay, I'll end up drinking more, and I know I'll make a decision that I'll regret in the morning. A night with him might be fun, but it's not going to fix things, and I'm fed up of putting a Band-Aid over my issues and hoping they'll be dealt with.

"Thanks for ... tonight. It was fun."

"Not fun enough to make you stay?" The little bit of hope in his eyes kills me. Maybe he is different, but going home with him tonight after just meeting him isn't the way to test that. Finding a man is nowhere on my to-do list right now.

"I'm sorry, I just got—"

"It's fine. If you need to go, you need to go. Can I at least give you my number?"

I chew on my bottom lip as I consider what to say, but

before I know what I'm doing, I'm reaching into my purse for my cell.

I swipe the screen to wake it up, but nothing happens.

Well, I guess that's fate telling me this isn't meant to be. "I'm sorry," I say, holding my cell up to show him. "Battery's dead."

I drop it back into my purse, not noticing he's moved until I look back up and find him waving to the bartender.

"Do you have a pen?"

The second one is handed over, he starts scribbling something down on a scrap of card. "Here," he says, passing it over. I stare down at the number scrawled across it and wonder if it'll be one I ever call. Probably not.

"No pressure, but I'd love to see you again." He smiles almost shyly, and it makes him look so endearing. I wonder for a brief moment if it's really him or just an act he's pulling to try to get what he wants. Hell knows, guys have done worse to get a girl into their bed for the night.

"Thanks. Well, I'm gonna ..." I point over my shoulder, and he nods.

"Until next time."

I walk away, wondering if that's a wish or a promise.

4

COREY

I roll over the next morning with a faint pounding behind my temples. It's much less than I deserve after the amount I drank with Milo once she left last night, but I can't say that I'm not relieved.

Cracking my eyes open, I stare at my phone on the bedside table, knowing that her number is sitting in it courtesy of a very drunk and very handsy Brooke. My fingers twitch to send her something, anything that might convince her to see me again. One dance and one kiss with her was nowhere near enough.

It's just because she turned you down, a little voice says in my head. I must admit, it doesn't happen all that often—especially not after the way she was moving her body against mine on the dance floor.

My cock swells as the memory of her arse moving against it resurfaces. Fuck, it felt so good to have a woman in my arms again. I can only imagine how it might have felt to get her into my bed. I look around the room I'm currently in. Okay, so maybe not my bed, but hers. Or any other, to be fair.

I drop my hand under the covers and wrap my fingers around my length. I pump a few times, her dark eyes, light pink lips, and sinful curves filling my mind as I do. The tingles she caused within me last night reappear, and in embarrassingly few minutes later, I come to the memory of us locked together in our kiss.

Fucking hell, my dry spell is turning me back into a damn teenager again. Jacking off to a fucking kiss? Pussy.

Jumping from the bed, I ignore the boxes around me and go straight for the shower. It's late and I need to be at the studio, not sitting here, dwelling on what could have been and if I should call her. I already know the answer. She wasn't interested, despite what her best friend drunkenly slurred at me before she left.

"She's scared, Brit boy. She needs someone to chase her because she won't hand herself over willingly. Me, on the other hand ..." She ran her hands up my chest, but she didn't get very far before I physically removed them. She might be attractive, but I had someone else in my sights.

I don't bother walking into my kitchen—it's pointless. Instead, I head straight out once I'm dressed. The diner a few doors up from the studio has quickly become my second home.

"Morning," Laura, the owner, sings as I walk through the entrance, making the little bell chime. "You want the usual?"

"Please," I say with a smile, hopping up onto one of the empty stools at the counter as she calls my order through to the kitchen.

"So, how're things?" she asks, pushing my first mug of coffee toward me.

"Same as."

"My brother still giving you shit?" She laughs as she

grabs a cloth and starts wiping down the already spotless counter.

"When isn't he?" That's not true. Oz, or Oscar, to his family, is possibly the best fucking artist I've ever seen. Convincing him to come and work for me—for Zach, really —was the biggest achievement I've had since taking over here. He's got an amazing reputation, and he doesn't half help bring the clients through the door. His on-and-off girlfriend who came with him, JJ, doesn't put them off either. She's a part-time model, part-time artist, and almost every guy in LA wants her leaning over them as she inks their bodies.

We chat away about nonsense, the weather, the busy summer days, and the upcoming hockey season—all the usual mundane stuff that completes my morning routine right now—before my first coffee is empty and Laura passes me my sausage, egg and bacon roll and a large takeout coffee. This breakfast is my little bit of home and part of the only thing I miss, aside from family and friends: a proper full English fry-up. I might love the Californian sun, but I can't get on board with waffles and pancakes to start the day. It's just not happening. I walk out with my cup and roll in hand and make the short journey to the studio to open up, dropping onto one of the sofas in the reception to enjoy my breakfast in peace before the guys arrive.

There are four of us, or three and a half, seeing as JJ is only here part-time. Snake is the only original artist from before Zach took over. The place was on the verge of going under, and it was purely by chance that I found it when I came here last year to get away from home for a few weeks when things were getting on top of me.

It was my last night here, and I had the urge to add to my ink to finish the holiday off right. Milo had mentioned this place, so I took the chance. And fuck am I glad I did. Snake and I hit it off immediately, obviously helped by our joint passion, and Snake was soon explaining how he was about to be unemployed as the owner was selling up.

I was on the phone to Zach the second I walked with my latest ink. The rest is history, I guess. He bought the place almost there and then. He didn't even fly out; he just took my word for it and jumped in head-first.

Although the idea had floated around my mind about me relocating to run this place, I didn't think it would happen. I was needed in Manchester. That was my studio after I escaped London the year before, but the second the call came from Zach to ask if I'd move here, there was only one answer. And that's how I found myself here, living on the sunny Californian coast, as far away from my troubles as I could get. It's just a shame it's impossible to leave my nightmares behind me for good. It seems those motherfuckers will haunt me no matter where I am on the planet.

"Morning," Oz sings as he joins me with his own coffee in hand, courtesy of his sister.

"Morning. Your better half not with you today?"

"Ugh," he grunts, rolling his eyes. "Don't. Just don't."

I can't help but chuckle. "Ah, domestic bliss. It's a sight to behold."

"Fuck off," he barks, disappearing to his room.

Much like the studios in both London and Manchester, each artist has their own room to work in. Zach has had the place fitted out the same way as all his other studios, so his Rebel Ink branding is strong despite the differences in location.

Once I've finished my breakfast, I head to my room. It's much more homely than the flat I'm renting—which is good, because if things continue the way they have been, then I might be moving into it sooner than I'd like to admit.

With just under an hour before my first client of the day, I power up my computer to get some admin done before pulling my phone from my pocket. Knowing her number is sitting there waiting for me taunts me. My thumb hovers over the contacts as I debate shooting her a message. I know the wisest thing to do would be to forget and move on, but there's something about her that's still under my skin.

Instead, I find the number for another woman who occupies a lot of my headspace. Sadly, it's in a totally different way to Harlow.

"Hey, son. How's it going over there?" Mum asks in a joyful voice that I know she's putting on for my benefit.

"It's fantastic." It's not a lie, I love my new life here, but speaking to her is always a stark reminder of the disaster I left behind. "And how are things there?"

"Yeah, yeah. They're good. The electric company has finally sorted the power out."

"That's great. What about everything else?"

She pauses and lets out a large sigh. "We're getting there. Natalie has a new bar job, so that will help. Sadie is looking, but with her studies, it's not easy. It'll all be fine though. I'm stronger than I look. I won't let him break me."

"I know you are, Mum."

"Plus, I've got you, my guardian angel." A smile curls up at one side of my mouth.

"It's the least I can do, seeing as I'm not there."

"How was I so lucky to get you as my son?" She asks me this often; my constant answer is that I'm only what she made me, but the words are getting boring.

"It's how it should be. Anything else from debt collectors?"

"No, not since the last lot of letters."

"That's good. Hopefully, they're coming to an end."

"I'm sure they are. There's only so much bad luck that can land on me, right?"

I agree, because I'm not sure what else to say. Mum chats away before I tell her that I've got to get to work and bring our conversation to an end, promising to ring her in a few days but insisting that she reaches out before then if she needs me. She agrees like always, but she's stubborn, and it's usually one of my sisters who ends up ringing with bad news.

Mum and Dad had been happily married all my life. I often questioned Mother's choice in men, seeing as he was so controlling. He'd enlisted in the army at fifteen, and every single part of his life was run like a military operation, including his marriage. I always assumed Mum was happy with that, because she never complained. Although I'm now learning it was more because she was afraid to than anything else.

Everything was ... bearable, I guess, until one day it all came crashing down around Mum's feet. Dad came home one night and announced that he'd met someone else and that he was leaving. Mum was shattered. Everything about life as she knew it ended with those few words, but she never imagined what was to follow, thanks to my father.

A knock at the door pulls me from my thoughts, and I pocket my phone and welcome my first client of the day. It's a guy who turned up a few weeks ago for a consultation. I've been working on finalising his design since, and I'm excited to be able to put some ink to skin at last. Hopefully, it might just rid me of some of my stress.

5

———

HARLOW

"Are you ever going to get that thing done, or do you just intend on staring at it for the rest of your days, wishing you were brave enough?"

I glance at the sketch tacked to my mirror before lifting my eyes over my shoulder to Brooke, who's now made herself comfortable in my bed.

"Something wrong with your room?"

"Yeah, actually. It stinks of vomit."

"So you thought you'd spread it to my bed, too? Great, thanks."

"I've showered; you're safe."

That doesn't exactly make me feel better, but I look back to my mirror to finish getting ready. My stomach bottoms out the second I remember what exactly it is I'm getting ready for before I have a chance to push it aside.

"I'll get it one day," I mutter, looking at the design I came up with a few years ago for the day I was brave enough to be inked. After all the shit I did in my teen years, you wouldn't think getting a tattoo would be all that wild,

35

but every time I think about it, I chicken out. I've even gotten as far as a waiting room a time or two, but each visit ended with me walking back out through the door with my skin as bare as when I walked inside.

"You've been saying that for years. Pull the Band-Aid off and just do it. I guarantee you'll feel better after."

"Says the expert," I mutter. Her knowledge of tattoos is limited to the tramp stamp on her back.

"I'm too hungover to argue with you."

"And for that, I'm truly grateful."

"Bitch."

"Yet still you love me."

"That I do, sista. That I do. You look nice," Brooke says, her eyes running the length of me.

"Dress for the news you want, right?"

"It'll be fine. I'm pretty sure you've had your fill of bad luck over the years."

"She's been called in on a Saturday. Do you really believe that?"

Dread passes through her eyes, and my stomach twists. I'm about to be told that I'm losing someone else I love. They're words that one should only hear once or twice in their lives, but for me, it's a more common occurrence than I'd like to admit.

Brooke's slightly green face pales. She knows I'm right.

"It will be what it will be. I've just got to do my best to support her through it."

"She's lucky to have you."

I shrug. I can see how Brooke might see it that way, but really, I'm the lucky one. My aunt is my lifeline. She came for me when I was at my lowest, and without her, I've no doubt that I wouldn't be here right now.

Pushing from the stool I'm sitting on, I stand and pull my purse from the bed.

"Message me when you have news."

I nod, my breath caught in my throat and move toward the door. I've got to be strong for her. She might be all I have in the family department, but equally, I'm all she's got, and I need to be as strong for her as she was for me. It's time for me to pull up my big-girl panties.

My aunt's waiting at the window when I pull up to her home. In seconds, she's out of the front door and heading my way. A weak smile graces her lips, but she's just trying to put on a show for my benefit. I can see how she's really feeling in the depths of her dark eyes. She's terrified but doesn't want me to know it.

"Good morning," she sings in her usual cheerful voice which normally brings me joy, but right now, all I want to do is cry.

"Morning," I force out through the lump in my throat.

"You didn't have to come, you know. I'm a big girl; I could have gone alone."

"No chance. We're a team, remember? We do the hard stuff together." I repeat the words she said to me time and time again in my late teen years.

She reaches over and grabs my hand, squeezing tightly. "We both know what he's going to say, and neither of us wants or needs to hear it. But ..." She trails off.

"The unknown is worse than the reality." She nods, a tiny smile twitching at her lips.

"Exactly. Let's go and find out the reality. See what we're really facing."

My aunt was first diagnosed with breast cancer when I was nineteen. I'd just managed to sort my life out and then hers was falling apart.

She'd saved my life, and now she was going to lose hers.

Tears burn my eyes as I recall that first appointment when we heard the bad news, and everything that was to follow. The hospital appointments, the treatment, the sickness. She handled it all with such strength. I already knew that she was one hell of a woman, but watching her kick cancer's butt one day at a time was incredible. I was so proud of her and inspired by her resilience. She'd only recently lost the love of her life, and now she was fighting for her own. It takes a really special kind of person to be able to get through all of that unscathed—not to mention picking up your wayward niece and bringing her back to life along the way.

I back out of her drive and force down my fear. There's no point in jumping to conclusions. This is going to be bad, but we don't know how bad. People live with returning cancer for years. Maybe she'll be one of the lucky ones.

"I'M sorry to have to tell you this, but the scans show that your tumors are growing faster than we anticipated. That will account for the symptoms you've been complaining of. The headaches, the dizziness, the confusion, the seizures." I turn to look at my aunt, my eyebrows raised in accusation. All the while, my heart is shattering in my chest.

"You didn't tell me—"

"I didn't want to worry you unduly."

"Unduly? I'm thinking it was kind of important."

"It is what it is. There's nothing you could do to fix it."

"Maybe not. But he can," I say, gesturing to the doctor watching our exchange. "So, what next? What's the treatment plan? What's the prognosis?"

He swallows before opening his mouth, and my body turns to ice. "Well, we can discuss treatment options, most likely radiation. But you've already indicated on a number of occasions that you don't want any more treatment. Is that right Mrs. Winslow?"

"But that was before. When you thought it was all over. You can't still—"

"That's correct."

"No, no. It might help. It might give you more time," I beg, reality fast slipping away from me.

"More time for what, Lo? To be ill and have to be looked after by you, carers or nurses? If this is my time, then I want to go out with dignity."

I blow out a long breath, trying to absorb what she's saying. What she's always said. "I know you do." I take her hand in mine and squeeze. It takes every bit of strength I possess to say it, but I meet her eyes and allow the words to pass my lips. "I'll be there for you, whatever you decide."

"Thank you," she whispers, her own eyes full of unshed tears.

"So, the prognosis?" I ask again, turning to the doctor.

"It's all a guess at this stage, but at best I'd say a couple of months. At worst ..."

"At worst?"

"Weeks."

"Fucking hell," I say on a sigh, my body desperate to curl up into a ball in an attempt to block everything out.

I don't hear another word the doctor says. The only thing filling my ears is my blood racing through them, and my pounding heart that sounds like a drum.

I'm going to lose her, too, and then who do I have?

When it's time to leave, my aunt places her hand on my

shoulder. I flinch at the contact, so lost in my own world that I wasn't even aware the appointment was over.

"Come on, Lo. I think we should go and get cake."

A sad laugh falls from my lips, but I can't deny that eating my weight in cake right now sounds appealing.

She slips her hand into mine, and together, with our heads held high and tears in our eyes, we walk toward the car.

I drive us to our favorite place on autopilot, a little cake shop on the Malibu coastline. It's run by an old English couple, and it's the quaintest place I've ever seen. The homemade cakes are displayed on towering stands and the tables are covered in tartan cloths with small vases of fresh flowers.

My aunt orders us our regular: a pot of English tea for her and a large cappuccino with an extra shot for me, along with two huge slices of cake.

I poke my fork into the soft sponge, not really having the stomach for it now that it's in front of me. The silence between us is heavy, but it's not uncomfortable as we both attempt to come to terms with what we've just learned.

My uncle always promised that, should anything happen to him, my aunt would be looked after. He certainly pulled through. When I took her to her first appointment all those years ago, I was floored by the hospital she directed me to. It was a million miles from any I'd visited in my past. But sadly, it seems it doesn't matter how much money you have or how incredible the doctors who treat you are.

Cancer doesn't care.

It doesn't give a fuck what kind of person you are and what you can offer to the world. It just shits all over you and wipes you out before your time, leaving your loved ones behind, trying to figure out how to move on.

My lip trembles as I think of my future with no family.

"Everything will be okay, Lo."

"I know," I lie. "I'm just going to be alone. You're my last—" A sob bubbles up my throat, cutting off my words.

"Family isn't just blood. You've got Brooke and her parents."

"I know, but—"

"No buts. I'm not going to lie and try to tell you that the world hasn't handed you a pretty fucked-up few years, but you've gone through worse than this and you've come out the other side stronger. It's time, once again, to move on, to create your own family, and to think about your future."

At that moment, the song that was playing softly in the background comes to an end, and a male British voice fills the space. I'm immediately taken back to last night when Corey was whispering in my ear. My skin pricks and my cheeks heat.

"Lo?" my aunt asks, not missing my reaction.

Shaking my head, I drag myself back to my miserable here and now instead of the small escape I allowed myself last night.

"It's nothing," I mutter, finally lifting a forkful of cake to my lips.

"My dear, anything that makes you blush like that certainly isn't nothing."

"Perceptive much?" I grumble, making her laugh. "Brooke dragged me out last night and—"

"You met someone?" Her hopes rise along with her voice. She's been desperate for me to put myself out there— almost as desperate as Brooke has been, although I think their reasons might be slightly different.

"No, I haven't."

"Really?"

Rolling my eyes at her persistence, I give in, knowing she's desperate for something to think about other than the appointment we just left.

"There was just a guy I was dancing with. A British guy."

"Ohhh ... a British guy. You know what they say about those?" She winks, and my cheeks flame once again.

"Err ... no?"

"Me neither, but any man who turns your cheeks that color is worthy of a little of your time. So, when are you seeing him again?"

"I'm not," I mutter, focusing on my now half-eaten cake.

"He didn't give you his number?"

"Yeah, he did. I'm just not looking for anything right now."

"Harlow, the best things don't appear when we're looking for them. They usually hit you upside the head when you least expect it."

"I know."

"So, call him. He might be the perfect distraction." She winks, and I pray for the floor to swallow me up. My aunt isn't naïve to my past—she actually found herself dragging me from the situations I got myself into more than once, so she knows exactly the kind of *distraction* I used to rely on.

"I don't need a distraction."

"Harlow," she sighs. "Stop being so afraid. Meeting this guy again, going on a date, spending time with him is so far from anything in your past. A distraction can come in many forms. You're a different person now. You're strong. You know what you want from life. You make good choices. But you're letting your fear get in the way of really living your life. How many guys have you turned down over the years?"

"A lot," I mutter, not all that happy that this has turned

into a Harlow therapy session all of a sudden. Shouldn't I be supporting her right now?

"Love is worth being brave for. Trust me." Her eyes go all soft as she thinks about my uncle. He was the only man she ever knew, and their love was unbreakable to the very end.

"I'm not sure this is—"

"You'll never know if you don't call him and find out. Sure, there's a chance you'll meet a few frogs along the way, but some lucky people like me find their prince right away."

"I've already done the frogs. They're what I'm afraid of."

"Different kind of frog, Lo."

I think back to the guys of my past, and I can't deny that what she's saying isn't true. Corey is totally different from the wastes of space I remember, who only wanted me for one thing while I craved the mind-numbing bliss they offered in return. My stomach turns over with disgust.

I mull her words over as I finish off my cake. As much as I hate to consider that she might be right, it's better than thinking about our reality. In a few weeks, she might not be here to give me any advice, so I'd better enjoy it while I have it.

"I'll think about it."

"Good, because it's time you started doing something for yourself for a change. You spend too much of your life supporting everyone else around you."

"It's what I enjoy."

"I know you do, and I know it makes you happy. But you're important too."

She yawns, and it's the perfect reminder of what the biggest issue is right now.

"I should get you home."

"I'm sorry, I—"

"Don't. Don't ever be sorry. None of this is your fault."

"I know. I just hate that I've put that look in your eye once more."

"You don't need to worry about me. I'm stronger than I look, it seems."

"That you are, girl. That you are."

We pay our small bill before heading out to find my car.

"I could do with a few groceries, but I'm not sure I'm going to make it," she admits, resting her head back the second she's in the seat, her eyes heavy with exhaustion.

"Tell me what you need, and I'll run in. Unless you'd rather go straight home."

"I can wait in the car. I don't want you doing more than necessary."

I want to tell her that it's the least I can do, but she looks too tired for the inevitable argument that would follow.

"As long as you're sure. I don't want you to be uncomfortable."

"I'm fine," she argues, but I can see in her eyes that it's all lies. She quickly lists off a few things she needs before resting back once again and closing her eyes.

I look over once we're out on the freeway, and she's already asleep.

My chest aches with the knowledge that she's in constant discomfort, yet to an outsider they'd never know. She appears so strong, so healthy, especially with her perfectly applied make-up and styled hair. Underneath all of that is just a shell of a woman. Every time I see her, a little more of her spark has gone, and it kills me. I hate to imagine what the next few weeks—couple of months, if we're lucky—might be like as I watch her lose her fight against this disease.

I grab all the items my aunt asked for before adding a new bottle of rum, some cola, and a bar of chocolate to the cart and heading to the register. That's my night sorted.

"You should call him." My aunt's words ring out in my mind as I join the line, and my stomach twists uncomfortably. He's probably forgotten all about me by now. For all I know, he found a replacement the moment I left and spent the night with her instead.

Pushing aside the thought, I pay for our groceries and head back to the car.

The rest of the ride is in silence, and I'm glad. My head is spinning with everything the doctors said alongside my aunt's advice. I know she's right. I need to stop worrying about everyone else, but that's easier said than done. For as long as I can remember, I've put myself last. For a long time, it was easier to focus on others and their issues than it was to think about my own disaster of a life.

After helping her in, I put the few groceries away while my aunt changes and settles herself on the couch.

"Would you like me to stay?" I ask from the doorway.

"No, no. You get off and enjoy yourself."

"I'm not sure I'm really up for it."

"Harlow," she says on a sigh. "Take it from someone older and possibly a little bit wiser. Life goes by in the blink of an eye. It's too short not to enjoy yourself. So put on your dancing shoes and drag Brooke out for a night of fun, if you're still insistent that you're not going to call your mystery man."

I nod, her hopeful expression too much to deny. "I'll see what I can do."

My aunt smiles, but I'm not sure if she believes me or not. Honestly, I don't believe myself either.

"Just don't waste time, Lo." I drop a kiss to her cheek

and promise to call her in the morning, leaving her house with a heavy heart, wondering how many more times I'm going to get to do so.

Tears burn my eyes, but I refuse to give in to them until I'm in the safety of my car.

The second I close the door behind me, everything I've kept bottled inside since walking out of the doctor's office explodes.

I cry, sob, and wail for everything I'm about to lose. My aunt is all I have now. She's picked me up time and time again, and I don't know what I'm going to do without her.

I sit there for the longest time, trying to imagine what's in the future for us and how my life is going to change once again when the time comes to say goodbye to her.

Movement in her living room window catches my eye and forces me to turn the engine on and pull away from my parking spot. The last thing I need is her knowing how much this is ripping me apart. I can't imagine how she's coping; she doesn't need to be worrying about me as well.

I slam my foot down on the accelerator and speed off down the street. The bottle of rum and the chocolate call to me from the trunk, and I fully intend on pulling on some yoga pants and sitting my ass down on the couch with both at the first possible opportunity.

I pull up on the driveway to the house Brooke and I share and let out a large sigh. I wipe any remaining tears from my eyes, although I know it's pointless. The second she sees the redness surrounding them, she'll know. She always does. That's the thing with us; we might be polar opposites with everything, but our connection runs deeper, stronger than any differences in opinion or taste.

With my grocery bag of goodies in hand, I push through the front door. She's there immediately.

A sob erupts from my throat, and she rushes for me. Somehow, she takes the bag from my hands before it crashes to the floor and pulls me into her arms.

"I'm so sorry," she whispers in my ear as she holds me.

"She ... she might only have weeks, B."

"It's going to be okay," she soothes.

"How?"

"Because it will. You're stronger than this."

"What if I don't want to be?"

"I'm sorry, but that's not a choice right now. She needs you, and I know you'll do everything you can for her. But I'm here for anything else you need. I know you're freaking out that she's about to leave you alone, but that's not true. You've got me. You've got my parents. We're all here for you."

"I know you are. She's just—"

"I know, but she needs to know you're okay. That you're going to be okay. She'll never tell you, but she's terrified too."

I pull out of my best friend's arms and narrow my watery eyes at her. "She called you, didn't she?"

"Of course. Come on."

I follow her through to the kitchen where I find a big glass of rum and Coke already waiting for me. I should have known that Brooke would have seen the empty bottle and been on top of it.

"Thank you," I mutter, happily accepting the glass as she passes it over.

"Drink that and then go and sort yourself out. We're going out."

I groan. "No arguments. I'm not allowing you to sit around here and stew on things you can't change. We're not doing anything crazy, just food and a few drinks. Anyway, you can't say no, because I promised your aunt I would cheer you up, so ..." She gives me a faux innocent smile.

Although fake, and the fact that "nothing crazy" is probably a lie, I feel the first bit of excitement I have all day. I could argue and continue with my plan to drink my misery away alone on the couch, or I could go out with my best friend who's going to do everything she can to put a smile on my face.

"Okay," I say, having a large sip of my drink. "Whoa. How much rum did you put in this?"

"Enough." She shrugs. "I've got to be honest," she says as she follows me from the kitchen. "I thought you would take a little more convincing."

"A night with you sounds like exactly what I need. And do you know what?" She lifts a brow as I spin around to face her. "I'm even going to let you pick what I wear."

"Who are you and what have you done with my best friend?"

"Funny. I don't want to think, so just point me in the right direction and make sure I have a drink at all times."

"Done. Go get in the shower, and I'll work on the wardrobe."

With my drink still in hand, I walk into my bathroom and turn the shower on. My aunt was right about something: I need a distraction, and although I might not be willing to find a man to do so, my best friend fits the bill.

I shower, take off what's left of today's makeup, and wrap a towel around both my body and my hair before walking out of my bathroom.

I find Brooke standing in the middle of my room in just her underwear with two dress options hanging from her fingers. The first one is a definite no—I think I've got skirts that are bigger—but the second one is perfect.

"Okay, this is gorgeous," I say, taking the soft floral fabric between my fingers. "Why have you never tried making me wear this one before?" I notice the tag still hanging on the back.

"Because I bought it for your birthday. I just thought you might need it tonight instead."

"How many times do I need to tell you not to buy me anything for my birthday?"

"Every year. But equally, every year I'll ignore you. So, happy birthday," she says despite the fact it's still over a month away, holding the hanger out for me to take. I do so eagerly.

It's a stunning navy wrap dress with bright pink flowers covering it. Granted, it's a good few inches shorter than I'd usually choose for myself, but it's got full sleeves to make up for it.

"You've got thirty minutes. I've booked us a table."

"Where?"

She taps her nose before walking out of the door, holding the other miniscule dress to her body. God help me if she's wearing that; the guys will trip over themselves just to get a look.

I pull out one of my nicest sets of underwear in the hope that it, along with the dress, will cheer me up before spritzing myself with perfume and pulling it all on.

I dry my hair and make quick work of accentuating my natural curls, allowing it to hang down over my shoulders before going for my makeup. My mood has me applying it a little heavier than I usually would, but when I sit back and look myself over, I can't help but be pleased. I look a million miles from the girl who broke down in the hall not so long ago. My armor is firmly back in place, and I'm ready to spend some time with one of my favorite people.

"Are you ready?" I call to Brooke as I slip my feet into a pair of wedges and swipe a clutch from my closet.

"Almost. You?"

I drop my gloss and cell into the small purse and walk to her room.

"Ready."

She glances over her shoulder at me, her eyes going wide as she takes me in. "Whoa, girl. That dress was made for you."

"I love it. Thank you so much."

"You're more than welcome. I wish you'd let me shop for you more often." She stands, revealing her tiny black bodycon dress, and I remember why she shouldn't be my personal shopper. "Oh shush," she says with a wave of her hand, knowing my exact thoughts about the scrap of fabric she calls a dress. "Let's go."

Her hand slips into mine and she pulls me through the house. Outside, I find an Uber waiting for us, and after locking the front door we climb in.

Brooke confirms our destination, off we go.

It's only a few minutes later that we pull up in front of my favorite tapas restaurant.

"You got a table last minute?"

"Sure did," she says with a wink.

"Oh God, who did you promise what to?"

"Moi?"

"The innocent look doesn't wash with me, B."

Rolling her eyes, she huffs out a breath. "I might have agreed to a date with Todd."

"You did not!" I squeal.

"See how much I love you?"

"Oh, like it's really a hardship. He's not exactly bad looking." Todd's been a waiter here since it opened, and he's hit on Brooke every single time we've been. And every single time, she's knocked him back. I don't know the real reason; she comes up with some pathetic excuse each time before deflecting the conversation.

"If it puts a smile on your face, then it'll be worth it."

"Thank you," I say sincerely as we walk toward the entrance. As if he was waiting, Todd pulls the door open and greets us—okay, Brooke—with a wide smile. Credit where credit's due, his eyes don't drop in favor of her body for almost a whole minute.

"I secured you both the best table."

"Thank you, Todd. I really appreciate it."

"No problem. I can assure you that the pleasure is all mine," he mutters almost absently as Brooke walks ahead, giving him full sight of her ass.

I laugh at him before following her lead.

"You want the usual?"

"You got it."

Todd nods and walks away to place our order. We've spent so much time here in the past year that he doesn't even need to write it down now.

Brooke chats away about a guy she's been messaging that she met the previous night after I left, and I'm grateful that she keeps my mind on less depressing matters. Todd arrives with a giant decanter of sangria and two glasses. The place is packed, so he doesn't hang around long, even if it's clear he would like to.

"I don't know what your issue is with him. He's sweet."

"Exactly. I don't want sweet. I want a bad boy."

I roll my eyes at her. "Of course you do."

"And what about you? Is there a reason that you're avoiding talking about last night?"

My temperature rises just thinking about it. "No, there's just nothing to talk about."

"Oh right. Yeah, sorry, I forgot that getting all up in that hot Brit's business was a totally normal thing for you to do."

"It was the tequila," I argue, much to her amusement.

6

COREY

I'm pretty sure that I should feel some sense of relief or comfort as I walk into my flat after my shift at the studio, but with all my shit in boxes and my looming eviction, I can't find it in me to want to be here. I should be living the life right now. That's exactly what I tell everyone I'm doing, and it's what they believe.

When Zach flew over to check the place out a few weeks ago, I was terrified he was going to discover the truth and demand he help, and I knew he wouldn't have stopped until he did. But I don't want help. He already pays me healthily for my position here. He was the one who believed in my dream and allowed it to happen in the first place. Without him, I'd still be stuck, drowning in my own miserable life. At least here I get to see the sun and the sand every day.

I pull my fridge open and stare at the empty racks. Not even a block of moldy fucking cheese. I fucking hate this, but what choice do I have? I can't leave Mum and my sisters; they need me, and I might be all kinds of fucked up, but I'm not *him*. I won't abandon them when they're at rock bottom. They sure as hell didn't leave me.

With a sigh, I pull the one bottle of water from the fridge and fall down into the chair, contemplating going to find some dinner.

I'm just about to leave the flat once again when my phone dings with a text.

Pulling it from my pocket, I find an unknown number staring back at me.

> Hey! It's Harlow (from last night). I'd love to see you again. Meet me at The Underground. I'm downstairs x

I reread the message again and again, my brows drawing together. Did her friend give me a fake number? Good job I didn't message her earlier.

It might be totally unexpected, but fuck if it doesn't have a little excitement filling my veins. I've hardly stopped thinking about her since the moment she made her excuses last night. The way her body felt pressed up against mine on that dance floor ... damn. My cock's getting hard just thinking about it.

> Corey: I'll be thirty minutes.

The message shows as read, but she never replies. Excitement and anticipation race through me. This is exactly what I fucking need.

Without putting any more thought into dinner, I stand and march straight towards the bathroom. If she's giving me this second chance, like fuck am I going to screw it up.

With the intention of doing everything I can to ensure I end today buried deep inside her and pushing away any thoughts of my reality, I step out of my clothes to freshen up.

After running a little wax through my hair, I slip my feet into my shoes and drop both my wallet and phone into my pocket. At the last minute, I turn back and grab a few condoms from the dresser. A smile twitches at my lips as I imagine her laid out before me, her red hair fanning my pillow and her curves on full display.

I look around the room on my way out and tell myself that it won't be happening here. Fuck the expense; I'll book us a hotel if I have to. No one needs to see how I'm living right now.

Stepping from my building, I find the Uber I booked waiting for me.

"Evenin'," I say as I climb in and quickly confirm my destination.

He chats away about my plans, and it only builds my hope that I'm about to end my dry spell with a girl who captured my attention the second she fell into my lap last night.

I could have easily gone and found some pussy since I arrived, but something has stopped me. The stress from getting the shop off the ground and everything else in life that tries to keep me down, I guess. This isn't about romance; I don't sign up for that shit. This is about getting what I need—what we both need, if the way her body reacted to mine last night is anything to go by.

The place is packed when the car pulls up out the front, and I end up having to wait to even get inside.

By the time the bouncer lifts the rope and allows me in, I'm desperate for a fucking drink. I make a beeline for the bar and order a scotch. I swallow it down in one, enjoying the burn and waiting for the warmth to hit me.

"Another?" the bartender shouts when I slam the glass down.

Shaking my head, I spin around and go in search of who I really came here for.

I locate the stairs and head down. As I descend, the chaos from above begins to quiet, and when I push through the doors to this section, I find the music is completely different. Gone are the fast-paced club tracks that were filling my ears, and instead a low, sexy R&B vibe sounds out.

It's quieter down here, but it still takes me longer than I would like to find her. She's dancing with her friend, who's in another minuscule dress. I smile as I watch them letting go to the beat of the music.

I walk to the bar and order myself another while I watch them. Harlow has a wide smile on her face as she moves her hips and lifts her arms above her head.

As her friend dances, I get my first proper look at Harlow. Her floral dress might be almost as short as her friend's, especially with her arms up, but that's where the similarities end. She wasn't wrong last night when she said they couldn't be more different.

I down my drink and wait a few seconds, but I can only hold off for so long. She pulls me in in a way I've never experienced before. My need to run my hands over her, to sweep my tongue against hers and taste her once again is all-consuming.

I take two steps forward before her friend sees me approaching over Harlow's shoulder. Her eyes run the length of me. Her interest is obvious, but my body doesn't react to her attention one bit. It might have been a while, but she's really not my type. Her friend, on the other hand ... I'm only a few feet away when Harlow stills. She stares at her friend, who's still smiling at me, before turning to look over her shoulder.

Her eyes land on me immediately as I continue my approach, but it takes a few seconds for Harlow to register that it's me. When she does, her eyes go wide in shock, but to my delight, a smile curls at her full, red lips.

"What are you doing here?" she shouts over the music when I'm close enough.

"You invited me." My brows pull together in confusion. "No, I—" A thought hits her and her lips purse, but sadly, it's not in preparation for a kiss. "Brooke," she accuses, turning towards where her friend was just standing, only she's gone. "What the ..." We both find her at the same time, dancing with a guy only a few feet away. She notices our attention and smiles and waves, a cheeky glint sparkling in her eyes.

Blowing out a breath, Harlow turns to me. "I'm so sorry. As you can tell, it wasn't me who invited you."

"Well, I'm here now. Fancy a drink?" Harlow looks from me to her now very distracted friend.

"Sure, why not?" She takes a step around me, and I place my hand on the small of her back as we make our way towards the bar. Her movement stills for a beat when my warmth hits her, but she doesn't push me away like I first feared she might.

"Rum and Coke, right?" She smiles and nods beside me as I repeat our order to the bartender.

I don't allow her to take the glass; instead, I pick both up and turn. "Let's go and find somewhere to sit."

"There's a quieter section around the corner."

My eyes drop to her cleavage for a second, and my mouth waters. "Sounds perfect," I mutter, my eyes finding hers once more. Her head tilts to the side, her brows rising in amusement, but she doesn't say anything. Instead, she spins and leads the way. I could swear there's more of a spring in her step than there was earlier.

She comes to a stop beside a sofa that a few people are vacating.

"Here?" she asks.

"I'm easy."

"Is that right?" The music is quieter back here, so I hear her as I fall down onto the sofa beside her.

"I guess that's something you're going to have to find out." Her cheeks heat, but I don't miss the darkening of her chestnut eyes.

I slide over so we're close enough that her bare thigh presses against mine, and I rest my arm over the back of the sofa, temptingly close to pulling her into me.

"So, what's the occasion?" I ask, changing the topic for fear of coming on too strong and ruining my chances.

"Uh ..." She stalls. "No occasion, just a night out to ..."

"To?"

She sighs. "Forget."

"Oh?" I ask, wondering if she's about to open up. I'm usually not one for all the talk; I'm more of an action guy. But as a conflicted look passes across her face, I can't help but want to listen to all her worries. "It's n-nothing. Just family stuff."

"Ah, now that is something I know all about." Reaching forward, I grab both of our drinks from the small table in front of us. "To forgetting." I lift my glass, and after a second, she taps hers to it.

I watch as she brings her drink to her lips and sips. Her eyes shutter slightly as the taste hits her, and I find myself captivated.

"Not thirsty?" she asks when she lowers it once again and notices that I've not had any.

"Not so much." Her eyes run over my face and focus on my lips when I run my tongue over my bottom one. "Last night wasn't the same after you left."

"No? Brooke didn't keep you company?"

I laugh, because I'm sure she happily would have given the chance, but everyone kept her busy chatting and drinking before she had to be escorted into a car to get home.

"No. I was pretty lonely, to tell the truth." I down my drink before placing the glass on the table and turning my attention to her.

"My heart bleeds," she says with a smile.

"Maybe we could make up for it tonight." Not able to keep my hands to myself any longer, I reach out and take her drink from her before I tuck a lock of her hair behind her ear. The connection I remember all too well from last night crackles between us the second our skin touches.

"I'm ... um ... not sure ..."

"I thought you wanted to forget." My hand wraps around the side of her neck, my fingers twisting in her hair and my thumb brushing her cheek.

"I do. But—"

"Let me help you," I interrupt. "I know the perfect way to distract you from whatever it is putting that frown on your pretty face."

"Corey, I—"

I lean forward and cut her words off with a brush of my lips. She stills, her breath coming out in a rush and tickling over my face. "Shush. Don't think. Just feel."

She nods ever so slightly, and I make my move. My fingers tighten in her hair as I tilt her head to the side and seal my lips over hers. She shudders beneath me, and it's all the encouragement I need.

My tongue sneaks out to tease her, and her lips part almost immediately, allowing me entry.

The taste of her mixes with the rum and Coke she just had a sip of, and my need for her quadruples.

She turns to me, allowing me to run my other hand up her bare thigh. I push my fingers slightly under the hem of her dress, my addiction to her too much to deny.

Everything around us disappears as her tongue twists with mine, but it hardly satisfies my need, which continues to grow by the second.

"Jesus, Harlow. You're addictive," I admit when my lips brush her ear. Her increased breaths rush past mine, and I shiver.

"Corey, I—" She can barely get her words out, she's breathing so fast, but I help her by cutting her off.

"Dance with me?"

"O-okay."

I pass her drink back, and she immediately tips it to her lips and drains the lot before reaching for my outstretched hand and allowing me to pull her up and back towards where I first found her.

We pass her friend, who's grinding up against some guy, having the time of her life, but I pay her little mind. My entire focus is on having this woman pressed up against me again.

I come to a stop in a small bit of space and tug her arm gently, so she has no choice but to step into my body.

She looks up at me, her wide, chestnut eyes staring right into mine. I swear she can see deeper than most, and I'm not sure how that makes me feel. I don't need anyone seeing into the reality that is my life.

Taking her wrists, I lift her arms so they rest over my shoulders. Her breasts press against my chest, and I fight the need to growl. My hands drop to her hips and close any last space between us as we move in time with the music. Her curves fit the hard planes of my body perfectly, and I can't help my mind wandering to just how we might move together when we're naked.

My cock swells in my pants. Fuck, I want this woman something fierce.

Her eyes still hold mine, the hesitation in them from when I first arrived vanished. I drop my head, my lips brushing over hers gently to see how she'll respond. Thankfully, she accepts my kiss. My tongue sweeps into her mouth. Her taste along with her drink mixes and only adds fuel to my raging fire.

My hands slip around to her arse, and I press my hardening cock against her belly, so she knows exactly what kind of reaction she stirs in me.

"Corey," she moans as I kiss down her neck, and I damn near lose my shit.

"We should probably either stop or get out of here before I do something that will end with me in a police cell."

Her shocked eyes find mine, but the small smile on her lips gives me hope that she's on my wavelength. She searches my face for a few seconds. I've no idea what she's looking for, but she must be happy with what she finds because she reaches up, her lips brushing my ear, and whispers, "We should probably leave then. You're no good to me locked up."

Fucking hell. This woman is going to be the death of me.

"Okay ... oh ... yeah." She laughs at my obvious shock,

and although it's the pounding beat of the music that's filling my ears, the sound of her chuckle hits me right in the chest. "Come on then." I take her hand once again as we make our way from the dance floor.

She pauses when she catches the eye of her friend. Harlow points to me and then the door—much to Brooke's delight, if the smile that stretches across her face is anything to go by.

"Where to then?" she asks once we step away from the noise and commotion behind us.

"Uh ..." I look up and my eyes land on a fancy looking hotel across the street. "Right here?"

She follows my line of sight. "Sure. It's probably better than having to spend the night listening to Brooke and whoever she's pulled."

With a smile, I wrap my arm around her waist and pull her into me. Her sweet, floral scent fills my nose, and a wave of desire washes through me so strong I worry it might take me to my knees. Hopefully, she'll be naked by the time that happens.

7

HARLOW

One moment we're at the reception desk asking about a room, and the next we're in the elevator watching the doors close. The air is electric, desire flooding through my veins. The second we're alone in the enclosed space, he turns to me, closing the gap between us.

My breath catches as his blue eyes stare down into mine. Dirty thoughts play out as clear as day in his eyes. The memory of his body pressed against mine pops into my head, and a thrill runs through me, pushing me forward and reminding me that it's okay to let go for a night. To take the escape I need and just enjoy myself.

Doing this, getting a hotel room with a somewhat random guy, isn't me reverting to my past mistakes. I'm an adult now, and I'm making an informed—okay, somewhat slightly drunk—decision.

I know that if I walked away from him for a second night, I'd only lie in bed later and regret it. Regrets are good for no one. I've got enough of them lurking in my past to prove it.

"You're so beautiful," he murmurs, the heat of his body

warming mine. His hand cups my jaw, and he tilts my head back to give him the access he needs to my lips.

This time, there's no caution when he kisses me. There's no sweet, gentle brush of his lips against mine, and there's certainly no hesitation.

His tongue parts my lips the second we connect, and he dives straight in, demanding mine to join, which it does immediately.

He steps forward, forcing me take one back so that I'm pinned between the mirrored wall and his hard body.

His hand skims down my body before finding the bare skin of my knee. He hitches my leg up around his waist, then runs his hot palm down my thigh until he can grab my ass, rocking me against him.

"Oh God," I groan into his mouth as his erection rubs against my heated core.

It's been so long that I'd almost forgotten just how good this could be.

He grinds his hips slowly, and the sensation makes my head spin as the elevator rises through the building. The unfiltered lust mixes with the alcohol I've consumed tonight, and all of it together helps to drag me from my own head and forces me to enjoy the moment.

Fuck, I can't even remember the last time that happened.

Sadly, the elevator chimes, and we're forced to part.

After a beat, Corey takes a step back. His blue eyes are so dark they're almost black, his lips are swollen from our kiss, and his wide chest heaves as he drags in some much-needed air.

"Come on. I need you out of that dress."

Desire pools between my thighs, knowing that he wants me so badly. That I turn him on this much.

The walk to our room is short, but it seems to take forever for Corey to get the door to unlock.

"Fucking thing," he mutters frustratedly as he frantically pushes the card in and out of the small slot.

"As much as I like your eagerness, let me." I place my hand on his and he pauses.

Taking the card, I slide it into the machine with a little more grace, and the light immediately flicks to green.

"How'd you—"

"Do you really want to discuss technique right now?"

"Oh," he says, taking hold of my hips and pushing me through the door. "There's a few of your techniques that I'm really quite interested in. Opening the door, however, is not one of them."

I begin to laugh, but the second he presses his crotch against my ass, and I once again feel his hardness, all amusement leaves me.

The door slams behind us, signaling that we're alone for the first time. A shudder runs down my spine as the silence of the space fills my ears.

Corey leans forward, his increased breaths tickling my ear. "I've been dreaming about this since you fell into my lap last night," he whispers, his rough voice making my panties even wetter.

I groan in response.

"Then I find you tonight in this sexy little dress, and the only thing I've been able to think about is getting you out of it. Discovering if what's beneath is just as breathtaking."

My teeth sink into my bottom lip as his fingertips trail across my collarbones before dipping into the cleavage my dress exposes. He runs a line around the swell of my breasts before teasing my nipples beneath the fabric with his thumb. My back arches, my body silently begging for more of his addictive touch. We're both still fully clothed, yet I'm pretty sure I've never felt more desired. More wanted.

His hand drops to the tie that's knotted at my waist. He pauses, giving me a chance to change my mind. But when I don't say anything, his fingers make quick work of undoing it. My dress falls open and my skin erupts in goose bumps as the cool air surrounds me. His fingers continue with their exploration. They run over the lace edging of my bra before descending over my ribs, circling my belly button before tickling along the top of my panties.

"Are you wet for me, Harlow?" he groans, his fingers dropping lower over the lace. I gasp, expecting them to connect with where I need them most, but at the last minute he moves them away.

"Fuck," I breathe in frustration. He chuckles, but the sound is cut off as I'm suddenly spun around and pushed up against the wall.

"Jesus fucking Christ," he mutters, staring down at my black lace–clad body. "You should be fucking illegal."

His hand reaches for my waist, and his lips find mine once more. My fingernails run down his back before clinging to the fabric of his shirt.

Unhappy with him still being fully clothed while I'm here half naked, I make my way to the buttons and begin undoing them. The second the fabric parts, my hands dive inside, desperate to feel his hot, taut skin against my palms. And fuck if that's not what I find. I knew he was cut—it was obvious even covered in fabric—but as my fingers trail across the definition of his abs, I realize I hadn't given him enough credit.

My hands slide to his shoulders, and I hurriedly push it away. With a little help from him, the fabric flutters to the ground, and, after pulling my lips from his, I get my first look at his sculpted, tattooed chest. It's pretty mind-blowing. His ink is stunning. It's intricate, captivating, and clearly holds so many memories and stories. My eyes flick over it, but I don't get a chance to fully absorb everything because his hands drop to his waist and his fingers flick open the button before his pants fall to the floor, leaving him standing in just a pair of tight black boxer briefs. The fabric strains against his steel length, and my need to reach out and take it in my hand is almost too much to bear. I suck on my bottom lip as my fingers twitch to feel how hot and smooth he is.

His thumb presses against my chin and successfully pulls my lip free. "Save the sucking for later, eh?" he says with a wink before his lips crash to mine once again.

My dress is pulled from my shoulders before I'm lifted from my feet. The coldness of the wall bites into my back, but the second Corey's lips trail down over my collarbone and toward my lace-covered breasts, I forget all about it.

"I want to fucking devour you, Harlow. You taste so fucking sweet."

Arching my back, I offer myself to him, desperate for him to release my swollen, heavy breasts.

"Fuck," he barks, slipping his hand around my back and releasing the clasp.

The relief is instant, and in another second the item of clothing is discarded, and Corey is staring down at my chest like it's the first pair he's ever seen. We've not discussed our sexual history, thank fuck, but I highly doubt this is his first showing.

With his hips pinning me to the wall, he palms my breasts. Then, dropping his head, he sucks one of my nipples into his hot, greedy mouth. My head bangs back against the wall, but I don't feel anything other than the electric bolt that shoots straight between my legs.

"Oh fuck, that's good."

"Yeah?" he mumbles, smiling around my peak.

"Yeah. Ooooh," I groan as he begins licking around my breasts and nipping at the sensitive skin while pinching my other nipple almost painfully hard.

Everything he's doing feels incredible, but it's not enough. My hips grind, and he groans as I rub against him.

"Harlow, fuck." Every time he speaks, his voice is deeper, rougher, more desperate, and it only helps to feed my desire.

I moan in frustration as his hands leave my heavy breasts in favor of my ass, but the second I'm pulled from the wall, I know it's going to be worth it.

He walks us directly to the bed and drops me onto it. I bounce a couple of times, and he watches in fascination before reaching out and pulling my panties down my legs. I lie before him, totally bare, but my lust and the remaining alcohol in my system stop me feeling exposed. I'm too desperate for what comes next to care that he's the first man to stare at my naked body for longer than I'm willing to admit.

His eyes pause for a second on my breasts before he makes his way down over my stomach, hips, and all the way to my knees.

I'm enjoying the tingles his stare brings, but his eyes on me alone aren't enough. As he slowly starts to make his way back up, I lift my feet to the bed and spread my legs.

"Fuuuuck," he groans, his eyes flying to my core.

He drops to his knees, throws my legs over his shoulders, and drags me to the edge of the bed.

"I need you on my fucking tongue. Right now."

He's barely finished the words before his fingers open me up and his tongue licks up the length of my pussy.

"Oh shit." My hands fist the sheets beneath me, and I fight the need to buck away from his mouth. I'm so sensitive that his leisurely strokes verge on being too much to handle.

He must sense it because he keeps his movements slow and measured for the longest time, driving me higher and higher toward the mind-numbing bliss I'm desperate for.

My hands release the sheets in favor of his hair. I pull, probably painfully, but now I can almost taste what's coming for me, I need everything he's got.

One of his fingers teases my entrance and I moan his name, shamelessly pleading for more.

"Corey, fuck. Please."

At my encouragement, his fingers dive inside me. My walls ripple around the invasion. It's uncomfortable for a beat, but the second he bends them and finds that one special spot, I forget everything, even my own goddamn name as I fly towards ecstasy.

"Oh God. Oh God," I chant before a loud cry falls from my lips as I freefall over the edge.

I thrash on the bed, but at no point do I release his hair and allow him to pull away from me.

When I've finally come back to Earth, he strokes me a few more times, enticing a series of aftershocks to rock my body.

"Fuck," he mutters when he eventually emerges, his mouth glistening with my arousal.

My chest heaves as I fight to get it under control, but watching him push his thumbs into the waistband of his boxers and drop them to the floor doesn't help one bit.

His hard length springs free, and I'm powerless but to lick my lips as I stare at it.

When I eventually rip my eyes away and back up to his face, I find a sexy smirk gracing his lips. He knows he looks good, and he knows I very much like what I see, but I don't find the level of arrogance I've experienced in the past, and that fills me with joy. I can only hope that's a good thing.

After collecting a condom from his pocket and dropping it to the bed beside me, he crawls between my legs, and, with his hands on my waist, he pushes me up the bed so he can settle.

"Just one?" I tease.

"For now."

I don't get to respond, because he leans over me and takes my lips. I can taste myself on his tongue, and it only makes me slicker for him.

My back arches as he teases my breasts before he heads south and plunges two fingers deep inside me.

"So wet."

"So hard," I counter, reaching down between us and wrapping my fingers around his steel length. His skin is burning hot but so smooth as I begin stroking him.

"Fuck, baby," he groans in my mouth before blindly reaching for the condom.

Regretfully, he removes all touch as he rolls it down his shaft. I bite down on my bottom lip and tilt my head to the side as he completes the simple task.

"I'm going to watch you get yourself off one day." I don't realize I've said the words out loud until he replies.

"Only if you do the same for me. I want to watch these delicate fingers work your pussy into a frenzy." He takes one of my hands in his and laces our fingers together. He then lifts it above my head and begins teasing me with the tip of his cock. He circles my clit, drops to my entrance and pushes just an inch inside before pulling back again. It drives me fucking crazy, and if the smirk on his lips is anything to go by, then that was his plan.

He pushes inside me just that little bit more. My muscles contract, trying to pull him deeper, and he takes my other hand and lifts it to join the first.

"Corey, please," I beg. "Oh Jesus. Fuck," I cry as he thrusts forward. One single move and he's so incredibly deep inside me.

He stretches me open in a way I barely remember, and it's so fucking delicious it makes my eyes cross. He pulls out slowly before slamming back into me.

"You're fucking heaven, baby. Heaven."

He continues for a few more thrusts before his movements start to get more and more frenzied. Both our bodies are covered in a light sheen of sweat as the temperature of the room seems to explode as he moves against me.

Taking both my hands in only one of his, he drops his fingers, first to my breasts and then down to my clit. That extra pleasure mixed with him hitting so deep inside me sends me headfirst into another blissful release.

He groans out my name, the sound so erotic I immediately fall straight into my third orgasm before he twitches violently inside me.

His weight drops onto me as we both try to catch our breath.

"Wow." He's so breathless that the word is no more than a whisper.

"Yeah," I agree.

"Again?" He doesn't need to say it; I can feel his hardening cock already growing against me once more.

"I thought you'd never ask." He barks out a laugh before rolling onto his back and taking me with him.

8

———

COREY

I stare up at her. Her once smooth and styled hair is a mess, her previously red lipstick is now smeared around her face —along with mine, I would imagine—her chest heaves, and her nipples are pert and begging me to suck them into my mouth once again.

This woman is surprising me at every turn. I was shocked to receive her message earlier, which turned out to be warranted. I'd half expected her to dismiss my sudden appearance, but that's the furthest from what happened.

She trails her fingertips down my chest and onto my abs. My muscles bunch and twitch as she moves, my cock hardening even more against her pussy. Her heat burns, and I have to clench my teeth in an attempt to stop myself thrusting up into her bare.

It's so fucking tempting to feel her skin on skin. But I can't. I never, and I mean never, go bareback. I know all too well that the risk is too fucking high.

"There are more condoms in my jeans pocket."

"You came out with a plan, huh?"

"I used to be a boy scout." Her brows furrow. "Always be prepared."

"Oh, right. Well, I'm grateful." She climbs from my waist. I miss her weight immediately, but the sight of her arse as she walks to my discarded trousers and shoves her hand into the pocket makes up for it.

She spins on her tiptoes, holding the concom packet between two of her fingers, and smiles at me. If I weren't already lying down, it would knock me on my fucking arse. She's so beautiful. Her red hair hangs haphazardly around her shoulders, her curves are sinful, and her smile and eyes do shit to me they really shouldn't.

No one needs to find their way into the darkness I hold in on a daily basis. I spend most of my time wishing I could escape it.

"So, tell me," she starts, slowly moving toward me. "Just how prepared are you?"

"Well, enough to ensure you're unable to walk in the morning."

"I think you'd better order us some room service then, if we're in for a long night."

I stare at her, my chin dropping. Who is this woman? She seemed so shy, innocent even when I first met her last night, yet here she is, a red-headed goddess who's rocking my fucking world.

"Uh ..." I say as I roll towards the phone. Psyching myself to spend money I don't have. "Bottle of wine?"

"On second thought." She grabs the handset before I get anywhere near it. "Hello, yes. Please could we get a bottle of Macallan." If I thought I was shocked at her suggestion of room service, then I'm flabbergasted now. "Yeah, and do you do a smorgasbord of some sort?" She listens for a few seconds, allowing me to run my eyes over her. "Yeah, that's great. Room 608. Just knock and leave it outside. Thank you."

She places the phone back before turning her eyes on me. The hunger in them makes my cock twitch. Fucking hell; I haven't had anywhere near my fill yet.

"You think we've got time for another before it arrives?"

"Too fucking right, I do." I hold my hand out for the condom, but she doesn't hand it over. Her eyes flick down to my hard length, and she licks her lips. "Be my guest."

I sit myself up against the headboard so I can watch, my hands hanging limp at my sides. She climbs onto the bed and sits across my thighs as she rips the packet open using her teeth and pulls the condom out. Her delicate fingers roll the rubber all the way down my length like a pro, and the gentle touch is enough to have me craving my next release like a fucking junkie.

Looking up at me through her lashes, she lifts up and guides me to her entrance.

We both groan as she sinks down on me until she's fully seated.

I want to say that I've missed this feeling, but if I'm being honest with myself, I'm not sure it's ever felt quite like this.

Her walls ripple around me before she sits up and places her hands on my shoulders to give her some leverage.

"Fuck," I groan as she almost releases me before sinking back down. "Harlow, fuck."

She keeps moving, both of us finding our rhythm. My hands roam up her thighs and clamp down on her hips to help move her. As she gets closer to her release, her head falls back and she arches, thrusting her tits towards me.

Releasing her hips, I take them in my hands, pinching

her nipples between my fingers and making her moan in pleasure. The soft mewl is like music to my ears.

"Oh God." Her hips circle, taking exactly what she needs to get herself off, her pussy squeezing me impossibly tight. "Corey," she cries as she begins tightening around me, her nails digging into the skin of my shoulders, dragging me right along with her.

Dropping one hand, I press my fingertip to her clit and circle at the same speed she is with her hips. Only seconds later, she clamps down on me and makes the most erotic sound I've ever heard as she falls over the edge.

She squeezes down on me so hard I've no choice but to give in to my orgasm. My cock twitches violently as I release everything I have on a loud groan.

She falls down onto me moments before there's a knock at the door. Both our chests heave as we fight to catch our breath and calm our racing hearts.

"Perfect timing, Brit boy." She winks at me before climbing off, swiping my shirt from the floor and going to collect our room service. Her legs look fucking unbelievable, sticking out the bottom of the fabric, and I can't help but stare as she bends down to pick up what's been left for us.

If I thought the sight of her from behind wearing my shirt was incredible, then it's nothing compared to when she comes back and walks towards me with the front hanging open, giving me just a hint of what I know is hiding behind it, the bottle of Macallan in her hand.

She twists the top and lifts the neck to her lips, taking a large swig.

"Mmm ... that's good." She holds the bottle out for me to have a drink. I almost pass it up to get another taste of her instead.

The rest of the night is a haze of sex, whisky, and

orgasms. I swear I've died and gone to fucking heaven with this woman.

It's almost dawn before we fall onto the bed after having christened the shower and washed away the sweat and scent of sex that was clinging to both of us.

I swear my head doesn't even hit the pillow before I'm out like a light.

WHEN I WAKE a few hours later, the sun from the curtains we were apparently unable to close properly in our drunken stupor burns into my eyes, making the pounding at my temples worse.

How much did we fucking drink last night?

Thoughts of the woman I got to know very well fill my mind, and I reach out to find her. What better way to push away this hangover than to slide inside her once again? Only, when I move my hand to the other side of the bed, I'm met with cold sheets.

Dragging my eyes open, I look over to confirm what I already know.

She's gone.

Motherfucker.

I roll onto my back and blow out a breath. So, this is how it feels to be the one who's humped and dumped.

Something pulls at my chest. I tell myself that it's just disappointment that I didn't get to start my day inside her, but the reality is that I'm mostly just disappointed she's not here.

I guess it's karma for all the women I've left barely minutes after getting what I came for. I can't say it doesn't sting, though.

With a sigh, I swing my legs over the edge of the bed and move to stand—only my foot doesn't hit the carpet first; it lands on the bottle of whisky. Reaching down, I lift it to find there's not a drop left. How the hell did she make it out of here without me noticing when we consumed the entire bottle between us? She must have been trashed. I know I was.

Placing it on the side, I notice all the empty wrappers and used condoms littering the floor.

A smile pulls at one corner of my mouth. She and all her belongings may be gone, but there's plenty to remind me that she was here, that last night wasn't just a very vivid dream.

I make the most of the shower that is significantly better than the one in my flat. It could be a while before I experience another this good, seeing as every penny I'm earning right now is going back home to my mum and sisters, and to pay for our night of passion. They need it more than I do. I tidy up the mess we made, and with one last look at the room where it all happened, I make my way down to reception to check out, leaving with only memories and a lingering hangover.

I have my credit card ready, hoping like hell it won't decline, but when I get to the front of the queue, I discover the room and our late-night delivery have already been paid for.

Feeling a little used and abused by the red-headed goddess, I head out into the late morning sun and set about finding myself some food.

9

———

HARLOW

I sit surrounded by white fluffy bubbles as the hot water burns my skin and tears track down my cheeks, but I don't cry. I can't. I'm numb.

My head throbs, reminding me of the colossal mistake I made last night and the whisky that fueled it. I never should have agreed to go to that hotel with him. Being inside that small room brought out a side of me that I'd rather never meet again. The weak girl who'd do anything for a distraction.

It worked. I forgot about my daily stresses, about what I'm about to face with my aunt, and my past that haunts every second of my life. All of it was gone with one skilled kiss and caress of his fingers. But that's not how it should be. That's how I used to deal with things. I'm stronger, or at least I hoped I was.

Everyone keeps telling me that I'm a different person now. But one thing goes wrong in my life, and I fall back into old habits. Habits that took too long to break and a lifetime to regret.

I'm done with regrets. I've got a truckload that weigh

me down on a daily basis. I do not need any more. Especially any that include a smooth-talking man with an addictive British accent.

Everything was fine until he rolled over and fell asleep, and all that was left was the girl I hated.

So, I did what I thought was for the best. I somehow got myself dressed and stumbled from the room. I liked to think it was somewhat elegant, but the reality was that I'd drank half a bottle of Macallan, so I probably bounced off each wall as I made my way toward the door.

I know what I was to him. A one-night stand. If he was interested in anything else, he wouldn't have taken me straight to a hotel room. He'd have brought me home, given me a kiss to remember him by, and asked me out on a date. But he didn't. He got me to the closest bed and allowed me to dive headfirst into the perfect distraction: alcohol and sex.

I'm such a fucking idiot.

"Harlow?" Brooke's voice calls through the house seconds after the front door slams shut.

I wasn't surprised to find it empty when the taxi dropped me off sometime before dawn. Brooke makes a hobby out of spending her weekends in anyone's bed but her own.

Her footsteps thunder up the stairs as she calls out again, and I know my solitude is coming to an end.

I rush to wipe the tears from my cheeks, expecting her to come crashing in at any moment. I don't think for a second that it'll cover up the fact that I've been crying. I'm sure my red-rimmed eyes will tell her everything in a flash.

She gets closer before the door handle twists and she pokes her head inside.

"Here she is. Did you have a—fuck, what's wrong?" She races over, sitting on the edge of the bathtub, her brows pulled together as she looks over my face, trying to find signs for why I'm so upset.

I blow out a breath as I try to figure out how to answer that question. Brooke has been by my side through everything. She knows all my dark and dirty secrets, but watching it is very different to actually experiencing it. She tries to understand, but it's hard. She can tell me all she likes that things are different now, that I'm different, but it's hard to believe it when I can so easily fall back into old habits.

"N-nothing. I'm just regretting last night."

"Do not tell me that he was bad in bed. That man screams sex god. If my sex-o-meter is off, I'm going to be seriously pissed."

"No, it's not that. He was ..." Her eyes widen in excitement. "Fine. I just shouldn't have done it."

She moves after a second and sits on the floor with her back against the wall.

"Why not? You deserve to have some fun. And it's not like you did it with some random guy who was only interested in one thing."

"Didn't I? I feel like I've just taken five giant steps back."

"Harlow, stop," she begs. "This is nothing like that. You are not that person anymore."

"I had a one-night stand in a hotel, B."

"You're making it sound like you did something seedy. You didn't. Corey wasn't just some random guy, and he clearly didn't just want to get his leg over and move on."

"How'd you figure that out?" I ask, interrupting her.

"Because he was at that bar thirty minutes after I messaged him. He wanted to see you again, even though you ran out on him the night before. If he only wanted a quick roll in the sheets, I'm sure there would have been some hussy he could have picked up without the threat of being kicked to the curb once again."

"I guess."

"There's no 'I guess' here. He wanted you. He jumped at the opportunity of a second chance."

"But he took me to the closest hotel with only one thing in mind."

"So? There could be a million reasons why he didn't take you elsewhere. He might live with his mother or something." I raise a brow at her. "Okay, yeah, he doesn't seem like a mommy's boy, but you never know."

"So, what are you suggesting here, exactly?"

"I'm saying you shouldn't write him off. Call him. See if he wants to meet up again."

"I don't think—"

"Don't forget him before you have any solid evidence. He could be the one—"

"I highly doubt that."

"You didn't let me finish. He could be the one to help remind you how good men can be."

I bark out a laugh and flick some bubbles at her when she stands and steps toward the door.

"I'm just saying, have an open mind. Everything happens for a reason. You fell into him for a reason."

She slips from the room, leaving me with that little bit of advice to dwell on.

I sink back into the rapidly cooling water and close my eyes. My head spins with everything that's happened in the last twenty-four hours. I should be focusing on my aunt right now, not have my head in the clouds over some Brit with a body built for sin.

BY THE TIME I emerge from the bathtub, the bubbles have long disappeared, and the water is uncomfortably cold.

I remove what's left of last night's make-up and cover myself in my favorite body lotion in an attempt to perk myself up a little before making my way back to my room.

I pull on a pair of leggings and an oversized hoodie with the intention of spending the day chilling out in front of the TV and hopefully catching up on some much-needed sleep.

As I descend the stairs, the familiar sizzle of frying bacon hits my ears seconds before the smell surrounds me. My mouth waters and I pick up my pace a little.

"Hungry?" Brooke asks when I join her in the kitchen and pull out a carton of orange juice from the fridge.

"Starved."

"That would be all the exercise you had." My cheeks heat despite the fact that she's not looking at me.

"Hmm ..." I mumble, pouring us both a drink and taking a seat at our table.

Brooke finishes up our sandwiches before placing a plate down in front of me.

"You do know that you're not getting away with it, don't you?"

"I don't know what you mean," I say with a mouthful of delicious salty, smoked bacon.

"I want all the details from last night."

"I already told you, it was good. Fun ... while it lasted."

"Oh, come on, you need to give me more than that."

"He was ..." I pause to think of the right word. "Mind-blowing."

She stares at me for a beat, and I can almost see the excitement building behind her eyes.

"You rode him all night long, didn't you?"

My face flames red. "Might have."

"Yes, get in there, girl!"

"What about you?" I ask, turning this on her, not wanting to give her a play by play of my regretful evening. "You've only just got in; how was your night?"

"It was fine." I narrow my eyes at her. It's so unlike her to withhold any details about her conquests.

"It was fine? Wow, he must have really rocked your world. Was it the guy you were dancing with?"

"No, he disappeared not long after you left. It was just some guy. There won't be a repeat."

"When is there?" I ask, pushing my empty plate away from me.

She shrugs, totally unfazed.

"So, have you decided if you're going to call him?"

I open my mouth to respond but soon discover that I don't have the answer—at least, not the one she wants to hear.

"I'm going to lie down. Leave the washing up; I'll do it later."

"That's it?" she calls as I leave the room. "Fine, run away." Her voice is light, but I can't help wondering how true her words are.

She ignores my parting comment, because by the time I get to the top of the stairs, she's crashing around in the kitchen, tidying up.

I don't make it to my bed. Instead, I come to a stop at my dressing table and fall onto my stool as I stare at the photograph of me standing with my parents and little sister when I was a kid.

Reaching out, I run my fingertip over each of them. I desperately try to remember what it was actually like to touch them, how warm their skin was, how they smelled, what their voices sounded like. Some days it feels like only yesterday they were taken from me, but others, I almost feel like I've lived my entire life without them.

My eyes drift to the frame slightly behind them of my aunt and me the day I graduated college—something I never thought I'd be able achieve during my last few years at high school. She was the only one who was able to break through the dark haze I was drowning in and make me look forward. I'll forever be grateful for what she gave me.

I blow out a breath, making the piece of paper stuck to my mirror flutter. I stare at the drawing I did so long ago.

"Today could be the day, you know." I didn't hear her join me, so the sound of Brooke's voice startles me.

I look over at her to find her resting her hip against the doorframe with her arms over her chest.

"Maybe," I say, but it's sarcastic at best.

"You should go and see Snake."

"Who the fuck is Snake?"

"The guy who inked Fletch and Reese. A few of the others, too."

"You are aware that they're going to take a restraining order out on you soon, right?"

"Ha ha, you're funny. I wasn't at the window watching or anything. Reese was telling me about it at work one day. I'll message you the address in case you get brave."

"Thank you." I'm not sure if I'm actually grateful or not. I know that I should either pluck up the courage and do it or just forget about it. Maybe having this address sitting on my cell will be the kick up the ass I need.

Deciding against lazing in bed all day, I pull my hoodie off, remove my leggings, and open my closet. I grab the first thing I put my hand on, a black T-shirt dress, and pull it over my head.

After running my fingers through my now-dry hair, I grab my purse from the dresser and slip my feet into my flip-flops. At the last minute, I turn and pull my sketch from the mirror, just in case Brooke is right.

"I'm going out," I say as I pass Brooke's door.

"Do you want company?"

"No, I need to clear my head."

"Okay, have fun."

I climb into my car and start the engine. The music is still on low after my devastating drive home from my aunt's yesterday.

Jesus, how was that only yesterday?

Grabbing my cell, I quickly shoot my aunt a text to check in with her before turning the volume up. I back off the driveway and press my foot on the accelerator.

I don't have a destination in mind—I just intend to drive until I feel the need to return home once again, but I'm not surprised when I pull up to a parking lot that I've become very familiar with over the years.

Ignoring the benches, I walk up to the top of the hill and drop onto the grass.

This is my happy place. The spot I come to when things in the town below get too much. All I can hear is the sound of birdsong and the very faint crashing of waves in the distance.

Lying back, I close my eyes and allow the afternoon sun to warm my skin.

I think back to last night and how easily I followed Corey to that hotel and cringe at my behavior. One suggestion of a good night and I follow his lead like he's the fucking pied piper.

My stomach clenches uncomfortably. I've spent years finding other outlets to help me deal with everything that happened, but one threat of losing another person I love, and I fall straight back into old ways.

I hate myself for it. It doesn't matter how many times Brooke tells me that it's different, that I'm different. I still feel the same as I used to back then after making yet another bad decision.

Children playing somewhere in the distance force me to sit up. I look down the hill slightly to see them running around and laughing. The sight is like a baseball bat to the chest.

This place is where my parents used to bring us to play. We learned to ride our bikes without training wheels here, we flew our kites, and it was where we'd spend hours chasing butterflies.

I sigh as tears burn the backs of my eyes. There are so many memories of them in this town that I've often wondered if I should have left, if it would have made it any easier. But then I think of Brooke and her parents, and my aunt. I could never leave them.

Without any family to take me in, I found myself being bounced around foster families and group homes after I lost them.

Each one was worse than the last. I'd assumed it was karma. It was my fault they'd died that day, so it was the universe punishing me for being so selfish.

My final family was totally different from any I'd experienced before, and I had no idea how to handle it. I'd left behind the ones who only cared about the money they got for taking in an orphan and found myself inside a loving one, which, for some fucked-up reason, genuinely wanted me there.

I couldn't believe it the day I was dropped off to find this lovely house with seemingly happy and normal parents. There had to be a catch. I'd spent the past few years in hell —enough to know there was *always* a catch.

But I was welcomed into their family as if I were their own and shown to a bedroom bigger than I'd experienced in a lot of years. It was unbelievable, but I couldn't handle it.

To this day, I have no idea why they put up with me. They did everything they could for me, but I pushed back at every opportunity. I'd skip school and end up being returned by the police when they found me off-my-ass drunk somewhere. I'd climb from my bedroom window to escape, to find a distraction I so desperately craved. I was the teenager from hell, I know that, but they stood by me, and Brooke and I struck up a sisterly bond that to this day hasn't been broken. We are the most unlikely of friends, but she's seen me at my darkest, and, just like her parents, she never let me go. For that, I'll forever be grateful.

The light wind blows and movement at my feet catches my eye. Reaching out, I pull the dandelion from the ground and hold it up in front of me, inspecting the seeds.

Sucking in a deep breath, I purse my lips and blow. The seeds are immediately released and dance off into the warm afternoon air, floating away to find a new life elsewhere.

My heart clenches at the same time my cell pings.

Pulling it from my purse, I find my best friend's name staring back at me. How does she always know?

Brooke: If you need me, call me x

Scrolling up slightly, I find the address she promised to send me.

Could I?

Her words from earlier come back to me. *Today could be the day, you know.*

Placing my cell back into my purse, I stand. After taking one last look around and breathing in the fresh air, I head back to my car.

The address is for the other side of town. I have no idea if they're open or where exactly it is, so I decide that while I've got nothing better to do, I'll have a little road trip before going home and getting another grilling from Brooke.

I stop off at a coffee place and grab myself an afternoon snack and one very strong cappuccino that will hopefully help keep me awake before I carry on.

When I get closer, I put the address into the GPS and allow it to guide me to my destination.

It has me pulling into a dark and dingy parking lot which looks less than appealing, but as I drive around, I spot the neon light from the studio in the distance.

Something flutters in my stomach, but I have no idea if it's nerves or excitement.

After killing the engine, I sit there staring at the tattoo studio for the longest time. I've learned the location—I could leave, knowing that one day, when I feel ready, I could return.

But that isn't what happens. Instead, I find myself pushing the door open and stepping out. I look around, feeling a little uneasy about the parking lot, before making my way toward the glowing sign. It looks familiar somehow, but I don't know where I might have seen it before.

A few doors down, there's a bar. The temptation to go and get a drink to give me a little courage is strong. That's exactly what the old me would have done.

I tell myself that I'm stronger, that all I'm going to do is go in and ask about getting an appointment.

As I get closer, a pink "Open" sign glows, putting an end to any chance I had of not being able to go inside.

I push the heavy door open, and I startle when a bell chimes, alerting whoever is here that I've joined them.

As nerves assault me, I glance around the space. There are huge black couches in the center of the room with an elaborate chandelier hanging from the ceiling, the light casting unique shadows around the walls that are covered in ink designs. But they're not like the ones I've seen before. There are no simple love hearts, or images of Tigger. It's artwork. I take a step toward one of the walls, my eyes not knowing which bit to focus on first as a heavy pair of footsteps approaches me.

When I turn around, I find a middle-aged man with short hair and quite possibly the biggest beard I've ever seen. Of course, he's covered in ink.

"Afternoon, how can I help you?" There's something in his voice that relaxes me immediately.

"Um ... I'd like to see about getting a tattoo."

"Well, you've come to the right place." He winks at me, and the twinkle in his eye makes me smile.

"I've got a little time now, if you'd like to discuss your plans?"

I start to believe that I can do this, that he'll be able to keep me relaxed enough to go through with something I've spent years dreaming about.

But then everything changes.

"Don't even think about taking her back to your room, Snake." My entire body jolts at the sound of his voice a beat before my skin erupts in goose bumps.

He's here.

My eyes dart around, but I can't see him. That doesn't

mean that my body doesn't immediately react to his proximity.

I back away from the desk, my heart pounding uncontrollably in my chest, my hands trembling.

Of all the fucking places for him to be, why does it have to be here?

Just when I thought I was going to take control of just a small part of my life, there he is, turning it upside down again.

Snake's chin drops as I move toward the door, but the second Corey steps out from the shadows, my body freezes.

"I've got this."

Snake looks between the two of us, concern written all over his face, and for a moment, he refuses to move.

"Snake," Corey barks, effectively forcing him to leave. "Well, well, well, look who it is."

Dread fills my stomach, thinking that he's angry with me for leaving like I did. I don't know why I care, and that pisses me off more than anything.

"I had a feeling you wouldn't be able to stay away."

"What? No, that's not what ..." He rounds the desk, his eyes running the length of my body. I can read his thoughts as if they're my own. He's imagining last night.

Fuck. This was a massive fucking mistake.

"I ... I ..." I stutter, wishing I was closer to the door so I could escape.

Sadly, Corey has other ideas.

"I think we should go and discuss that tattoo you want."

"N-No, it's okay. I just stopped in on a whim aaaand—" I squeal as his fingers wrap around my wrist, and he pulls me into him.

He stares at me for a beat before his head moves closer.

For a second I think he's going to kiss me, but then he moves to the side, so his lips brush my ear.

"I'm not letting you run so easily this time."

I try to swallow, but there's something clogging my throat.

"Come on." He doesn't allow me to argue. Instead, he tugs me toward his room, giving me no choice but to follow.

He shuts the door behind him, and I find myself in an almost identical room to the reception, only instead of a couch there's a tattoo chair. Artwork still covers the walls, and in my need to look away from him, to break what's crackling between us, I focus on it.

My eyes flick over the incredible work before landing on something very familiar. I remember tracing this heart engulfed in flames last night. It's on his chest. I reach out to run my finger over it, but his words stop me.

"I thought I was going to have to work harder to find you again. You really are making it easy for me."

"I had no idea you'd be here."

"Really?" he asks, his voice accusatory, making me turn to look at him.

His eyes are wide with suspicion, but they're also full of heat. My cheeks flush, my temperature soaring, but that's not the most noticeable thing. That's the desire that races through me, begging me to give him another shot.

My hands continue to tremble as my head and body war over what I should do. My head says leave, but my legs refuse, and I stay exactly where I am.

"W-why would I know you were here?" I ask, confused. Clearly, last night's whisky is still having an effect, because it should be obvious.

"My job isn't a secret, Harlow. Most people here know what I do."

The image of Brooke so helpfully giving me this address pops into my mind.

She fucking knew.

"I've been set up, haven't I?"

"I don't know. But I'm glad to see you." His expression softens, giving me little choice but to believe him.

"Really? Why?"

He takes a step toward me and doesn't stop until I bump up against the wall and he's right in my personal space. His woodsy scent fills my nose, and the heat from his wide chest burns into me.

"Because we have unfinished business."

"D-do we?" I thought my actions this morning would have drawn a line under anything between us. Maybe I was wrong.

"I woke up this morning with one thing on my mind. But when I opened my eyes, you weren't there."

His eyes search mine. I have no idea what he's trying to find, or if he manages it or not. To be honest, I think I'd rather not know.

"Our time was done."

"Huh," he says, taking a step back and turning away from me. "I thought maybe I'd left a little more of an impression on you than that."

I miss his closeness the second the cool air surrounds my body.

"It was what it was," I admit, regret flooding me.

"An hour or so ago, I was on my way to believing that. But now here you are. Do you believe in fate, Harlow?"

"Yes."

"Well then, we clearly aren't done, are we? Now, you came here for a reason, and I'm more than happy to give you what you need. Hop up on the chair."

"No."

"No?"

"I ... um ... I'm not sure about ..."

"Do you know what you want?"

"Y-yes but—"

"Do you have a reason for it?"

"Yes."

"A reason good enough that you'd never regret it being permanently on your skin?"

"Yes."

"Good. Now, hop on," he repeats.

I take a hesitant step toward his chair as he drops down onto a little wheeled stool. His jeans stretch across his wide thighs before his inked arms rest on his knees as he waits for me to make a decision.

I've wanted this tattoo for years. I know I'd never regret it. But one, I'm scared of the pain, and two, I'm even more scared of the man who might deliver it.

"Jesus, Harlow, it's like I've just committed you to the death sentence. I'm not going to force this thing on you. I've got plenty of other uses for this chair, you know."

I run my eyes over the black leather and picture myself laid out on it while he ... *Nope, stop it.* Those kinds of thoughts are not going to help right now.

I sit on the edge, as far away from him as possible. He chuckles at my attempt to keep some space between us and rolls himself over until his knees cage my legs in.

He drops his hand to a lever beneath his ass and lifts, so our eyes are in line.

"So, what did you have in mind?"

My breath catches at his deep, rumbling voice. He almost makes me forget my reason for coming here in the first place.

"I've ... um ... got a drawing."

"You really have planned this."

"It's been some time coming," I admit. "I'm scared of needles, so I usually run out of the studio before I get that close."

"It's probably nothing like you're expecting." His large, burning hand lands on the bare skin of my thigh. "I can't promise that it won't hurt. But I've got ways of making up for it after." His hand pushes higher.

Desire burns through me, and I have to bite back the suggestion of forgetting the tattoo so he can just distract me instead.

No, Harlow. Not again.

What is it about this man that makes me forget everything I've tried so hard to overcome and throw myself head-first back into a life I regret?

It's not the same. You are not the same. He wants you, and not just for a quick fuck. Brooke's voice pops into my head.

"What do you want from me?" The question is out before I even realize it. Embarrassment burns my cheeks as his eyes widen in shock.

"I ... uh ..." He hesitates as he tries to figure out where I'm going with this. "Honestly," he says, holding my stare, "right now, I'll take whatever you'll give me."

10
___

COREY

"Right now, I'll take whatever you'll give me." I rear back a little. Did those words just actually come out of my mouth?

Fucking hell. Get your shit together, man.

She stares back at me, shadows clouding her eyes, but they lighten slightly as my words register.

If I had time to think about an answer, I would have told her that I just wanted a little more of last night. That's what I'd usually say, and all I'm usually willing to give, but my subconscious has clearly decided that's not everything I'm willing to give this woman.

"So ..." She hesitates, and I hate that I'm making her question herself right now. "You didn't just want me for one hot night?"

"Fuck," I grunt, remembering last night and just how hot it really was. Do I want more of that? Fuck yeah. But is that *all* I want?

The fact that I'm asking myself these questions pisses me off. I should be screaming that yes, sex is all I want. It's all I've got the time and energy for. But the thought of her walking away because that offer isn't good enough has me panicking. Last night wasn't enough, I've come to terms with that, but I'm not in a place where I can seriously consider anything more.

"If you're asking if I want a repeat, then hell yeah. Last night was mind-blowing. If you're asking if that's all I want, then … honestly, I don't know. My life is … complicated."

"Right." She pushes to the edge of the chair, and I panic.

"But …" She looks up at me, hope filling her eyes, "I'd like to spend more time with you," I admit, and really, it's not hard to do so. This woman is pretty incredible. On the outside, she seems like one thing, but close that bedroom door and she's someone else entirely. I can't lie and say I don't want to find out exactly what makes her tick.

"Not just in the bedroom?"

"Shall we do what we need to do here, then I'll take you for dinner. How's that sound?"

A smile tugs at the corner of her mouth before she remembers something. "I might run before we get that far."

I lean forward, both my hands running up her thighs, my fingers dipping under the hem of her dress and whisper, "It's okay, I've locked the door." I must admit that it comes out sounding a little more sinister than I was expecting, but when she shudders beneath my palms, it seems she took it as intended.

She nods, turning to her bag beside her.

I sit back as she pulls a battered piece of paper from inside and unfolds it. She stares at it for a moment before finding some courage and passing it over.

I love nothing more than doing a tattoo for someone that means something. Some of them are so personal that it's like they're exposing a piece of themselves to me just for that small amount of time, even if they're too scared to do it to anyone else. And that's exactly how I feel when I take hold of the paper.

I didn't need to hear the conviction in her tone when she responded to my question about this being important to her earlier. I could sense it.

I hold her eyes for a second before ripping them away and down to her drawing.

It's a dandelion with the seeds drifting off, nothing too out of the ordinary, but as I look closer, the seeds that are flying away have names in them.

Looking back up at her, I find tears pooling in her dark eyes.

"It's okay. I'm not going to make you talk about it if you don't want to. I'm not a therapist, although not all my clients are aware of that," I add, thinking about the weird and wonderful things people have told me over the years.

"I'm sorry," she says, looking to the other side of the room and lifting her hands to wipe her eyes.

"Hey, it's okay." Reaching out, I gently press my fingers to her cheek and move her eyes back to mine.

"We don't have to do this now if you don't want. We could always plan it for a future date." The fact that I've just offered to date this woman in a roundabout way isn't lost on me, but it doesn't panic me like I thought it might.

"No. I need to do this. I've run scared too many times. And ... rightly or wrongly, I trust you."

My chest constricts at her words, making my breath catch. I haven't heard those words for years, and they take me back to a time that needs to stay locked in the box I've put it in.

Swallowing the lump she's caused in my throat, I focus on the task at hand.

"Okay, so where are we doing this?"

"On my back, up my spine, with the seeds on my shoulder blades."

"That's probably going to hurt."

"I know. I can handle it. Just promise me you'll be gentle."

My eyes bounce between hers. "Always."

"So ... what's next?" she asks nervously.

"You're going to need to show me some skin." I wiggle my eyebrows as a wicked grin curls at my lips.

"Ah, I see. This is all a ploy to get me naked again."

"It's your fault. You could have asked for it on your leg."

She stands before me, my knees still either side of hers. There are only inches between us, but it seems her inner goddess has found its way past the nerves.

Wrapping her fingers around the hem of her dress, she pulls it upwards.

I'm powerless but to watch as she reveals her perfect, milky skin to me. Biting down on my bottom lip, I run my eyes up the curve of her hip, over the black lace covering her and up her slim waist.

My cock swells as she lifts it higher, revealing her bra-encased breasts. I curse the padding that's stopping me from seeing her perfect rosebud nipples. I bet they're pert right now.

As the fabric clears her head, her red hair falls back down around her shoulders.

The silence in the room is heavy as we stare at each other with chemistry crackling between us. She's right there in touching distance. All I'd have to do is lean forward, and I could feel her soft skin.

"C-Corey?" The slight waver in her voice proves that she's maybe not as confident right now as she appears.

"Fuck." I scrub my hands down my face and over my rough jaw.

"Don't you want to ..." She reaches for her dress that's been discarded on the end of the chair.

"No," I say, standing and wrapping my fingers around her wrist, stopping her from picking it back up. "I'm just really fucking glad Snake didn't get to do this."

I lean forward and she gasps, her pupils dilating. I know she thinks I'm about to kiss her, but as much as I might want to do exactly that, I know I can't. Not yet, anyway. I've got a job to do, and I need to keep my head in the game and not just think with my cock.

Reaching out, I hit the button on the chair to flatten it.

She jumps in front of me as the movement startles her.

"Lie down on your front," I whisper in her ear. She shudders as my breath tickles down her neck, and goose bumps prick her skin.

"O-Okay," she breathes.

Reluctantly, I take a step back and watch as she does as I say. My fists clench with need, but I stay put. I've got a job to do. So what if I want to fuck my client into next week? I'm a professional.

She pulls her hair over her shoulder and looks at me. I drop my eyes down her back and stop on her lace-covered arse.

Jesus fucking Christ. Why couldn't she have at least been wearing trousers? I hate to do it, but I turn around and grab a blanket that I've got folded up on the side. I shake it out and cover her from the waist down.

"I don't want you getting cold," I mumble as an excuse. Of course I want her to be comfortable, but this is as much for my own comfort as it is hers.

With her eyes still on me, I make a show of rearranging

myself just so she knows exactly what the sight of her almost-naked body does to me before turning around to sort out my kit.

I'd tidied up after my client left, thinking that I was done for the day. How wrong I was.

After settling myself beside her, I look over her smooth, flawless skin. Excitement tingles just below the surface. I love getting my hands on a virgin.

"I'm glad I get to be your first," I murmur, much to her amusement. "So, starting here," I press my finger against the skin of her lower back, and I swear to fucking God that an electric current shoots up my arm. If her surprised gasp is anything to go by, I'd say she felt it too. "And then finish about up here?" I walk my fingers up her back and delight in the shudder that runs through her.

"Y-yes."

Let me stencil it on and you can check that you're happy.

"No," she blurts, making she pause. "Just do it. I trust you."

My heart beats a little faster as her words settle into me.

"You're going to need to stay still."

"Then you'd better stop tickling."

Silence descends as I get her ready for the needle.

"Did you draw this?" I ask, looking at her sketch.

"Yeah. I know I won't be winning any awards anytime soon."

"I've seen a lot worse," I chuckle, picking up my machine and turning it on. She tenses beneath me at the sound. "So, if art's not your thing, what are you good at?" I ask, hoping I can distract her a little.

"Um ... I'm not sure I have a talent, to be honest. Ow, fuck," she moans as I touch skin for the first time.

"I'd beg to differ. I think you're very talented."

"I'm not sure that's a compliment," she mutters.

"Why not? I think you're a fantastic dancer." She laughs, and I'm forced to stop what I'm doing as her body jiggles. The soft sound is too good to make her stop.

"Shit, I'm sorry," she says when she realises she's making my life hard.

"Are you doing okay?"

"Yeah, I'm not regretting it yet."

"Life's too short for regrets." I don't know why I say it, because the reality is that I spend most of my days drowning in mine.

"So you'd think." The sadness in her voice pulls at something inside me.

"Sorry, I fucking hate that saying."

"Me too."

We both fall silent while a million questions hang in the air between us. I can see in her eyes that she wants to ask about my regrets just as badly as I want to know about hers. I might have suggested one date after this, but I've certainly not signed up for all the feelings and shit, so I force my mouth to stay shut, no matter how much I want to get to know what she's hiding.

It's two hours later when I finish off the drifting seeds and write names into three of them.

"Who's this for?" I ask, although I'm not sure it's a really good idea. If she wanted to talk, surely she'd have offered up the information?

"My parents and my sister. They were killed a few years ago."

"Fuck. I'm sorry."

She shrugs. "It is what it is. Nothing I can do about it now."

"Ain't that the fucking truth," I say, thinking of the people who I've lost that had a hand in my move over here. "What doesn't break us only makes us stronger."

"Jesus, you're all about the one-liners today, huh?"

"Can't help myself. That one I kinda believe in, though."

"Me too. So now what?"

I blow out a breath, thinking of what I'd really like to do with her laid out here before me. "I can show you, and then we wrap it and go for dinner."

I push my kit to the side and hold my hand out to help her up.

The sight of her in her underwear threatens to floor me, just like it did when she first pulled her dress off.

"Over here." I pull her to stand in front of the mirror and grab another to hold behind her.

"Oh my God," she gasps when she gets her first look at her ink.

"It'll look better once your skin settles." Where she's naturally so pale, the redness around the ink looks extra angry right now.

"It's incredible, Corey. Thank you."

Lowering the mirror, I give in to my need to touch her. I step up behind her and place my hand on her waist, meeting her eyes in the mirror. They're full with tears, but delight sparkles within them.

"Is it what you imagined?"

"No." My heart drops that it's not what she wanted. "It's better."

"Yeah?"

"Yeah. Thank you so much. And it wasn't as scary as I thought it might be."

"I've got magic fingers. That's why." She chuckles but soon stops when I move them across her belly.

"Corey," she half-warns, half-moans.

"Do you have any idea how sexy you are?"

"On the verge of tears with a raw back? I'm sure I'm anything but sexy."

"That's where you're very, very wrong." My fingers drop to the edge of her lace knickers, and her eyes narrow. "Last night wasn't enough," I whisper in her ear, edging my fingers lower.

"Corey," Her voice is barely a whisper, so the last thing I expect is for her hand to wrap around my forearm to stop me.

"H-how much do I owe you?"

The question damn near gives me whiplash.

"Uh … n-nothing."

"You're not doing it for free."

"You can buy dinner."

Taking a step back and turning into the room, I put some space between us. By the time I look back at her, she's holding her dress against her front, seemingly shy all of a sudden.

"Let me wrap that and you can get dressed."

"Your artwork is stunning," she muses as I work. "I'm assuming you've drawn all this?"

"Yep, all mine."

"Have you always been an artist?"

"No, actually. I was in the army. I only got into this because of a friend. He used to spend all his time drawing when we were on tour together. I loved art in school but never really thought about it as a career. He gave me one of his sketchbooks and I've never looked back."

I focus on wrapping her up and not thinking back to those times. They only make my chest ache with loss.

"Okay, you're good. Let me tidy up and we can head out."

"You've got no more clients today?"

"Nope, just one earlier before you showed up."

"Brooke gave me this address," she admits. "I'm assuming she knew you'd be here."

"For someone who apparently wanted me, she's doing a good job of pushing us together."

"She's a good friend."

"So, you're admitting that she's doing the right thing?"

She blows out a breath. "I have no idea. She wants me to ..."

She trails off like she's not going to explain, and I can't help prompting her. "To ..."

"Live, be happy, take some risks."

"And I do all of those things?"

"You can certainly help. I'm the only one holding me back."

"Why?"

She pauses as I put my last few bits away. When I look up, I find her hovering by the door, chewing on her bottom lip, deep in thought.

"I—" she starts, but I cut her off.

"You don't have to tell me. I was just being nosey. Shall we ..." I gesture to the door at her back and follow her out.

Snake is back at the reception desk, faffing around with something, when we emerge.

"Was he gentle with you, sweetheart?"

"The perfect gentleman."

I think about how I almost had my fingers between her legs and smile to myself.

"I'm glad. You happy with the result?"

"It's perfect. Thank you for your help earlier."

Snake nods at Harlow before turning and winking at me.

"I'm done for the day. See you in a few?"

"Sure thing, man. Enjoy."

I wait until the door shuts behind us before wrapping my arm around Harlow's waist and pulling her into my side. I drop my lips to her ear, and she shudders at my closeness.

"I'm not sure I've ever been described as a perfect gentleman before."

"I was just being polite."

I bark out a laugh. "I was going to say—if what happened in there was me being a gentleman, I'd hate to know how other men treat you." She tenses in my arm, and I panic. "I … uh … didn't mean …" I'm not entirely sure what I'm going to say, but thankfully, she cuts me off.

"It's okay. And you were a gentleman. Mostly. Where are we going exactly?"

"Do you have a car?"

"Yes."

"Fancy a drive?"

"Sure."

She leads me to a silver Audi, but instead of going for the driver's side, she opts for the passenger door.

"You can drive, right?" she asks when I hesitate.

"Yeah, of course. I just wasn't expecting to."

"Well, you know where we're going." She shrugs and drops down into the seat.

"What if I'm a terrible driver?"

"Only time will tell."

I rev the engine and back out of the space.

I navigate us out of town before pulling onto the freeway and gunning it.

"Holy shit," she squeals, her fingers wrapping around the edge of the seat, her nails digging into the leather.

I put the windows down and breathe in the fresh ocean air as we head towards the shore and bark out a laugh. I've been dying to do this since I arrived, but it's kinda hard without a vehicle.

I feel her stare. It burns into the side of my face, but I keep my eyes on the road, not wanting to kill us both before we've managed this date.

"What?" I ask when her attention stays on me.

"Nothing. Just watching you enjoying yourself."

I fill my lungs with air once more and appreciate everything I've got here. So what, I can't afford this month's —or last month's—rent? I've got a perfectly good studio to sleep in. It'll get better once Mum and my sisters are sorted. I'm meant to be here. It feels more like home than London, or England, for that matter, has done in a very long time.

"You like seafood?"

"Love it."

"Good. I know the most incredible place."

I turn her radio up—not because I don't want to talk, but because I want to relax and enjoy the moment. I'm not sure I'm going to feel this free again for some time, so I need to make the most of it.

11

———

HARLOW

I might only be able to see him in profile, but it's enough to know that the smile on his face would knock the wind out of me if I were to see it face-on.

We're only in the car for a short time, but it's enough to know that he really needed it. By the time he pulls off the highway and into the parking lot of a small surf shack, the muscles in his shoulders have relaxed and he has a totally different aura about him. Yeah, he's still the cocky Brit I first met, but it's like the ocean breeze coming from the windows blew down a couple of his walls—or at least I hope that's the case, because I'm dying to find out more about this man.

"They do the best seafood in all of LA."

"Is that right?" I ask, climbing from the car and looking out over the bright blue ocean beyond. It's a sight I don't think I'll ever tire of.

"I don't know," he laughs. "I've not been here long enough to test out all the competition, but it's pretty bloody fantastic."

He jogs around the car to meet me, and, to my surprise, he laces his fingers through mine.

Was Brooke right? Is he in this for more than just a good time?

After opening the door, he gestures for me to enter. My eyes widen as I step inside.

"Oh wow, this was not what I was expecting," I breathe as I take in all the sports memorabilia covering the walls. All of LA's teams are represented, but none more so than the LA Vipers.

"It's a surf shack with a difference," Corey says, standing close enough behind me that his breath rushes over my ear, sending a shiver down my spine.

I'm still distracted with the decoration when a woman approaches. I don't pay her much mind until she speaks.

"Corey! I was beginning to think you'd abandoned us," she says with a friendly smile on her face, her eyes fully focused on his.

Something stirs deep in my belly. Something I don't like, and something I certainly shouldn't be feeling.

"Just been busy—you know how it is," he says nonchalantly, although his attention remains firmly on hers.

"Sure do. Things still going well down there?"

"Yeah, it's doing good. Harlow, this is Kat. Her dad owns this place."

"Hey," I say politely, forcing a smile onto my lips.

"Table for two?"

"Please," Core says, placing his hand on my lower back. A move that Kat clocks, but she doesn't look pissed or jealous. Just ... happy.

"Right, this way then."

We follow her out onto the patio area, and she seats us at a secluded table in the corner.

"I'm assuming you'd like a beer and ..." She looks to me,

but despite the riot of emotions bubbling up inside me, she doesn't look anything but professional right now.

"A rum and Coke, please."

"Perfect. Here are the menus—not that he needs one. I'll be back in a few moments."

"Thank you," we say in unison as she disappears around the corner.

Silence falls between us as I battle to banish the jealous that erupted from nowhere.

He's not yours, Harlow. Reign it in.

Corey's brows pinch as he studies me, already able to read me well enough to know something is wrong.

"This place is nice. How'd you find it?" I ask, hoping to distract him from asking questions I don't want to answer.

"One of my first clients recommended it. I've been addicted ever since."

"I can see why."

Silence returns with only the chatter of the other patrons and the crash of the waves below filling our ears.

"So, how come you left the army?" I ask, needing to know more about him and how he came to be here.

"Medical discharge."

"Oh?"

"We ended up somewhere we shouldn't have been. Things didn't go too well. Only a few of us made it out."

"I'm so sorry."

"It is what it is," he says, using my line from earlier. "I lost some great friends that day. But it got me back to civi life."

"You didn't want to be in the army?"

He looks out to the ocean, getting lost in his memories. "I didn't have a lot of choice. The day I was born a boy, my dad decided I'd follow in his footsteps and enlist the second

I left school. He had dreams of me becoming an officer, making a difference to my country and all that."

"You weren't interested?"

"It was more that I didn't want to do what I was told," he says with a laugh. "I can't say I never would have signed up of my own accord—it was in my blood, after all. My father, grandfather, and great-grandfather were all military men. But I didn't take well to being told."

"I can understand that."

"So, what about you? Have you always been a hockey fan?"

A soft smile plays on my lips.

"No. I was a teenager when Brooke and her father opened my eyes to it. It was a few years later that I knew I wanted a career that allowed me to give back to the community."

"Because of losing your family?" Corey guesses.

I nod as a lump of emotion crawls up my throat.

"I can't imagine how hard that must have been."

I shrug, not really wanting to talk about it when we should be enjoying ourselves. Thankfully, Kat chooses that moment to reappear with our drinks and take our orders. I haven't even glanced at the menu, so when Corey immediately places his order, I ask for the same, trusting that he knows what's good.

"So, why LA?" I ask once we're alone again, hoping to turn the conversation away from my past. Nothing good can come from that.

"I needed a chance, and the lure of the sun and the ocean was too much."

"Fair enough." I can't really argue; we do live in a beautiful place.

The meal is incredible, just like Corey promised. The

conversation between us after touching on our pasts was light, and just being with him made me feel so comfortable. As we make our way out, I can't help butterflies erupting in my belly. What's next?

His fingers lace with mine, but no words are said between us. Knowing that he's also lost people he loved helps me understand why we might have the connection we do. Unlike most people I meet, I think he actually understands. I know it's not unusual for people to have lost their parents young, but the way it happened isn't all that common, or for them to all be wiped out at the same time. Everyone is sympathetic, but they don't get it, not really. Even Brooke, who lived through some of the aftermath with me, can't possibly understand.

We climb into the car and Corey heads back onto the highway. Silence fills the space, but it's not uncomfortable—totally the opposite, in fact. If anything, his presence is soothing.

"I ... uh ... don't know where I'm going," he says after a few minutes.

"Hang on." I wake up the GPS and hit the home button so he can follow it before sitting back in my seat and watching the sun setting into the ocean.

"Penny for your thoughts."

I sigh and turn back to look at him. The concern on his face makes my breath catch. His brows are pulled together, and there are creases in his forehead.

"I was just thinking about what you said about it being a great place to live," I lie.

He's silent for a beat, and I worry he's about to tell me I'm talking shit. Thankfully, after he turns back to the road, all he does is agree.

"Thank you for today. I never would have thought it, but it was exactly what I needed."

"Oh yeah?" His familiar cocky smirk appears, making his dimple pop up.

"I'm sorry I left like I did this morning," I say, addressing the elephant in the room.

"I'm sure you had your reasons, although I do hope they weren't due to my performance."

His grip on the wheel tightens until his knuckles turn white, and heat floods my core knowing that he's reminiscing about our time together.

"I don't think your ego needs me to tell you that wasn't the reason."

"It always likes being stroked."

"Oh my God," I laugh. "I'm sure it does."

He reaches over and places his large, burning hot hand against my thigh, and I tense.

"Relax," he mutters when he feels my muscles tighten beneath his touch.

"I'm sorry."

"Get out of your head and enjoy yourself."

"Trust me when I say that I've done that more in my short time with you than I've done in the last few years."

"Really?" he asks, glancing over, a smile twitching at his lips.

"Really."

"Then I think we should definitely spend some more time together."

"How'd you figure that?" I ask with a laugh.

"I'm clearly good for you."

"Hmmm ... so, what are you suggesting?"

"Another date? Say, Friday night?"

"I'll need to check my calendar. I might already have one."

His eyebrows rise in surprise. "Oh, I wasn't aware I was one of many of your conquests."

"Never assume, Brit boy. Never assume." I hate to make out like I might be playing the field when it's the furthest thing from the truth, but I'm happy to keep him on his toes.

He glances over as we turn into my street. His eyes are darker than before, but I can't get a read on him as to why.

He brings my car to a stop outside my house and pulls his cell from his pocket, hitting a few buttons before pushing it back inside the fabric of his pants.

I hesitate, not sure if I should get out or wait for what he has to say.

I'm about to reach for the door handle when he turns to me.

My breath catches at the look in his eyes. There's a familiar desire dancing in them, much like when he looked at me in only my underwear earlier, but there's also a hint of anger in them.

My stomach clenches for the briefest moment as I wonder if I've got him all wrong.

"I strongly suggest you cancel your Friday night plans."

"Oh," I squeak. "Why's that?"

"Because you're mine."

"Am I?"

"You are." His hand comes up, his fingers wrapping around the nape of my neck as he leans closer. Our noses brush before his lips tease mine. The touch is so light, yet it sends a shockwave through my body, causing my temperature to soar. My skin tingles for more, to feel his hands all over me once again.

"Corey," I moan when he doesn't move to kiss me properly.

"Mine," he whispers against my lips, his breath almost burning hot against me.

My heart pounds, trying to escape my chest as I wait for him to deepen the kiss, but it never comes.

After a beat, he frees me from the confines of the seat belt and pulls away. He climbs from the car like that moment between us didn't happen before walking around to my side and opening my door.

He holds his hand out, and although I don't want his help after the way he just teased me, I'm powerless but to slide mine into his larger one just to feel him once again.

Something happens when we touch, something I can't describe, but I know it's powerful enough to have me addicted.

I allow him to pull me from the car and slam the door behind me before he pins my hips against it. Movement from my left catches my eye, but I ignore our one-woman audience. I'm too consumed by the man who's pressed up against my body and stealing all my air.

"I'm so glad you found me today," he admits, his voice deep and gravelly as his dark blue eyes stare down into mine.

"It seems the universe—or Brooke—wants us to be together."

Something flickers in his eyes at my words, but he doesn't give me a chance to ask. "It seems that way. And who would we be to deny the universe what it wants?"

His hand slips up the length of my neck before his fingers tangle in my hair. He grips and tips my head back slightly so I'm at the perfect position for him.

"Friday night can't come soon enough," he mutters before his mouth crashes down on mine.

My lips part the second his tongue seeks entry, and I can't help a groan rumbling up my throat when they connect.

I sag back against the car, relying on his body to hold me up, and he renders me useless with his intoxicating kiss.

My head spins as he consumes me. His fingers grip tighter on my hair, his hard length pressing against my hip and driving me crazy with need.

His hand slips down from my waist and hooks my leg up around his hip. It causes him to press exactly where I need him.

Knowing how easily he could make me fall completely under his spell is like a bucket of cold water. I pull my leg from his grasp and press my palms against his solid chest.

He pulls back and looks down at me. His pupils are shot, the blue almost swallowed by the black of his desire.

"Harlow?" His chest heaves as he tries to catch his breath.

"Friday night?"

"Y-yeah. Can I ... call you?"

I nod, heat creeping up my neck. I was just basically dry humping him against my car for all my neighbors to see. Why is it that the suggestion of him calling me turns me into an excited teenage girl with her first crush?

"You can."

A car pulls up somewhere behind us, and, after a quick glance at it, Corey's focus is back on me.

"That's my Uber."

"Okay."

"Thank you for today. It was ... unexpected. From beginning to end."

A chuckle falls from my lips as he steps back and turns toward his waiting car.

"Hey, Brit boy," I call.

He looks back at me over his shoulder, a panty-melting smile on his face. A bolt of lust hits me as his eyes drop to my body.

"Sneaking out this morning might have been the best thing I've done in my life."

His smile lights up his entire face. He knows as well as I do that if I were still in that bed when he woke this morning, none of this would have happened.

"Until Friday."

I nod and smile at him, dizzy with excitement. It's a feeling that's eluded me for a very long time.

After watching his car speed off, I push through the front door before falling back against it and giving my heart a second to slow down.

"You're welcome," comes from the living room where I knew she was watching. I can't help but laugh. "Did you have a good afternoon?" she asks, appearing in the doorway.

"What do you think?"

"Well, from the fact that I just watched your little porno in the driveway, I'd say yes. But I never know with you."

I swat her shoulder as I walk past her and directly to the kitchen for a drink. I know I'm about to get a Brooke grilling, so I need a strong one.

I'm pouring the rum into my glass when I sense her behind me.

"I can't believe you sent me there, knowing he'd be there."

"I didn't know for sure. I was just hoping."

"You're an interfering whore, you know that?"

She barks a laugh. "Guilty as charged. But wasn't it worth it?"

My cheeks heat, knowing what she just witnessed.

"It was okay, I guess."

"Okay?" she echoes incredulously. "He had you pinned to the car. I thought I was going to combust just watching you. How you allowed him to walk away, God only knows."

"We've had a really great day. After he inked me, he took me for dinner at a surf shack by the ocean."

"Whoa, hold up a minute. You let him do it? Let me see. Let me see."

Putting my drink down, I lift my dress to show her my back.

"Ouch, that looks sore."

It's only as she says it that I feel it. "I had a good distraction."

"True that. It's stunning."

"He's really talented."

"Oh yeah? Tell me more about those talented fingers."

"Nothing happened beyond what you just saw."

"But you've been with him for hours—practically naked, I'm assuming, to get that done. How—"

"Because it was the right thing to do. This might sound crazy to you, but we just spent time together. Actually got to know each other."

"You make me sound like a sex maniac."

I raise a brow at her.

"What? I have more than first dates."

"When?"

"Err ... about four months ago."

"And you came home complaining that he was too boring because he didn't try to touch you up after date two."

"Well, he didn't. I like to know what I'm working with and if they're good in the sack."

"Whatever," I mutter, pushing past her in favor of the couch.

"So, are you seeing him again?"

"Friday night."

She squeals in excitement as she curls herself onto the other couch where she must have been before we interrupted her evening, if her half-empty bottle of wine is anything to go by.

"Book Friday off. I'm not working, so we'll spend the day getting you date ready."

"I can't, I've got too much to do."

"Too much to get a fresh wax?"

I throw a cushion at her and turn the TV up in hope of drowning her out.

"Don't do this to me," she warns. "I tell you all about the guys I spend time with."

I groan. Don't I know it.

"I don't ask for most of the shit you share, B."

"Maybe not, but I was hoping to get the same in return when you eventually found someone."

"I wouldn't describe one date as 'finding someone.'"

She shrugs. "Not important. Is he as perfect and dreamy as he looks?"

"He's a good guy."

"A *good guy*? My dad is a good guy. James," she says with a sigh, naming the LA Vipers head coach, "is a good guy. You gotta give me more than that. Does he give you tingles when he says your name in that accent?"

"Tingles, yes," I admit, much to her delight. "And I don't know him well enough to give you much else."

"You've seen him naked. What more do you need to know?"

"You're a fucking nightmare."

12

COREY

"What the fuck is up with you?" Oz asks after seeing his afternoon client out of the studio.

I wasn't aware that how I was feeling was written all over my face.

"I've got a date tomorrow night," I admit.

"Yes, man. Get in there. Wait ... why is that making you look like someone just drowned your puppy?"

"I've never been on one before, let alone planned one."

"Huh." He drops down on the sofa in front of me and puts his feet up on the coffee table. "So, I'm assuming you want to end the night fucking this girl?"

I open my mouth to respond. Usually, I wouldn't hesitate in giving anyone the details of my plans for ending the night, but with Harlow in mind, it seems wrong.

"I wouldn't be against it."

"Oh fuck, man," he says excitedly.

"W-what?"

"She's got you fucking whipped. Is this the girl Snake was telling me about?"

Fucking hell, I forgot those two spend their time

gossiping like they're at a fucking Women's Institute meeting.

"Yes," I admit reluctantly.

"So, is she your forever girl, or what?"

I sit forward, my eyes wide. "Definitely *or what*. There is no forever girl for me. I don't sign on to that shit."

"That's what we all say, until she sucks you in and never lets go."

I think about just how tight she sucked me in on Saturday night. She definitely made her mark on me, that's for sure.

"Anyway, what's she like? Is she a party-all-night kinda girl or a quiet, romantic dinner and stroll on the beach kind?"

"Dinner and beach," I say without even having to think about it. I might have met her twice in a club, but anyone with eyes could tell it's not her ideal night out.

"Find a nice restaurant, something fancy. Treat her. Then take her to the beach once the sun is setting and see what you can get in the dunes." He wiggles his eyebrows suggestively.

"Is that how you got JJ?"

He barks out a laugh. "No, that girl wouldn't know romance if it hit her in the face."

I can't really say I'm surprised; she definitely isn't the kind who'd expect flowers every Friday night. "Glad I didn't ask her, then."

"You'd get nowhere, man."

The door chimes and Oz's next client walks in.

"You need any more help, just shout." I nod as he walks off to his room, trailing behind his client.

My head falls back on the cushion. I feel totally out of my depth right now. If it were anyone else, I'd have bailed, but there's something about Harlow. Even after not seeing her for four days, my skin still tingles with awareness when I think about our parting kiss. There's no question in my mind that I want to spend more time with her. I just somehow need to figure out a way to not let her get the wrong idea about what I want. I'm all for enjoying ourselves, but there will be no serious future between us.

I don't do promises, and I certainly don't do forevers.

I'M STILL in the dark as to what to do when evening rolls around, and if I weren't so desperate to see her again then I'd have cancelled already. Oz texted me some restaurants to check out after his client left, and when I looked them up, my eyes almost popped out of my head at the prices. I can't afford shit like that, no matter how incredible Harlow might be. By the time I finish up for the night, I'm not exactly in the mood to head to my aunt and uncle's for a family dinner I agreed to weeks ago.

I call myself an Uber and head to their side of town. They live in the picture-perfect house with a wraparound porch and swing seat out the front. White picket fence and all. It's the exact kind of upbringing I'm sure I'd have loved. My aunt and uncle are both incredibly kind and gentle people—unlike my father who's an uptight, controlling arsehole.

I walk up their driveway to find my uncle's arse sticking out from their campervan.

"Corey, there you are. Sandy was starting to think you'd bailed on her lasagne."

"Never," I say with a laugh, thinking of the home-cooked food I'm desperate for.

He pulls me in for a one-armed man hug, allowing me to see the inside of the camper. It's almost in its original state. It's like a time-warp.

"Whoa, this is impressive," I say, continuing to look around.

"Yep, she's a beaut all right."

"You getting ready to take her out?"

"I wish. We haven't had a chance to get away in months. I feel guilty she hasn't moved an inch off the drive."

Ideas start popping up in my head, but when my aunt spots me from the kitchen window and comes running from the house to pull me into her arms, I soon get distracted.

"It's so good to see you," she cries as she flies at me.

She's a petite woman, and her arms barely close around my middle as she holds me.

"The LA sun looks good on you, boy."

With one final look at me, she pulls me inside, telling me that Milo is already here. We find him in the kitchen, prepping a salad to accompany the lasagne. This house is covered in his accolades, from winning a championship in high school to the day he got drafted to his dream team.

It's clear how proud of Milo they are, and it makes my heart ache every time I see it.

No matter what path Milo chose in life, they'd have supported him without question.

"Hey man. How's it going?"

"It's good. Quiet. Looking forward to the season starting and getting back at it."

"You're gonna kill it. Gonna watch you lift that trophy, man."

"Here's hoping."

Spending time in this house is a reminder of the kind of family life I'd have loved as a kid but never got to have. We never had one home. We were dragged from military base to military base, mostly across Europe, wherever Dad was posted, and we just had to make the best of it—until we started secondary school. Then, we were abandoned in London at a private school and mostly left to do our own thing. There were certainly no family dinners or enjoying each other's company after that.

We sit and chat as the food is laid on the table, and I eat as if I haven't done so all week, much to their amusement.

We chat about our lives, and they ask about the studio as if they really care. It makes me regret not wanting to come. I always tell myself it'll be just like being with my family, but it's never anything like it, and I always enjoy their company.

"Did you have fun at Milo's birthday Friday night?" my aunt asks.

"Yeah, I've been meaning to talk to you about that," Milo muses, his eyes locked on me.

A knowing smirk appears on his lips, ensuring his parents give me the same attention.

I was waiting for this. Not for a second did I think that Brooke would have been able to keep her mouth shut about Harlow and me spending time together.

"Oh?" both my aunt and uncle say at the same time.

"How is the lovely Harlow?"

"I ... uh ..." My aunt's eyes widen at the possibility of me finding a girlfriend. "I haven't seen her since Sunday."

"So I heard. I also heard that you've got a date tomorrow night and that she has no idea what you have planned."

"She's not the only one," I mutter as they all stare at me. "I was actually going to ask you for a favour," I say, looking at my uncle.

"Go on."

"You said your camper hasn't been out. I wondered if I could possibly borrow it?"

He opens his mouth, I'm assuming to deny me his beloved baby, but my aunt beats him to it.

"Of course, sweetheart. It's just sitting on the driveway doing nothing."

My uncle narrows his eyes at his wife, but all she does is laugh.

"Come on, I'll show you around." She winks at me. "These two can do the washing up."

A few hours later, I leave my aunt and uncle's house, driving his beloved camper with a smile on my face.

This is going to be perfect.

HARLOW

This week at work with my upcoming masquerade ball is crazy. It almost means I forget about the fact that I hear nothing from Corey until almost midnight on Thursday, by which time I'd pretty much decided he'd bailed and that anything between us was done. It was probably the way it should have been. I have enough on my plate with my aunt's health and work, but I couldn't help but be disappointed.

I look down at his message again.

> Brit Boy: Be ready for seven. I'll pick you up.

That's it. No other instruction, no hint as to what we could be doing. Nothing.

"So ..." Brooke says, staring into my closet.

"I don't know. I'm sure whatever we choose will be wrong."

"Choosing something that will make you look like sex on legs could never be wrong."

"This is a date, not a hook-up."

"They can be the same thing. You want to be prepared for the best outcome, always."

"Just grab me a denim skirt and top."

"Har—"

"No," I say, holding my hand up to halt her. "You can do the hair and makeup. I choose the clothes."

"Fine, fine," she concedes, pulling my favorite skirt from the closet, closely followed by a couple of tanks.

"Black and this," I say, grabbing a light floral cardigan.

"Okay, yeah. That's cute."

"Thank you."

I allow her to curl my hair, and to my delight, she doesn't go too heavy-handed with the makeup for once.

I sip away at an overly strong rum and Coke Brooke made to help settle my nerves, but when my head starts to swim before he's even here, I regret it.

I want to make decisions I won't regret in the morning.

The beeping of a horn has us both jumping up. Brooke runs to the window like someone set her ass on fire.

"Oh my God," she gasps.

I take a step toward her, but she pulls the curtains closed so I can't see anything.

"No, go and meet him and find out for yourself."

"But—"

"Nope. No buts. Just go and enjoy yourself."

I blow out a breath in the hope it'll calm my racing heart. It does nothing.

"Okay. I've got this."

I'm almost at the stairs when I hear her again

"Have you got condoms?"

I don't answer, although my cheeks do heat as I recall sliding a box into my purse earlier today. Like the man said himself: always be prepared.

My legs are like jelly as I make my way to the front door, my heart hammering in my chest.

Pulling my purse up higher on my shoulder, I open the door and close my eyes for a beat in an attempt to prepare myself for what's waiting for me.

"Oh my God," I breathe, repeating Brooke's reaction. I can honestly say that this was the last thing I was expecting to see.

I step from the house as Corey drops down from the driver's seat of the vintage Volkswagen camper. But the second he emerges, the vehicle vanishes into the background. All I can see is him. He's wearing a skintight white T-shirt that stretches across his wide shoulders and shows off his pecs and abs to perfection. My mouth is watering long before I drop my eyes to take in his denim-clad thighs.

When I find my way back up to his eyes, he seems to be looking at me with a familiar heat in his blue depths.

"Hey," I say, dragging his attention back to my face.

"Hey yourself. You look stunning."

My cheeks burn at his compliment. "T-thank you. You don't look so bad either." He smirks, and I swear his cheeks heat a little. "So, what are we doing?"

"Fancy a little drive?"

Excitement races though me. I've always wanted to have a camper vacation but never had the chance. The trips we had when I was a kid were usually abroad in fancy hotels. I've never done anything like this—well, aside from passing out somewhere random in my former years that I'd rather not think about.

"Yes," I squeal, moving for the passenger door.

"Let me," Corey says, reaching for the handle and opening it for me like a gentleman.

"Thank you."

I strap myself in as he jogs around to the other side. Movement in my bedroom window catches my eye, and when I look up, I find Brooke still watching us. She makes a heart gesture with her hands before blowing me a kiss.

He backs out the drive, turning the music down a little so we can talk.

"Does she interfere with every part of your life?" he asks with a laugh.

"She just wants me to be happy. Have you had a good week?" I ask, not wanting to talk about Brooke and her best intentions right now. Wanting to know why it took him until Thursday night to message is much more pressing.

"Yeah, really busy." He chats away about some of his clients. The passion and enthusiasm for his job is infectious. "I had dinner with Milo and his parents last night. Seemed he knew all about us."

My heart thuds in my chest. Does he think there is an us?

"I'm not surprised. I'm sure we were the hot topic of conversation at the arena."

"Fantastic," he mutters lightheartedly. "What about you? Any epic fundraisers on the horizon?"

"Yes, actually. I have a ball coming up. Black ties, ballgowns, silent auction, the whole shebang."

"Sounds impressive."

"It's my first big event. I've only done a few fun runs and some work with the local schools so far. I'm kind of terrified."

"It'll be amazing."

"Reese is supporting me, and she's incredible. It should raise a lot of money for the Foundation, if it goes to plan." I tell him about the team having to attend along with longstanding season ticket holders and other wealthy figureheads in the community, as well as the entertainment for the night as he drives to wherever it is we're going. I don't bother asking; I trust him.

We approach the ocean at roughly the same time we did on Sunday night. The sun is beginning to set, casting a gorgeous orange glow across the bay.

The beach is almost empty, just a couple walking along the water's edge and the odd surfer attempting to catch the last of the sunlight.

Corey drives the length of the parking lot before continuing onto the sand.

"Are we allowed to drive out here?"

"Do you always follow all the rules?"

"Uh ... yeah, actually."

"Well, maybe it's time to reconsider. Things can be much more fun when you break them."

"You'd better show me, then."

He glances over, mischief dancing in his eyes, and a wave of desire hits me.

He pulls the camper to a stop on a secluded bit of the beach. The few people we could see when we first arrived are no longer visible, making it seem like we're the only ones here. It's a heady thought, knowing that we're totally alone once again.

"Do you want to eat inside or out?"

I glance over my shoulder at the stunning old-fashioned fittings, but as tempting as they are, I want to watch the sun make its final descent for the day.

"Outside. Definitely outside."

"Come on, then."

He hops out of the camper before coming around for me, but my feet are already heading for the sand below.

His need to help must get the better of him, because he steps forward and wraps his arm around my waist. Our chests crash together, his hard lines against my soft curves, and I just about manage to swallow the groan of pleasure that threatens to rumble up my throat at his contact.

Slowly, he lowers me until my feet hit the ground.

"I've been looking forward to this all week," he whispers, his deep voice hitting right between my legs.

"Oh, and here I was, thinking you'd forgotten."

"Never. You're all I've been able to think about." To make his point, he presses his already hard length against me.

"Oh," falls from my lips, but it's no more than a breathy whisper.

"Every time I look at my chair, I see you laid out on it in your underwear. I'm pretty sure the guys I've seen this week all think I'm gay."

I can't help but bark out a laugh. "Whatever turns you on, Brit boy."

His hand slips around the back of my neck as he drops his head slightly. Desire pulls at my lower stomach, and I lick my lips in preparation for what I hope is going to come.

"You, Lo. Only you." His lips brush mine, as my stomach flutters with the way he says that nickname, but he doesn't give me what I need.

When I give in to temptation and move toward him, he pulls back, a wicked smile playing on his lips.

"We should eat."

He takes a huge step away as I fall back against the van, trying to catch my breath, and drag my head from the clouds.

I stand, feeling a little lost as he grabs a few things from the back of the camper and places them down on the sand.

"Help me with this," he says, holding a blanket out toward me.

I grab one corner, and together we shake it out and set up our picnic. He places a wicker basket in the center before throwing a couple of cushions down and re-emerging from the camper with a chilled bottle of wine.

He passes it over, and the label makes my heart race. I feel ridiculous that the sight of a bottle of wine can affect me, but I can't help it.

"D-do you have anything else to drink?" I ask, wishing I could just suck it up and enjoy it.

"Oh shit, I'm so sorry. I forgot you don't drink it."

"I-It's not that. It just reminds me of my parents." My cheeks flush, feeling ridiculous.

"Oh ... um ..." He jumps back into the camper and pulls out a bottle of rum.

"You brought some as well."

Heat creeps onto his cheeks. "I was trying to be all romantic and shit."

I can't help but chuckle. "Everything is perfect, Corey."

"I borrowed my aunt and uncle's camper and made a picnic. It's not exactly the date of the century."

Once he's settled beside me, I reach over and place my hand over his.

"It's perfect."

"Really?" He glances over at me, and I love the little bit of vulnerability in his eyes.

"Really."

We fall silent for a few seconds as a young family walks across the beach. We're not close enough to hear what they're saying, but I can't help smiling as I watch their toddler attempt to chase their dog.

Corey sighs, dragging my attention back to him. "Hungry?" he asks before I can ask if he's okay.

"Starved."

He opens the basket and reveals the contents. Bread from a deli, cheese, meats, olives. It's almost a replica from our midnight snack at the hotel, and my cheeks heat as I remember eating some of that from his body.

Jesus, I was such a hussy that night.

Noticing my flushed state, he lifts the hem of his shirt, cheekiness twinkling in his blue eyes. "Want a repeat?"

"A plate will be fine, thank you." I lean forward to take one of the plastic ones he brought out, and he drops his shirt. It's a shame, but I'm on my best behavior tonight.

"I'm pretty sure you concluded that anything would taste better if my abs were the plate."

"I did not say that," I mutter into the palms of my hands as I try to hide my embarrassment.

"I guess you'll have to do it again to test it out. Here." When I part my fingers and look, he's holding out some bread for me.

"You know, I don't do what happened on Saturday night."

"You don't have sex? I think you'll find you do. And I can also confirm that you're really quite good at it."

"Quite good?" I ask but regret the question the second it passes my lips. "Forget I asked that. And no, I meant I don't go to hotel rooms with guys I've just met."

"You didn't just meet me. We met the night before."

"You know what I mean. I just needed you to know that it's not something I make a habit out of. I'm not a ..."

"A...?"

"Slut," I mumble around a bit of my bread.

He shakes his head. "That's not ... no, Harlow. Just no.

If I had any questions about your morals or behavior, do you think I'd be here right now?"

I shrug. He has a point.

"I just needed to get it off my chest."

His eyes drop to my breasts at my words, his pupils dilating as if he's remembering what they look like with no clothing covering them.

"I could sure use you getting something else off your chest." His voice is low, and it causes all kinds of flutters to erupt down below.

"Eat up. If you're lucky, you might need your stamina later."

His eyes fly back up to mine, a smirk spreading across his lips. Placing his food onto the picnic blanket, he leans over, resting a palm beside my hip and forcing me to lower my plate as he closes the space between us.

The fingers of his other hand gently brush against my cheek, sending a shiver down my spine. His eyes stare deep into mine. It's like he sees me—the real me, cracks, dents, regrets and all—despite the fact that he's barely scratched the surface of my life.

"You're incredible," he muses, his eyes bouncing between mine. "I've never had a first date before." His admission hits me right in the chest. How? How is that possible? "So, rest assured that if I didn't want to be here right now, if I had any doubts about you, then I wouldn't be."

"Y-you've never had a date before?" I ask, utterly astounded.

He shakes his head.

"Why?"

He opens his mouth to respond but must change his mind at the last minute because he closes it again.

"It's okay," I encourage, desperate for him to open up just a little. It's totally hypocritical of me, because I'm not exactly an open book.

He sits back, sucking in a fortifying breath. "I'm not looking for forever, Harlow," he admits as he stares out to ocean, his voice a little colder than before. "I'm not some kind of Prince Charming that you're going to be able to gallop off into the sunset with."

"But—"

"No. No buts. It's who I am. I can't be tied down."

"Why?"

He closes his eyes and drags in a deep breath. For a moment, I don't think he's going to respond, but then his lips part and he confesses, "Bad shit happens to those around me. I'm like a fucking curse that doesn't stop striking. I refuse to drag anyone else into my fucked-up life."

He pulls his knees up and rests his arms across the top as he focuses on the waves crashing.

"I'm no princess, Corey."

The silence hanging between us is heavy, yet the pull I feel toward him never dissipates as he loses himself in his own head.

Pushing my plate aside, I do the only thing I can think of to drag him back from wherever he's gone: I gently lift his arms and nudge his legs down before straddling his lap.

I take his cheeks in my hands. "Did you hear me?" I lean forward, the tip of my nose brushing his. "I said I'm no fucking princess." I squeal as his hands grab onto my ass. He flips me over and stares into my eyes for a beat before crushing his lips to mine.

His kiss is hard, passionate, frantic, as if he just can't get enough of me. I take everything he gives as my fingers grip tightly to the fabric at his back.

Our tongues duel and our teeth clash. I completely forget that we're in a public place where everyone can see, and I lose myself to this tormented man.

He might think he's a curse, but he has no idea that I'm the true poison here. But I fear that now I've had a taste of him, I'm not going to be able to release him.

When he eventually pulls back, both our chests heave for air as our breaths mingle. He stares down at me from his position with his hands either side of my head.

"Fuck," he barks. "Why are you so fucking tempting?" I expect him to kiss me again, but I'm disappointed, because, after running his thumb along my bottom lip, he falls to the side and pulls me into his body.

His fingers trail around the softness of my stomach as we lie in silence. It's not like it was earlier; it's now comfortable with desire crackling between us. That kiss was amazing, but it was nowhere near what either of us needed.

"This is why I moved here," he suddenly says, breaking the silence. He nods towards the empty beach and the orange and yellow sky. "I craved this kind of peace. This solitude. I had to get away, and here seemed like paradise."

"And how's it working out for you?"

"Good and bad."

"How's that?"

"Turns out you can't run away from problems or nightmares. They follow you wherever you go."

I may not have moved all that far from when I was a child, but I still know exactly what he means. "It doesn't matter how much you try to drown them out, either. They're always there."

He looks down at me, and I'm powerless but to turn to him.

He searches my eyes as if he's trying to find something. "You know. How do you know?"

"A lifetime of mistakes."

"Tell me about it," he says sadly, dropping back onto the blanket and resting his arm on my stomach. Together, we stare at the sky as it darkens, and the twinkling stars appear.

"Harlow?" he whispers so quietly I almost think I imagined it.

"Yeah?"

He twists so he's on his side and staring down at me once more.

He bites down on his bottom lip as he considers his question, and I want to release it and bite on it myself. Lust shoots down my body as I remember what those lips are capable of. Of how alive he made me feel.

"Spend the night with me?"

My lips part to answer, but no words come out. Instead, my mind goes crazy.

He's already admitted he doesn't do forever. Is this just a fancy hook-up? Was this date just a way to ensure I'd get in his bed?

"It's okay. Forget it. Let's just take you home."

The thought of leaving him is worse than any of my previous concerns. If I go home, I get to climb into my cold bed and let my mind run crazy with thoughts of what could be. Or I could go with him and take a chance. The kind of chance Brooke has been begging for me to take for years.

"No. I want to stay with you."

The muscles in his neck ripple as he swallows.

Leaning forward, he captures my lips, proving just how right my decision is.

14

COREY

I glance over at her as I drive the camper back to my flat. She says she's no princess, and she's right. She's a fucking angel.

She should have run at the first hint of the darkness that follows me around, yet she's here, holding my hand as I drive and agreeing to spend the night with me.

Going back to my place could be a mistake. All my shit is in boxes. It's nowhere near a home. But I can't bring myself to go back to her house, knowing that we'll have company. I need this woman all to myself. I need her in my bed.

We pull up outside my building, and I park in my allotted space, which is a novelty.

"Stay there," I warn, jumping from the camper and jogging around to her side.

I pull her door open and step up to her.

"Last chance to change your mind."

She shakes her head, a shy smile playing on her lips. My cock swells, knowing just how those full lips feel wrapped around it.

"Argh, Corey," she squeals as I lift her from the seat and throw her over my shoulder.

Slamming the camper door, I march toward the building.

"This isn't necessary," she shouts as I unlock the front door and head for the stairs. "Your neighbors will think you're abducting me."

"Let them."

I run my hand up the back of her exposed thigh and enjoy the feeling of her shuddering in my hold.

When she crawled onto my lap earlier, it took all my restraint not to take her right there and then, where any fuckers could have walked by.

She deserves more than me. It's one of the reasons I admitted what I did. I don't want to put her off, but equally, I need her to know what she's getting involved with. If she's got images in her head of a white wedding, a picket fence and two point five kids, then she really needs to walk away.

I know the pain that comes with plans like that falling apart, and I refuse to put myself in that position again.

Alone is better.

No one can leave.

No one can betray you when you're all alone.

I carry her up to my flat as if she weighs no more than a feather before finding my keys and letting us in.

The second we're inside, I kick the door closed and drop her to her feet. She wobbles a little and takes a step back while all the blood rushes from her head.

"That really wasn't necessary." Her eyes hold mine, and I'm grateful she didn't look around the place the second she opened them. I'm ashamed that I've been here all these weeks, yet I have no real home to show of it.

"I haven't got much to offer, but would you like a drink?"

I take a step toward her, and she takes one back, a teasing smile playing on her lips.

"No."

"No?" I step toward her again, and she takes another back until she bumps up against the island.

"No."

"Well, I don't have a TV, so that's out. Is there anything else I can interest you in?"

Her eyes drop from mine in favour of my chest, and, in my need to get closer, I lift my arm behind me and drag my shirt up and over my head. Her eyes feast on me, getting darker and darker by the second.

She bites down on her bottom lip as I step right up to her. Her soft breasts brush against my chest, and my cock hardens for her.

"Corey," she moans, reacting to the simple touch in the same way.

"What is it you want, Lo?"

"Y-You."

"Fuck."

Taking her cheeks in my palms, I tilt her head back and slam my lips to hers. They part immediately, her tongue coming out to dance with mine as if she's as desperate for this as I am.

It's been almost a week since I was inside her, and that's too damn long. She's been the only thing I've thought about since I met her; not having her again was never a question.

My hands drop to her arse so I can lift her onto the counter. Her legs wrap around my waist, lining us up perfectly, and we both moan into our kiss, desperate for more.

I push the fabric from her shoulders before wrapping my fingers around the bottom of her tank and pulling it up her body.

Our lips part, but only for a second. The moment the fabric is clear of her face, she's reaching for me once again.

I kiss along her jaw and down her neck as I palm her still lace-covered breasts. She moans above me as I pinch her already pert nipples through the fabric.

My name is a plea on her lips, and it makes my head spin with desire.

"Fuck. I need you."

"Yes. Yes," she chants as I slide my palms up her thighs, taking the fabric of her skirt with them until it bunches around her waist.

"These are pretty," I say, running my finger over the damp lace between her thighs as she squirms about on my kitchen counter.

"Oh God. More. Please." Her legs widen as she tries to find my friction.

"That's it, my little goddess," I encourage. "Tell me what you need."

"I-I need you. I need everything."

Slipping the fabric aside, I run my finger through her wet folds, and her head falls back in pleasure. Making the most of the opportunity, I fix my lips to the sensitive skin of her neck and suck and lick as I slide my fingers deep inside her.

"Oh God. Oh God."

With a hand on the small of her back, I slide her forward to allow me to push up higher into her. I want to find the spot that makes her scream.

"Corey," she cries when I hit it and start to up my tempo.

I kiss down her chest and over the swell of her breasts, but I need more. Releasing the clasp of her bra, I watch in delight as the fabric falls from her body, revealing her tits to me. I waste no time in leaning forward and sucking one of her rosy, pink peaks into my mouth.

She tastes even better than I remember. I lick and bite while I fuck her into a frenzy.

"Come for me, Harlow," I demand between kisses. In only seconds, her walls clamp down around my fingers so tightly that it makes my cock weep, and she cries out my name into my empty flat. Suddenly, this place doesn't feel so cold, so depressing. She's only been here a few moments, yet she's already brought colour and life into a place I avoid at all costs. It's a stark reminder of my reality. I might look like I'm living the high life in LA, running Zach's newest studio, but the man behind that mask is a very different story.

She's barely come down from her high when I pull her into my body. Her legs automatically wrap around my waist, and her arms cling to my shoulders as I move us toward the back of the flat and my bedroom.

Once again, she doesn't take any notice of her surroundings as her lips land on my rough jaw and kiss down my neck. She grinds her hips, knowing full well that she's pressed up tightly against my length, and a growl rumbles up my throat.

The second we're in my room, I throw her down on my bed and watch as she bounces a few times before I reach out to remove what's left of her clothing.

"I need you naked. Now," I warn as I pop the button on her skirt and drag it down her legs. Her knickers follow, leaving her gloriously bare and waiting for me. "Much better."

She pushes herself so she's sitting and resting back on her palms, allowing me the time I need to get my fill, although I already know it'll never be enough. I could stare at her all night, but I know the second she leaves in the morning that I'll want to do it all over again. It's fucking unnerving.

Before I'm ready, she scoots over to the edge of the bed. I want to tell her to go back, but the moment her fingers brush the skin above the waistband of my jeans and boxers, all thoughts leave my mind.

"I think it's your turn, don't you?"

I open my mouth to reply, to tell her that I want nothing more than to watch her suck my cock deep into her mouth once again, but all words leave me when she releases my jeans and pushes everything down my hips. My cock springs free and she licks her lips as she stares at it like it's her next meal.

She doesn't bother fully removing my remaining clothes. Instead, she wraps her fingers around me and leans forward.

"Fuuuuuck," I groan as she licks the tip of me. I thread my fingers into her red hair and hold her in place. Her huge, chestnut eyes find mine, and something happens in my chest. Something that tells me that I'm never going to be able to let her go.

Fuck.

My thoughts are lost when she leans forward, sucking my length into her mouth. I hit the back of her throat before she pulls back and licks around the tip once again.

"Fuck, Harlow." She smiles around me at my praise and, thankfully, keeps going.

Long before I'm ready for it to end, my balls draw up

and my cock twitches violently in her mouth. She doesn't miss a beat in swallowing me down.

Fuck, this woman has me on my knees, and she has no idea.

Unable to bear not touching her, I crawl over her body, forcing her to scramble up the bed.

"You're right," I mumble against her neck.

"Oh yeah?"

"You're not a princess. No princess sucks cock quite like that."

She barks out a laugh, the sound making tingles erupt in my body. "Have a lot of experience with that?"

"Oh yeah. I was a regular at Buckingham Palace, back in the day." I tickle down her side and she squirms beneath me.

"I can just picture you having afternoon tea with the Queen."

Looming over her, I take one of her nipples in my mouth before kissing down her stomach.

Pushing her legs wide, I lick up her seam as she sighs in pleasure.

"I much prefer dirty princesses." The vibration of my voice makes her moan seconds before I seal my lips around her.

She's crying out once again in seconds. It seems sucking me off got her all worked up.

No sooner has she come down from her release than I grab a condom from the bedside table and slide into her scorching, wet heat.

Now this place really feels like home.

"PROMISE ME SOMETHING," I ask when we both fall onto the bed with heaving chests after our second round.

"Sure."

"Promise me that you'll still be here in the morning."

She turns to me, her dark eyes going all soft. I hate that my words might be giving her ideas about the future, but for the first time in my adult life, the prospect of waking up to a woman doesn't freak me the fuck out. The last thing I want is her running off again. I'd much prefer her to be right here so we can start our day properly.

"O-okay."

"Yeah?"

"Yeah. You'd better make it worth my while though," she says with a wink, making me laugh.

"Oh, you can fucking guarantee it."

Rolling her over, I press my lips to hers. If she thinks she's sleeping yet, then she needs to think again.

15

HARLOW

A pain in my side drags me from my sleep. I blink a couple of times in the darkness, trying to figure out what it was and where I am. When it happens again, everything comes back to me.

"No," Corey cries, his arms flailing around like he's trying to grab something. "No, let me help. No, let me go." His voice is deep with emotion as he continues to fight his imaginary demons.

I scramble so I'm sitting on my knees beside him.

"Corey," I say gently, reaching out to touch him.

He throws his arm around once more and it connects with mine, making it go dead immediately. Understanding the pain he's in right now, I rush to try to drag him from his nightmare.

My heart aches for him that whatever it is that causes shadows in his eyes during waking hours also disturbs his slumber.

"Corey," I repeat louder in the hope of dragging him from his nightmare. "It's okay." I put more pressure onto his chest as I shake him awake.

"I'm sorry," he mumbles, his voice broken and distant. "I'm so sorry."

"Are you awake?" I ask, although I'm not surprised when he doesn't respond. That apology wasn't meant for me. It's for whomever he's dreaming about.

I lie back beside him once he's settled, but I can't switch off. Just those few simple words from whatever is haunting him stir up memories of my own. Of the people I couldn't save and who only found themselves in danger because of me.

A sob rumbles up my throat as my loss hits me full force. I'd hoped that after all these years it would have been easier, but it never is. I came to the conclusion a few years ago that the pain and regret are just something I'm going to have to live with for the rest of my life.

Pushing myself from his bed as quietly as I can, I grab one of his shirts that's been abandoned on the floor, but before I pull it over my head, I gather it in front of my nose. His smell takes me back to being encased in his arms as I drifted off to sleep last night. I've slept in a bed with other people more times than I can count, but I've never fallen asleep in a man's arms like that before.

It was as comforting as much as it was unsettling.

I've only known this man a week, yet he's somehow managed to wriggle his way behind the armor I wear on a daily basis. He's becoming an addiction I'm not sure I want to break anytime soon.

I look over at where he's sleeping. He's on his back with one arm thrown over his head. His lips are parted, and his dark eyelashes rest on his cheekbones. One leg is out of the covers, revealing the mass of ink down almost the entire length.

Dropping the fabric so his shirt falls around my thighs, I

walk over to him. I may have seen him naked on two occasions now, but I've never really had the chance to study his art. As I get closer, I notice something that's passed me by the last two times. The tattoos on his left leg aren't just artwork. I drop to my knees, feeling like a bit of a creep for studying him when he's unaware, but the rippling and stretching of the skin beneath the ink draws me in.

There are scars, and a lot of them.

I gasp at the severity. He's done a fantastic job of covering it. You'd never know from a distance that anything was amiss. Hell, I didn't notice, and I've slept with him twice. The artist that did all of this is incredible. There's a Union Jack, dog tag, a gun, and other army paraphernalia inked onto his leg along with a series of names. Most of the ink is in black, but laced through it all are bright red poppies and the script *Lest we forget.* My breath catches and tears burn the backs of my eyes at what he must have been through.

Standing, I silently back away from him and leave the room. When he told me about being medically discharged last weekend and losing some of his guys, he said it so lightly that I didn't really think about what that meant. But seeing that has reality crashing down. No wonder he's so closed off about love and his future. He's probably just trying to get through each day. My nightmares must pale in comparison to the things he's seen, the things he's experienced.

The small hallway is void of any furniture or possessions, and I wrap my arms around myself as I make my way down to the kitchen and living area.

I didn't have a chance to look at my surroundings when we first arrived here last night. I was too consumed by him. But now I see that this apartment isn't a home. It's just a place he exists in.

I chew on my bottom lip as I look around the bare space. There's an old couch and coffee table in the middle of the living area along with a small, empty bookcase. There's no TV, no photographs or ornaments, any of the things that turn a place into a home.

It's just empty. Cold. Sad.

A shudder runs down my spine despite the warm morning sun beginning to pour through the curtainless window. I take a step closer and inhale a deep breath. At least he can see the ocean from here.

With a sad sigh, I turn back to the kitchen. The only thing on the counter is a coffee machine. A small smile creeps onto my lips. I'm glad he has some priorities right.

I pause at the hallway and listen to see if he's awake, but when I hear nothing but his soft snores, I continue to the machine that's calling my name.

I stare at it, figuring out how it works before setting about finding a pod and a mug.

Pulling the first cupboard open, I find it empty, and the next, and then the next.

Corey's been here a couple of months. How has he lived like this?

I locate a solitary mug and place it under the machine before starting on my quest for pods.

As expected, the first few drawers are empty, but then I pull one open that has a few bits of paperwork inside. I'm about to shut it, not wanting to pry, but at the last minute the large red eviction notice stamp catches my eye.

Unable to help myself, I pull the letter out.

It's dated three days ago and has an eviction date of Friday.

I look back to where he is when I hear a noise before

quickly shoving the letter back where I found it. The last thing he needs is to catch me prying.

Suddenly the emptiness of the place makes sense. He's getting ready to leave. But why is he being evicted? He's got a good job. His eyes light up when he talks about it and his boss back in London. He's told me that he's getting paid well for setting it up like he has.

I stand motionless for a few minutes as everything settles in my head.

Something's not right here.

I desperately want to ask him about it, but I can't. It's not my place or my business. We've slept together twice, and he's already made it abundantly clear that there is no forever option here.

My need to help nags at me, but it's not my place. I barely know the guy.

Going back to my original mission, I locate the coffee pods and get the machine started. I definitely need caffeine now.

I take my mug and curl myself into the corner of the couch, staring out at the deserted beach beyond. I love my house, but a view of the ocean sure would make it better. I love watching the waves crash in. I could lose a lot of hours if I had it on a daily basis.

I have no idea how much time passes before I hear Corey padding down the hallway, but the mug in my hands is long empty and I'm starting to get a stiff neck where I'm craning slightly to get the best view.

"I thought you'd left again," he says, dejection clear in his tone, and it throws me for a loop.

Last night he was telling me he doesn't do forever, then he's disappointed that I might have left. Surely that's exactly what someone who isn't looking for long-term wants, right?

I sigh, feeling like I'm already spinning out of control with my confusion. But I really don't want to be one of those women who asks questions like 'where is this going?' because I already know the answer.

"Sorry, I couldn't sleep."

"Am I that bad a bed mate?" His voice is lighter as he jokes, and it makes me wonder if he remembers his nightmare.

"No, not at all."

"I see you found the coffee machine."

"It wasn't hard; there's nothing else in here."

"Yeah," he says, rubbing at the back of his neck. "About that ..."

"Are you moving?" I ask when I get the sense that he needs an out.

"Uh ... yeah, something like that."

"It's a shame. This place is nice. Great view." I nod toward the window.

"The bedroom has a balcony."

"Really?"

"Yeah."

"Well, what are we waiting for? Let's go have coffee out there."

"We'll have to share. I've only got one mug."

I shrug, passing him the empty mug in my hands.

I stand and take his hand as he walks away with his shoulders lowered.

"Hey," I say, stopping him in his tracks. "I don't care about this place."

"It's not exactly the kind of home I wanted to bring you back to."

"I didn't come back for your apartment, Corey. I came here for you."

"Yeah?" The beginnings of his signature smirk start to appear on his lips.

"Yeah. Maybe we should forget about coffee. I can think of something I want more."

He abandons the mug in the kitchen as we pass before taking both of my hands in his, and he begins walking us backward toward the bedroom.

Yeah, the coffee can wait.

IT'S two hours later before we're both dressed, and I manage to get him out of the door for breakfast.

"Do you have any preference?" he asks as he threads his fingers with mine and pulls me toward the stairs.

"Nope. I don't know this side of town very well. Where's good?"

"I know just the place."

Ignoring the camper that's sitting in the parking lot, we head out on foot. We walk in silence. I'm desperate to ask about his nightmare, but I'm scared how he might react. I know from personal experience that someone bringing up something you're trying desperately hard to forget about is almost worse than the nightmare itself.

"What's wrong?" he asks as we walk. "You're tense."

"I'm sorry. It's just ..."

"Just what?"

"Do you remember anything from last night?"

He pulls me to a stop and steps into my body, so I have no choice but to back up against the wall beside me. He ducks down and stares into my eyes.

"I remember you wrapping your lips around my cock. I remember you coming with my tongue inside you, then my fingers and finally my cock."

My cheeks burn up as oblivious pedestrians continue to walk past us as if he's not whispering these things to me in the middle of a public place.

"Corey." It's meant to be a warning, but it comes out more like a moan.

"You remember how good it felt?" He closes the space between us and presses the length of his body to mine.

A whimper falls from my lips. How could I forget? He reminded me less than an hour ago.

"T-that's not quite what I meant."

"Oh?"

His eyes bore into mine, and I stand no chance of getting myself out of this now.

"Y-you ..." His brows lift in curiously as I fumble around my words. "You had a nightmare. That's why I was up this morning. You woke me and I couldn't—"

"Motherfucker." His angry grunt and giant step back cut off my words.

"Hey, it's okay. I just didn't know if you could remember and ..."

"Can we not?" he pleads, his eyes begging me to stop before he breaks the connection between us and looks away.

"Yeah, sure. I just wanted you to know that I ... I understand, and it's okay."

"It's okay?" he asks incredulously. "It's not ... it can't ... Fuck." He lifts his hands to his hair and tugs. I fear I might have just ruined everything between us, and all because I couldn't keep my big mouth shut about his damn nightmare.

I stay where I am and give him a moment to compose himself. Even if he can't remember the nightmare, I'm assuming that he's aware of what it would have been about, and that me bringing it up is just as painful.

Tipping his head back, he stares up at the sky for a few seconds. His chest heaves as his breaths race out past his open lips.

I feel for him. I know how painful memories and regrets are, if that's what he's going through, but equally, I know that there's nothing I can do right now other than wait him out.

"Let's go," he says eventually before he begins marching down the street.

This time, he doesn't reach for my hand.

He comes to a stop at a diner and pulls the door open for me.

"Morning, Corey. Whoa ... who's this?" the lady behind the counter says, excitedly looking from Corey to me.

"Hi, I'm Harlow."

"I'm Laura, and I'm shocked."

"Leave it," Corey hisses. "We'll be over in the corner," he says to the woman who clearly knows him fairly well.

We take a seat, but the tension between us is palpable and I kick myself for ruining how easy things had been between us this morning.

"You know her well?" I ask in the hope of breaking the discomfort surrounding us.

"Kind of. She's one of my artists' sisters. I come in here most mornings for food. Here." He slides the menu over to me and effectively ends my attempt at a conversation.

"What can I get you both?"

"The usual, please, and ..."

"Um ... waffles and bacon, please," I say when my eyes land on the first thing on the menu.

"Thank you. I'll be back with your coffees in a moment."

The silence returns the second Laura steps away.

"Corey?" He turns his haunted blue eyes on me, and my breath catches in my throat. "I-I'm sorry. I shouldn't have said anything." I've got so many questions, from his nightmare to his scars, to how it's affecting him now, but I can't ask. I daren't.

"It's okay. I'm going to need to take you home after this. I've got to get to work soon."

"I can call myself an Uber. You don't need to ..." I trail off, hoping that he's going to refuse my offer and demand he takes me home, but all he does is nod. Something inside me dies. I know he warned me that there was nothing serious here, but it seems my heart ignored it and got carried away with itself anyway.

Tears burn the backs of my eyes, but I blink them away —not that I think he'd notice. He's too lost in his own head right now to pay me any attention.

He stares out the window as Laura fills our mugs, and the silence stretches out to us eating our food. Well, I say eating; I mostly just push mine around my plate. Any appetite I might have had vanished the moment I mentioned his nightmare.

The second we've finished, he pays the bill before getting up and stalking outside. I have no idea if it's me he's trying to escape from or his memories, but it stings nonetheless.

I call an Uber and make the most of the facilities before joining him outside when I know the car is about to arrive.

"Thank you for last night. And this morning.' Reaching up on my tiptoes, I place a kiss to his cheek, but he doesn't register the move. It's like the soft and gentle man that I know has left his body, leaving behind a cold shell of a person.

With a sigh, I step toward my awaiting car and pull the door open. I'm about to climb inside when his voice stops me.

"Harlow?" I turn back to him. The haunted look still covers his face, but his eyes are a little brighter than a few moments ago.

"Yeah?"

"I'm so sorry."

Before I know what's happening, I'm pressed up against his body, his fingers are in my hair, and his lips are on mine.

The desperation in his kiss is palpable. I recognize it because I've felt it myself on more than one occasion as I've craved the relief from my memories.

His tongue sweeps into my mouth as his arm wraps around my back and holds me tightly.

I start to think he's never going to release me, but then the Uber driver beeps impatiently forcing him to pull back from my lips and rest his forehead on mine. He keeps his eyes closed for a beat before dragging his heavy lids open.

"I'm sorry, I just—"

"I get it, Corey. I really, really do. Go and sort your head out. If you want to talk or ... not, call me." He nods before releasing me.

'Thank you,' he mouths before watching me get into the car.

I breathe out a tense sigh as the car pulls away. That wasn't how I was expecting our time together to end. I kick myself for not being able to keep my lips shut about that damn nightmare, but at the same time, I'm glad I mentioned it. If it gets him talking, whether it's to me or someone else, then it might help.

Jesus, I sound just like all the people who've given me 'helpful' advice over the years.

16

HARLOW

"Here she is, doing the walk of shame at almost lunchtime," Brooke calls happily through the house when I close the front door behind me, making me groan. "Get ready, because you know I want all the juicy deets."

Ignoring her, I walk past the stairs and go straight for the kitchen. The coffee Laura served might have hit the spot, but I need more caffeine if I'm going to have to give Brooke a play-by-play of our date.

I think back to our picnic on the beach last night. It feels like a million years ago after the tense morning.

My mug is almost full when Brooke's feet race down the stairs and she appears dressed in her robe with a white face pack on.

"Wow, you're looking ravishing this morning."

"Is that for me?" She swipes the coffee from the machine and turns to put some sugar in it.

"No, it wasn't, but please, help yourself." I roll my eyes at her and pull down another mug to start all over again.

"So ... from the beginning, please," she encourages once she takes a seat at our table.

"He took me for a picnic on the beach."

"Aw."

"We sat out on a blanket and watched the sunset. It was a pretty incredible date."

"I knew he was hot, but I didn't think he had that in him. Way to go, Corey." I laugh at her antics. "And then you didn't come home, so I'm assuming you got a taste of the goods."

"Yeah. We went back to his place."

"Where does he live?"

"An apartment building that overlooks the ocean."

"Sounds flashy."

I think back to Corey's place. Right now, flashy is not a way I'd describe it, although I must admit it does have potential.

"What? You've got a weird look on your face."

"I think he's got money issues."

"Oooooh. Now I get the face."

"What?"

"It's your I-must-help-and-be-a-good-Samaritan face."

"Shut up. I do not have a look for that. I just like helping people. Hell knows, I can't help myself most days."

"I know, H. And I love you for it, for your generosity. But should you be getting involved?"

I shrug, because she's most probably right.

"He's hiding stuff ..." I hesitate. "Dark stuff." That piques Brooke's interest.

"I'm guessing he's not the only one." She quirks an eyebrow. "He has no idea about your background or that you can help with this, does he?"

"What do you think?" Brooke knows that I don't make a habit of telling anyone who I'm connected to.

"I think that if you suddenly help him out, you're going

to have to come clean, and I know how much you hate talking about it."

"Maybe it's worth it." Her chin drops as she stares at me in disbelief.

"What do you mean?" she whispers.

"I don't know. He's a good person who deserves better in his life. But to be honest, we didn't exactly leave things on great terms." She opens her mouth to respond, but I cut in. "He's not in a good place. He's run away from some shit that I only know the basics of. I just want to do something."

"What shit? How damaged are we talking here?"

"He was medically discharged from service six years ago. He's been through things ..." I trail off, because I have no idea what those things really are, and I'd hate to do him and his past a disservice by guessing. "Pasts can be painful, B. I know that better than most. I just want to help."

"I know you'll do what you think is right no matter what I say, so I'm just going to tell you that I trust you and leave you to make the decision on this."

"I-I appreciate that," I stutter. I was expecting her to get more involved, but she's right: I need to stay out of it.

"I'm going for a soak. Hot date tonight." She wiggles her eyebrows. "You won't need to wait up. I've got a good feeling about this one."

She dumps her mug in the sink before disappearing.

"When don't you?" I call after her, but all I get in response is her laughter.

I make myself another coffee and take it up to my room.

Sitting myself in the middle of my bed, I open up the website the final notice for Corey's apartment was from on my cell and hover my thumb over the call button.

My need to help burns through me. I can make the

stress of his imminent eviction disappear with one quick call.

I hesitate, but in the end, I put my phone down and try to forget about it. Brooke is right; it'll only lead to me having to answer questions I'm not ready for.

In the end, I finish my coffee and jump in the shower. I need to go and see my aunt.

I stop at the store on the way to pick her up a few things before pulling up to her house.

My stomach drops. All the curtains are closed.

I glance at the clock. It's now past lunchtime This isn't right. Throughout all her treatment, even on her worst days, she always got up and got dressed.

I find her front door key on my keyring, and, with her bags in hand, I make my way to the house. My heart pounds in my chest at what I'm going to find on the other side of the door.

"Hey, it's me," I call into an equally dark house.

"Upstairs," a weak voice replies. I drop everything in my hands and take off running.

Her bedroom door is wide open, and I quickly round the corner to find her propped up in bed.

"Hey," I whisper, walking up to the bed and dropping myself to the edge. "You not doing so well?" It's a stupid question and one I regret immediately.

"My seizures have been coming more often." Everything in my chest tumbles into the pit of my stomach.

"Would you like me to call the doctor?"

"We both know what he'll say."

I stare at her. Her previously glowing skin is almost gray, and her eyes have lost their sparkle.

"I know, but if it's the safest place for you to be, where

you can be properly looked after, then it might be the right thing to do."

She lets out a sigh.

I've offered to move in with her time and again, but she's point-blank refused. I understand that she doesn't want to drag me into this, but I'm her niece. I'm the only one she has left, and I'd do it in a heartbeat.

That's probably the reason she always refuses.

She told me from day one that she'd rather go into a hospice than watch me put my life on hold again, and I know how much she hates them, so it really is saying something. Equally, I don't want to see her in one of those places either, but it's something the doctors have been recommending.

"I'm sure I'll be fine in a bit. I just need some rest."

I want to argue. She's got terminal cancer, not the fucking flu. But I understand that she wants to be in her home. I hate that, ultimately, I'm the one who's going to have to stop that from happening. And soon.

Despite the fact that she's only said a few words to me, her eyes begin to get heavy. I take her hand in mine and squeeze, so she knows I'm here.

"I brought your groceries and ingredients for soup. I'll make us some for lunch."

She nods slowly and squeezes my hand back, but it's so weak it brings tears to my eyes.

She drifts off to sleep, her light snores filling the room, and when her hand goes limp in mine, I stand from the bed and slip away, unable to just sit there and watch. I'm much better when I'm doing something.

I make quick work of cleaning up everything that's been abandoned in the kitchen. It's so unlike her to leave even a glass unwashed. I do a lap downstairs, picking up rubbish and making sure that everything is in its right place before putting the flowers I bought in some water and placing them on the coffee table where she can enjoy them.

They're roses, her favorites, and they smell incredible.

I take a second to breathe them in and try to relax. But it's impossible. The countdown clock is ticking, and I fear it's going faster than I can deal with.

Lowering myself onto the edge of the couch, I drop my head into my hands as tears burn up the back of my throat.

I won't cry. I won't. She could come walking down those stairs any moment, and the last thing she needs is me in a state. She needs me strong, to fight beside her, not to break down.

I wipe the few escapee tears from my eyes and push up. I've got a job to do, and I need to focus on that, not sit here and dwell on what's to come.

I'm just about to start chopping vegetables for the soup when my cell pings in my purse. I expect it to be Brooke, so my eyes widen a little at the sight of Corey's contact. The words are simple, but the message behind them isn't.

Brit Boy: Thank you.

But what is he thanking me for? There could be a whole host of things.

Is it a thank you for a good time? A thank you for understanding? Or worse, a thank you because things are done?

I stare at those two words for the longest time, and they only add to the ache in my heart. Yeah, he freaked out this morning, but I wasn't lying when I told him that it was fine, that I understood. If this is a goodbye, then I'm not afraid to admit that I'm not ready for it. I want to reply, but I have no idea what to say, so in the end, I close the message and slide my cell into my back pocket and continue cooking.

Thoughts of both my aunt and Corey spin in my head as I potter around. I make the soup as promised, but when there's no movement from upstairs, I also pull out some of my aunt's beloved baking equipment and make her favorite lemon slices.

The scent of them baking fills the room, and my stomach rumbles.

Plating everything up, I carry a tray to her room to see if she's up for eating.

To my surprise, she's awake when I round the corner.

"Harlow, that smells delicious," she says softly. She's still not as enthusiastic as she normally is, but thankfully, she's more awake than when I first arrived.

She doesn't make any effort to get out of bed, and I don't mention it. I just sit with her and chat. Corey might be the last thing I want to talk about right now after that vague message, but I tell her all about last night's date and she swoons over a guy she might never meet, telling me that anyone who goes to that much effort for a single date must be worthy of my time.

I love her enthusiasm and her simple way of thinking. If only reality was that easy.

The sun is beginning to set when I say my goodbyes. I promise to pop in again tomorrow in the hope that she's feeling better, although something in the pit of my stomach already tells me she won't be. This is a downward spiral. The only question is how long it's going to take to get to the bottom. The doctor might have said weeks to months, but we all know that this disease is unpredictable at best, so all I can do is what he suggested and try to prepare for the worst.

Brooke has already left for her date when I get back, so I

order myself some takeout and make myself a rum and Coke in the hope it'll push away just a little of my worries for a moment.

It's wishful thinking.

When I get into bed later that night, my head is full of concern for my aunt and confusion over Corey.

I have no idea how long I'm there tossing and turning before a noise outside has me fully alert.

Jumping from the bed, I peel the fabric back from the curtain as the doorbell rings through the house. I have no idea what time it is, but it's late.

I don't see anyone for a few moments, but then someone stands back and looks right up at me.

Butterflies erupt, and I run from the room to let him in.

17

COREY

The second Harlow's taxi turned the corner at the end of the street this morning, I took off in the other direction toward the studio.

I was numb, and the only thing I could see was the horror from my nightmare. I knew I'd had it. I always do. Whether I remember the actual images playing out in my sleep or just wake with the sick feeling in the pit of my stomach and my body covered in a sheen of sweat, I always know.

I could just about handle them when I first came back to England and was forced to embark on life as a civi, but then my already bullshit life got turned upside down once again. Now the memories, combined with my own imagination and the guilt, almost swallow me whole.

It's another reason why I don't allow women to stay over. They don't need to see the darkness that I manage to fight in daylight but that consumes me at night.

The day passes in a haze of memories and ink. I lose myself in my art.

The only contact I allow myself to have with her is that

one text. I typed and retyped it over and over, trying to find the right words. But there weren't any.

In the end, "thank you" was all I could come up with. I had no idea if I was thanking her for the time we spent together, or for her understanding this morning. Regardless, it just felt right.

If it weren't for meeting Jonathan, who discovered my hidden talent, and then him introducing me to Zach when we were on leave, I don't know what would have become of me. I'm pretty sure I wouldn't be here now. Without a way to vent, to lose yourself, there's no way that one person can deal with that much loss in such a short time.

My leg tingles just like it does every time I think of my boys and how lightly I came out of the explosion that day. Two of us walked away. Two. But six years on, I'm the only one who's still here to tell the tale. It's a sobering thought, and one I've clung to many times over those years. I want to keep their memories alive, even if I never talk about it.

I've lost contact with their families now, who I hope have managed to rebuild their lives, and my only connection to Jonathan is Zach. We always raise a toast to him when we get together. To our fallen friend, the one who helped to put us both on the right tracks and find ourselves in ink.

I sit on the edge of my bed, staring down at the tattoo covering my entire left leg. I remember Zach working on it as if it were yesterday. Then, I place my hand to the one covering my heart. I might not be able to see that one so clearly, but it doesn't mean it hurts any less as I think of the person it's for.

A lump forms in my throat. I can't stay here alone tonight, feeling like I'm about to drown in the memories of those I've lost.

Pulling on some clean clothes, I walk through my empty

apartment and out the front door. I don't have a destination in mind; I just walk. It's a hell of a lot better than lying in bed, waiting for my nightmares to claim me.

Eventually, I approach the surf shack. I glance up at the roof of the building and know exactly where I need to sit and think.

Up there is the most peaceful place in the world, watching the waves crash in.

"Good evening, Corey," one of the waitresses sings as I walk through the front door. "Table for one?"

"Actually, do you mind if I just go and sit up top for a bit?" It's not the first time I've done this, but usually it's Kat who greets me and allows me special customer privileges.

"Sure thing. You want me to bring you anything up?"

"Nah, I'm good. Thanks." She nods and stands aside so I can walk out the back and to the stairs that lead to the roof terrace.

The last thing I expect to find when I reach the top is another figure sitting with his legs dangling over the edge of the building, staring out at the inky night sea beyond.

"Shit, I'm sorry. I'll just ..." I trail off as he turns toward me. "Fletch?"

He narrows his eyes at me as he pushes to stand.

"Corey, Milo's cousin," I offer when I see him trying to place me.

"Oh, yeah," he says like he has a fucking clue. I'm sure he meets hundreds of people on a weekly basis; he has no reason to remember me. "Having a rough night?"

"Something like that. I'm sorry for intruding, I'll leave you to it."

"It's fine. I can share." He lifts a bottle of Macallan and suddenly things feel a little lighter. He passes it over and I take a sip from the bottle, foregoing a glass. "Let's shoot the shit, see if we can solve the world's problems."

Moving before he changes his mind, I dash back down the stairs.

"So, what has you up here, wanting to outrun the world?" he asks after pouring me a very generous amount of whisky.

A laugh falls from my lips.

"I'll take that as it being a woman?"

"When isn't it, man?" A self-deprecating laugh falls from my lips. If only it were that simple.

"You've got me there."

"You in the doghouse?"

He lifts his glass. "Guilty," Fletch jokes, draining his own glass in one. "Hit me with it then, man."

I think of Harlow and where I should start. "I met this woman," I confess quietly.

"I see."

"But it's more than just her. It's ..." I scrub my hand down my face as the need to say more bubbles up inside me. I've haven't spoken about this with anyone. But I trust Fletch. "I lost people. People I've loved and ... I'm not sure I have it in me to go through all of that again."

Fletch watches me closely as I keep my eyes locked on the ocean before us.

"I get that," he finally murmurs. "As painful as it is that you've lost them, can you imagine your life without having them in it?"

"No, never. They've made me who I am. There isn't a day that goes by where I don't think about them."

"Life is fucking hard, man. Relationships are complicated, and love even more so. Heartbreak is inevitable. But the joys ..." He trails off, and I know he's thinking about Reese. I've only ever known them as I couple, but it would be naive of me to think their story was easy and without a few bumps in the road.

"Do I worry about losing Reese? Yeah, I'd be lying if I said I wasn't. I'm away from her for half of the year, most of the time on the other side of the country. I've seen what my lifestyle can do to relationships. I've seen more than my fair share of teammates ripped apart when the woman in their life couldn't hack it. But when I'm with her ... fuck, it's all so worth it.

"I just have to trust in her, trust in us. She's it for me, and quite frankly, I'd give it all up just to be with her if I had to."

"It's going to take some time to get my head around all of this. To work through the past."

"That's okay. The right woman will understand. She'll support you. Hell, she'll help. You just have to trust her to stand by your side through it all."

"How will I know?"

He shrugs one shoulder, a smile pulling at one side of his mouth.

"You just know, man." He thumps his chest with his fist, right above his heart. "Listen to this."

"I thought it was broken," I mutter.

"Nah, maybe just a little battered. Memories and people never leave us, Corey, not really. And wounds heal. You just have to be brave enough to move forward."

I climb to my feet, suddenly knowing exactly where I should be right now. "You heading home to grovel?"

His smile grows. "I'll sit here for a while longer before I go back and apologize for being an asshole."

I laugh as I walk away. I'm just about to descend the first step when Fletch calling my name stops me.

"Yeah."

"Say hi to Harlow for me."

I shake my head as I descend the stairs. Of course, he fucking knew.

I have a car heading my way before I even get to the bottom of the stairs, my need for her now stronger than ever.

She's like the little bit of light I need to make everything feel more bearable. And unlike many that have come before, when she looks into my eyes, she doesn't see someone who's broken and fighting his way through life. She just sees me, and as unnerving as it is, she gets it. She's lost the most important people in her life; she understands the hell I've lived through without me even having to explain to her the reality of it all.

My feet crunch up the gravel on her driveway seconds after I step from the car. The house is in darkness. I hesitate as I lift my finger to ring the bell. She's probably asleep; I have no idea how early I woke her this morning, but she deserves her rest after having to deal with me.

Being the selfish arsehole that I am, though, my need is stronger right now.

I press my finger to the button and listen to the ring as it cuts through the silence of the night.

I don't hear any movement, and I begin to think she either isn't in, slept through it, or just doesn't want to see me.

Taking a step back, I look to the upstairs windows in the hope of finding my answer. The curtain twitches, and there she is. Our eyes lock for a beat, and something slams into my chest.

I've needed her all day. It's only now I've seen her that I realise just how desperate I am.

When I'm with her, everything falls away. It's just us,

two broken souls trying to deal with our losses and fighting to carve ourselves the lives we deserve. I might not have the details about her family, but she has the same pain in her eyes. The same daily fight.

Coldness washes through me when she slips back inside the room, but it only lasts a few seconds. A light comes on behind the door before I see her move down the stairs through the small piece of frosted glass.

My heart pounds and my fists curl in my need to pull her into my arms, and my cock stirs just at the thought of it.

Hesitantly, she pulls the door open.

"Corey, what are you—"

I don't give her a chance to finish her question or even bother with a verbal answer. Instead, my hand lands on her duck egg–blue door, and I push it wider before stepping inside the house.

Her hair is a mess from where she's been in bed, and she's wearing a white, almost-see-through tank with a tiny pair of shorts that I'm sure wouldn't actually cover her arse should she turn around.

I'm a selfish prick, turning up here and waking her to take what I need to make all the noise in my head go away, but I'm powerless to resist. I kick the door closed behind me, the slam echoing through the house as I take her cheeks in my hands and slam my lips down on hers.

She gives herself over to me immediately, and the second I seek entrance, her lips part and she hungrily sucks my tongue into her mouth, her arms wrapping around my neck to hold me close.

My little goddess.

A growl rumbles up my throat, and I lose all control.

My mouth claims and my hands take everything she's offering to me, the escape only she understands.

The distraction.

My fingers pull at the hem of her tank, and our lips part for the two seconds it takes for me to tug it over her head.

Throwing it to the floor behind me, I retake her mouth, my hand dropping to her breast, palming the softness and pinching her nipple until she groans.

"Corey," she moans as my lips drop to her neck. Her fingernails scratch down my back as I continue teasing her. "More, Corey. More."

"Fuck," I bark, unable to get my head around just how fucking perfect this woman is.

I lift her and then press her into the wall with my hips.

"Oh God," she moans when my solid length grinds against her clit.

"You feel that, baby?" I mutter against her collarbone.

She nods eagerly, her fingers in my hair tugging, the bite of pain making my head spin.

"So hard," she moans, licking her lips like the master seductress she is.

"All for you."

I pull her from the wall, not giving her a chance to respond. I've never been inside her house, so I have no idea which room is which, but I'm so desperate I'd take her in her fucking garage right now if it had a decent surface.

I find her living room and lower her to her feet. Slipping my fingers into the waistband of her shorts, I push both those and her knickers down her thighs until they pool around her ankles.

"Fuck. You're so fucking beautiful."

Colour hits her cheeks, and it only makes her that much more breathtaking.

She stands naked as I run my eyes over her, my body still fully covered, but she doesn't bat an eyelid. Her nipples are peaked and her chest heaves. I know that if I were to run a finger through her folds, she would be soaked for me.

When my eyes come back up to her face, she quirks an eyebrow.

"Are you just going to stand there staring, or …"

She hasn't finished her question before I reach behind me and pull my T-shirt over my head, quickly followed by toeing off my shoes and dropping my trousers and boxers to the floor.

I kick myself free of the fabric before crushing my body to hers. My hands are everywhere—I have no idea where I want to touch first. Our kiss is frenzied as we both try to take what we need, even though we already know that it'll never be enough.

Or at least, I hope that's what she's thinking, too.

She moans for more, and my cock weeps.

"Turn around," I demand in her ear. She shudders as my breath tickles her sensitive skin, but she does as she's told.

Resting her forearms against the back of the sofa, she sticks her arse out temptingly toward me and I groan at the sight.

"You're going to be the fucking death of me."

She chuckles before moving her legs wider and arching her back.

"Fucking shit."

Stepping forward, I run my fingers through her wetness before dipping them into her to ensure she's ready. My other hand slowly strokes my needy dick.

"Corey," she moans, grinding down on my fingers, trying to find more.

"Patience," I mutter, although I must admit that I'm feeling less than patient myself.

She groans and continues moving her hips until I remove my fingers.

"Please, Corey. You can't turn up here like this and not ... fuuuuck."

I thrust into her in one move, her hip in one hand with my fingers digging into her skin, the other sliding into her hair, pulling as her back arches.

"Oh fuck. Fuck. Fuck," she chants as I start moving.

Her walls ripple around me, squeezing me so tight I have to fight to get control of myself.

"So fucking good," I groan as I pull almost all the way out before thrusting back in.

I hit so deep inside her that my eyes damn near cross.

Taking the length of her hair in my fist, I pull so she has no choice but to arch farther into me. She cries out in pleasure as I hit her at a slightly different angle.

"Good, baby?"

"Fuck, so good."

Her fingers find mine at her hip, and she threads them together as I continue my punishing pace.

The only thing that exists in my world right now is her and discovering just how loud I can make her scream.

She is exactly what I need.

I don't allow the magnitude of that realisation to hit me. Instead, I sweep it under the rug to deal with at a later time, like so many other parts of my life. This right now is about pleasure and taking what we need. There are no feelings, no futures, not even any tomorrows. It's just skin slapping, chest heaving, lip biting pleasure to chase away the demons that lurk in our pasts.

"Corey, Corey, Corey," she begins to chant when her release gets closer. I don't need her words. I feel it. She grows impossibly tight as she races towards her orgasm, and

I already know that I'm going to be powerless to stop myself falling over the edge with her.

"Corey!" she cries as her pussy clamps down around me, and I lose all control, emptying myself inside her. The world falls away as I drown in everything this woman is.

My chest heaves as I come back to myself, and a trickle of sweat runs down my temple from the exertion.

"Fucking hell," I mutter, wiping at my forehead with the back of my hand.

"You can say that again," Harlow mutters quietly where she's half folded over the back of her sofa.

I'm still inside of her, my cock still semi-hard, and I know that in only moments I'll be ready to go again. The tingles my orgasm left behind might still be zapping around my body, but I already know it's not enough.

Pulling from her, I spin her and lift her into my arms—and realisation hits me.

I didn't use a condom.

My heart thunders in my chest, but the second her eyes find mine, I relax.

"Hey," she says, looking at me with soft, heavy-lidded eyes and pushing the thought aside.

"Surprise!"

She laughs, and my chest constricts once again in a way I'm becoming all too used to when I'm around her. "It sure was."

"I hope you don't mind me showing up like this."

A wicked smile curls at her lips. "It's a little late for that now, don't you think?"

I shrug. "You can still kick me out, if you like."

"Nah, I think I'll make use of you, now you're here."

"Oh?"

Reaching up on her tiptoes, she brushes her lips along my jaw until she reaches my ear.

"Would you like to see my bedroom?"

"It's not your bedroom I'm all that interested in, Lo."

"Let's take this upstairs just in case Brooke's date doesn't go as well as she hoped."

My eyes widen, my fingers sinking into my sweat damp hair. I hadn't even considered her roommate.

"You make me lose my mind," I mutter as she points to the stairs. I follow her instructions, carrying her up with me.

"The feeling is most definitely mutual." She falls silent after saying this into my neck before pulling back to look into my eyes.

"What?" I ask when she stares at me weirdly.

"N-Nothing," she stutters after a few moments but then clearly changes her mind. "Did ... how did you know?"

"Know what?"

"Nothing. It's this one." She nods towards the open door, and I step inside before kicking it shut.

Her scent surrounds me as I look around the pink, girly room.

"Wow, this is ... unexpected." Harlow tenses in my arms and tucks her head into my neck to hide. I cast my eyes around her sickly pink walls. It's like I've walked into a little girl's room.

"Hey." I thread my fingers into her hair and tug lightly to encourage her out as I lower us and put her on the bed. "Don't hide from me."

She looks up, and I slide my hand around the back of her neck.

"I'm sorry, I just don't make a habit of bringing guys here. Like, ever." She looks away, and I hate that she's trying to hide whatever it is she's so concerned about.

"Harlow, am I the first guy to come here?"

She bites down on her bottom lip, and a surge of desire consumes me. "Y-Yeah. I know it's childish, I just …"

"Shh," I soothe, resting my forehead against hers. "I don't care how you decorate your bedroom. All I care about is the woman inside." I tense at the admission, and she doesn't miss it.

Her eyes find mine once again, and she stares into them so deeply. Something crackles between us, and I fear that, no matter how much I try, I'm never going to be able to walk away.

"Why are you here, Corey?" she asks, suddenly looking so serious.

"Because there isn't anywhere else in the world I want to be," I answer honestly.

18

HARLOW

"Because there isn't anywhere else in the world I want to be."

Even after a handful more orgasms, I still can't get those words out of my head.

It goes against everything he said about not wanting a future or anything serious. He wanted to be here again with me, and he's still beside me with his arms locked around my body.

"Stop thinking," he whispers into the top of my head.

My fingers pause where they were trailing around the lines of his six pack, and I risk a glance up at him. His eyes are tired and hooded, his lips swollen from our kisses, and his jaw is covered in so much scruff it could almost be classed as a beard. My thighs clench as I remember just how it scratched them not so long ago. "I can't help it," I admit. "Today has been ..." I trail off, not really knowing how to describe it.

"A clusterfuck?"

I laugh, "Yeah, that's a good way to put it. When you sent me that text, I thought ..."

"That was it between us?" he guesses, regret darkening his eyes.

I nod, not wanting to say it out loud.

"Honestly," he says, blowing out a breath, "it could have gone either way at that point."

I move to push myself from his body, but his arms lock, keeping me in place.

"I don't know what I'm doing here, Harlow. I've never ... I've never done this before."

"And what is *this*, exactly?"

"I have no idea. All I know is that when I'm with you ..." He pauses, glancing over my shoulder, giving himself a moment to process his thoughts. "When I'm with you, everything goes quiet. My memories drift away. The only other time I find that kind of peace is when I'm working. I didn't think it existed elsewhere."

A giant lump forms in my throat and tears pool in my eyes faster than I can control. When he looks back at me, two have dropped and are making their way down my cheeks.

"Fuck. What's wrong?"

"Nothing," I whisper. "I just ... I get it." I wipe at my cheeks, embarrassed. "I spent a lot of years trying to drown stuff out. Years that I'm not proud of."

Corey rolls me over so I'm on my back. He brushes his thumbs across my cheeks to clear the fresh tears.

"Let me help." His lips find mine and, just like he described, everything falls from my head as I focus on him and the things he does to my body.

"I CAN GO HOME if you'd prefer," he whispers when I'm just on the verge of drifting off an hour or so later. "I don't want to keep you awake again."

"You're not going anywhere. I can handle nightmares. I have enough of my own."

He falls silent but thankfully, he doesn't move. His chest rises and falls steadily beneath my cheek. His arm is wrapped tightly around me, and his hand is locked on my hip.

I feel safe. Secure. And, I hate to say it, hopeful.

In just a short time, Corey has given me something I never thought I'd find.

Peace.

Clearly, we both still have a lot to deal with. But suddenly, everything feels that little bit more possible.

"Will you tell me about them one day?" he asks, shocking the hell out of me.

My knee-jerk reaction is to say no. I don't talk about my parents. I barely even mention them to Brooke and my aunt, but never to anyone who doesn't already know the story. It's always been too painful to drudge it all back up again.

"One day," I whisper. "How about you. Fancy talking about it?"

"One day," he repeats. I might hate that he's keeping things hidden, but I can't exactly argue because I'm doing the same.

I drift off in his arms and don't surface again until my name being called stirs me back to life.

I crack my eyes open to find the sun streaming in through the crack in the curtains and glance at the clock.

Shit, it's late.

I look at Corey, who's still sleeping soundly beside me.

He's on his back with his arm thrown over his head, the covers so low that it exposes his toned and inked chest and stomach.

I lose myself following the lines of his tattoos, so I don't hear the footsteps heading for my bedroom door.

Before I know what's happening, it flies open, and Brooke comes marching in.

"Harlow, why are your clothes all over the living room flo ... oh, fuck." Her eyes go so wide, I half expect them to pop out. "Is that the Brit?"

"Yeah," he grumbles, "and he's sleeping."

"No problem. Could you just push the sheets a little lo—"

"Out, Brooke."

"But—"

"OUT," I hiss. After rolling her eyes, she backs out of the room.

"It's not like I haven't seen one before," she mutters seconds before the door closes.

"Exactly. Your wealth of knowledge is vast. Use your imagination."

"Bitch," she calls, making both Corey and me laugh.

"I'm so sorry," I say, dropping my forehead to his chest.

"There's something wrong with your best friend."

"I'm well aware. You know she's not going to let you out of here until she's grilled you for at least an hour, right?"

"She can try. I'm not one to kiss and tell. Although, I'm not sure it's going to be necessary."

"How comeeee," I squeal as he flips me onto my back and looms over me.

"She's about to hear just how good I am." He pushes my legs apart and settles between them as his fingers find my sensitive center. It's deliciously sore as he pushes two fingers inside me, reminding me of everything that happened last night. "Always so fucking wet."

"It's your ink. I can't get enough."

"My ink, huh? You sure it's not the promise of my cock?"

"Nah. I can take or leave that. Corey!" I cry as he bites down hard on my nipple.

"Louder. Make her really fucking jealous, Lo."

By the time we roll out of bed sometime later, I have no doubt that Brooke—and possibly half the street—know exactly what was going on.

"I need to shower," I say, padding to my bathroom as Corey stands deliciously naked at the window, staring at the glorious spring morning outside. "Do you mind? You'll give the neighbors a heart attack." I run my eyes down his sculpted back and to his ass. I bite down on my bottom lip. It should be illegal to have an ass quite that peachy.

"Just checking out the neighborhood while you check out my arse."

"Well, if you don't move, you won't get a chance to check me out in the shower. But I understand if the old woman over the street is more fascinating." Before I have a chance to turn away from him, he's halfway across the room and has my hand in his.

"Let's go. There's nothing more fascinating than watching bubbles run down your body."

***

"OH GOOD, you're both still alive. I started to get worried when all the cries for God and the banging stopped,"

Brooke quips when the two of us make it down to the kitchen sometime later. Thankfully, I found Corey's discarded clothes neatly folded outside my bedroom door when I emerged to find them for him.

"Shut up, B. I might suggest you're just jealous, but seeing as you didn't come home until this morning, I'm assuming you had yet another successful Saturday night."

"I've had worse, that's for sure. But you have most definitely had a better morning. For someone who's been celibate for—"

"Brooke," I hiss. "Enough."

"What? I'm just saying that you seem to have remembered how to ride the bike perfectly well."

"Like a pro," Corey adds, wrapping his arm around my shoulders and pulling me back into his body.

My cheeks burn as Brooke barks a laugh, amusement and delight filling her features.

"Morning, Brit boy. I would say it's nice to see you, but seeing as you clearly spent the night in her bed and not mine, I'm not so sure it is."

"Who said we didn't spend any time in your bed?"

Brooke gasps in mock horror. "Fair play. It was time you got your own back for that night I spent with Harry ... Hugo ... Henry ... Ugh, I don't remember his name. All I know is he had this massive—"

"You'd better be joking," I snap, cutting her off from the inevitable.

She winks at me. "I guess you'll never know."

"Jesus, you're a nightmare."

She shrugs. Her ability to not care about anything is one of the things I admire the most in her. She's desperate to find the one, but even with her lack of success she still keeps her head up and continues kissing the frogs.

"Who's for bacon?" she asks, pulling the refrigerator open and poking her head inside.

"As tempting as that sounds, I really need to head off." Disappointment floods me, and apparently, he doesn't miss it. "Walk me out?" he asks before directing me from the room.

"What? No kiss goodbye?" Brooke calls after us.

"Maybe another day."

"Don't even think about it. She kissed Fletch once and she's never let me forget it. My life wouldn't be worth living if—"

"She kissed Fletch?" he asks curiously.

"Yeah, why?"

"No reason." He pulls me into his arms and closes the space between us. "I wish I could stay." He rubs his nose against mine, and I sigh.

"It's okay. I've got some stuff to do," I admit. I need to check on my aunt again.

"Meet me after I finish work?" Hope shines in his eyes.

"Hmm ... that depends on what you've got to offer me."

"Dinner and a bad night's sleep?" he asks with a naughty glint in his eye.

"I've got work tomorrow morning."

"Bring what you need. You can go from mine."

An idea forms in my head. "Don't worry about planning anything; I've got it covered."

"Okay." Intrigue fills his face, but I don't let on.

"I'm going to miss you," he murmurs before dropping down to capture my lips.

"I'll see you later." I watch as he walks down our driveway and climbs into the car I didn't realize he'd ordered.

After waving him off, I head back in to join Brooke in the kitchen.

She looks over her shoulder at me from where she stands at the stove, and a smile curls her lips.

"You look really fucking happy."

I sigh, dropping down into a chair and unable to fight my own smile.

"I know I joke, but he's really good for you."

"I think you might be right."

"So, what happened last night? You never said he was coming."

"It wasn't planned," I admit. "I was in bed trying to sleep, and he just turned up."

"Oh, I love a good booty call."

"Is there anything involving sex that you don't like?"

"Umm ..." She pretends to think for a second before she starts laughing. "So, is this thing getting serious?"

I'm desperate to say yes, but the reality is that I really have no idea. "I don't know," I admit. "He tells me he doesn't do serious or even consider the possibility of a future, but then he turned up last night and said he needed me and didn't want to be anywhere else in the world. I don't know what to believe."

She stares at me for a beat before a small smile appears on her lips. "You've turned that poor man's world upside down, H."

"What makes you say that?"

"Oh, come off it. He might have never wanted a future with anyone before—he was probably telling the truth there —but equally, he's never met anyone quite like you. He's freaking out. You're showing him something he never thought he wanted."

"Really?" I hate sounding so unsure, but while he'll

openly admit that this kind of thing is all new to him, I'm not exactly an expert either. I've never had any kind of serious relationship. He's not the only one in uncharted water right now

"Yeah, but it doesn't really matter. It's been what? A week? Do you need to put a label on whatever it is yet? Just enjoy it. If it continues, then great. If it doesn't, then you know you tried and enjoyed yourself."

Her words play out in my mind as we eat our breakfast. Brooke knows me well enough to know that I need time to process this huge change in my life. To anyone else, this might be nothing, but I've never opened myself up to this kind of possibility before. As exciting as it might be, it's equally as terrifying.

"How was your aunt yesterday?" Brooke asks once we've finished eating.

I give her a rundown of how I found her, and Brooke's face shows the exact concern I feel. I told her to call me if she needed anything or was feeling worse, and when I checked my cell when I got up, there was nothing. I can only hope that means she's feeling a little better.

Brooke disappears to do her thing, and after washing up our mess, I sit down with a coffee to write a list. Selfishly, I don't want to go out tonight. I want to spend the night in with Corey, so I'm going to treat him to a little of my home cooking. It won't be all that impressive, but I've got a few signature dishes up my sleeve, thanks to my aunt's teaching skills.

THANKFULLY, when I get to her, the curtains have all been opened, and even without getting inside the house, I can already sense that it's a much less depressing place to be today.

"Hello?" I call once I've poked my head through the front door.

"In the kitchen, sweetie."

I make my way through with bags in hand. "Whoa, you look better today."

"I feel it." I breathe a sigh of relief. We all know what's coming, but just seeing the twinkle of life back in her eyes makes me feel so much lighter. I didn't want to admit it, but I thought yesterday might have been the beginning of the end. The fact that she's standing here now has tears burning my eyes.

"I just needed a good rest. I'd been doing too much."

Rolling my eyes at her, I walk over, drop the bags onto the table, and kiss her on the cheek.

"So, enough about me. Tell me about you. Have you seen your British man again?"

My cheeks burn, giving her all the answer she needs.

"Oh goodie, I was hoping for some juicy gossip. How about you make us a drink and tell me all about it?"

"Sure thing. Go and sit down."

"There are cookies in the tin."

"You made cookies?"

"I fancied a treat. Don't worry, I did it in the mixer. I hardly moved a muscle."

I raise a brow at her, relieved that my moaning is finally sinking in. I can't chastise her for the cookies though, because they're too damn good.

"So, come on." She wiggles her eyebrows at me. "Make an old woman very happy."

"You're not old," I mumble around a mouthful of cookie.

"Maybe not, but it's been a few years, and it's not like I have any of that in me these days."

A spray of cookie flies from my mouth at her innuendo. To start with, she looks horrified that I've just covered myself in half-chewed biscuit, but after a second, she realizes what she said and barks out a laugh of her own.

"I didn't mean it quite like that, but if your mind is going there, at least I know you have exciting things to tell me."

My cheeks burn, and as much as I might want to deny it, to not allow her to think of all the things I've been up to, I can't. I realize right there and then just how incredible my time with Corey has been. Even his meltdown yesterday morning. If anything, that just showed me how strong he is, how he's just like me.

"He turned up last night just because he needed to see me."

My aunt swoons.

"Tell me what he's like. What does he do for a living? What about his family? Are they here too?"

I tell her everything I know before coming to what I think is the most important part. "He's lost people too. He ... he gets it. He gets me. Neither of us have talked about it yet, but I can see it in his eyes."

"That's good, Harlow. I mean, not that he's lost loved ones. But that you both have that understanding of loss. Maybe you're meant to be. Maybe he was sent to you to help you finally heal from everything and move on."

I'm not sure I entirely believe her, but I can't deny that it sounds pretty damn good.

"I hope so. Something just feels so comfortable when we're together."

"So ... when are you seeing him again?"

A smile breaks out across my face. "Tonight. I'm cooking for him, for when he finishes work."

"What the hell are you doing here then?"

"Um ... checking in on you."

"Have you got everything in the car?"

"Yeah, why?"

"Bring it in. I want to help." I stare at her. "I'll remain seated at all times and just give you orders. What are you making?"

"Moussaka and cheesecake."

"Right, well, let's make sure it's the best damn moussaka and cheesecake that man has ever tasted. You want to get back in his bed, right?"

My chin drops in shock. "You did not just say that."

She gives me an innocent shrug and sips at her teacup like a lady. Lady my ass.

"I was with your uncle all my life, my dear. Don't be thinking we were boring."

"Christ. I'm going to get the groceries."

I walk out of her house with a wide smile on my face and a new excitement for life that I haven't felt in a very, very long time.

WITH THE BEST moussaka and cheesecake ever made sitting safely in the footwell of my car. I make a quick pit stop at home to shower and dress for tonight.

I'm standing with one towel around my body and another bundled on top of my head when a knock sounds at my door.

"Is it safe to come in?" Brooke laughs.

"Like it would stop you."

"Seriously," she says, poking her head inside and looking around as if he's going to magically appear, "the last thing I expected to find this morning was a naked man in your bed."

I think back to what it felt like, having the hot skin of his body pressed up against mine, and my temperature soars. It's damn good after so long.

"Trust me when I say I understand." I let out a sigh as I continue staring ahead. "I don't know what to wear."

"Something easy."

"Easy?"

"Yeah, you've snagged the guy now, so while you still want to look sexy, you need to ensure easy access at all times. Don't make him work harder than necessary to get the goods."

"Jesus Christ," I mutter. "So, jeans are out, then."

"Unless it's a skirt or dress—panties optional—then yes, it's out." She comes to stand beside me. "This?"

I stare at the dress she pulled out.

"No, too dressy. We're just hanging out at his place."

"Okay, then ... this?"

"Yeah, actually. That's perfect." I take the hanger from her and hold the full-length maxi dress against my body.

"It's got a lot of fabric. I'm not sure how easy access that is," she mutters.

"Ah, but you're missing something." Reaching down, I pull the split in the dress open.

"Ahhh ... see, I was underestimating you," she laughs, reclaiming her seat on the edge of my bed. "Honestly, I think you could probably turn up in a trash bag and he wouldn't bat an eyelid. Have you seen the way he looks at you?"

"Um ..." I bite down on my bottom lip. I know how it

feels when he looks at me. Chemistry and desire crackle between us, butterflies erupt in my belly, and things I'm not sure I've ever felt before happen between my legs. I might be a long way from a virgin after my former years, but no one back then ever turned me on like Corey. That was purely about escape; there was nothing more to it.

"Well, let me fill in those gaps for you. He wants you, girl, and I don't mean just out of that dress. He might not want to admit it, but you've got that man under your spell."

"We'll see," I say, taking a seat at my dressing table.

"You will. And then, you'll teach me how you did it."

"I didn't do anything, B. I just fell into his lap. Literally."

She thinks for a few moments. "As if sent from above."

"Whatever," I laugh. "What are your plans for the night?"

"Going to see the parentals. I was going to invite you before you had a better offer."

I smile at the thought of her parents. I haven't seen them in ages. "Aw, I wish I'd known."

"Don't even pretend you'd have blown off your hot date." Okay, so she might have a point. "Anyway, you'll see them at your ball in a few weeks."

"They're still coming?" I ask hopefully.

"Of course they are. They want to support you and your first big event."

"Give them a hug from me."

"I will. And I'll even gladly fill them in on why you can't attend. They'll be thrilled you're spending a night with a Brit between your legs."

"Please don't say it like that."

"Can't make any promises." She makes her way to the

door as I groan. "Have a good night. Remember, if you can still walk in the morning, he didn't do it properly."

"Have a good night," I call back, ignoring her comment but blushing at the thought of dragging myself into work in the morning.

With thirty minutes until Corey is due to finish, I leave the house and head for his studio. I told him I'd meet him at his place, but my impatience has gotten the better of me.

19

———

COREY

Knowing I'm seeing Harlow again after work means my day drags. I used to crave my hours sitting on my stool and working on intricate designs for hours. But as I sit here now, all I want is her.

It's really fucking weird.

I've never wanted anything serious with a woman. I joined the army when I was sixteen and knew that would be my life for the following God knew how many years, so I just enjoyed myself. I had a couple of regular girls I'd spend time with but never one I made any promises to.

I grimace as I think about Carla and what became of her. She was one of my childhood best friends, and guilt eats me that I was a huge part of her downfall. If we hadn't had that drunken night together at fifteen, things could have turned out very differently.

I sigh, trying not to be engulfed by my memories and mistakes, when a knock sounds out on my studio door.

"Hey, man," Oz says with a beaming smile on his face. I'm just cleaning up for the day and am more than ready to get the hell out of here to meet Harlow.

"Hey, what's the grin about? Shit your pants or something?"

"Nah, man. I'm just happy for you."

"For me?" I ask, not having the fucking foggiest as to what's going on.

"Yeah. It looks like you've got a sweet night ahead of you."

"What are you—" It's in that moment he moves aside and allows me to see through to reception.

"Holy shit."

My eyes run over her light makeup and curled hair, and then the fabric of her dress that covers most of her body but reveals one hell of a cleavage and a hint at her curvaceous leg hiding behind the slit.

She throws her head back and laughs at something JJ says before glancing over to us.

Our eyes lock and electricity crackles between us. All the air rushes from my lungs.

Her lips curl into a wide smile and her hand lifts to tuck her hair behind her ear.

"Fuck, man. You need to get the hell out of here before I leave you with JJ," Oz jokes.

"Keep your fucking hands to yourself, man." He holds them up in surrender.

"Oh, you are so fucking whipped. Are your balls even still attached to your body?"

"Fuck off. Like you can talk. JJ has been wearing yours as earrings for fucking months."

He winces as the visual hits him, but he soon shrugs. "It has its benefits."

Suddenly, all the things I never wanted, the same woman every night, the thoughts of futures and all the serious stuff that comes with it, doesn't feel quite so intimidating.

"Right, I'm out of here."

"At fucking last."

I drop the last few things into my drawer before shouldering past Oz.

"Here he is," JJ announces as I fly past her. "Your girl here was just telling me—"

Her words fade off as I take Harlow's face in my hands and drop my lips to hers.

JJ and Oz holler behind us in excitement, but I ignore them. My only focus is on the woman in my arms.

"This is a nice surprise," I say, running my nose against hers.

"I couldn't wait any longer."

"You and me both, baby." Pulling away from her, I turn to look at my employees who both have giant smiles on their faces. "We're out of here."

"Have a good night."

"You wanna drive?" Harlow asks me as we make our way to her car.

She holds the keys out and I take them from her in favour of getting us back as fast as possible.

"What's that smell?" I ask when my arse hits the driver's seat.

"That's dinner."

"You cooked?"

"Sure did."

"You are aware that I have no dining table or more than one plate, right?"

"I've got it all under control."

I shake my head, wondering how the hell this happened.

Turns out that having it all planned means that, along with our dinner, Harlow's car is packed with everything we could possibly need. She's even got an old foldaway camping table.

Once we get it all up to my flat, she turns to me and runs her palms up my chest.

"I missed you today." The words are out of my mouth before my brain registers them.

"Yeah?" Her dark eyes light up as a shy smile tugs at her lips. "What happened to Mr. I Don't Do Tomorrows?"

"Suddenly tomorrow doesn't seem so scary," I say quietly, dropping so my lips brush against hers.

"What are you saying, exactly?" She tenses in my arms. Her need to put a label on us amuses me.

"One day at a time, baby. One day at a time."

"Okay," she whispers, nodding and playing with the hair at the nape of my neck.

I lower and take her lips again. She lifts up on her tiptoes and presses the length of her body against mine. A groan rumbles up my throat as her soft curves line up perfectly with my hard lines.

My fingers twitch to lift her into my arms and carry her to my bedroom, but I resist.

"You go and shower or whatever, and I'll get dinner sorted."

"You sure you don't need help?" I ask, finding the slit in her dress and slipping my hand inside.

"Distracting, you mean."

"Same thing," I say, dropping my lips to her neck and licking her sensitive skin.

"No, no," she giggles, squirming against me and making the situation a whole lot worse. "Go." She slams her palms down on my chest and attempts to push me away. She's nowhere near strong enough to move me, but after a few seconds, I take pity on her and step back.

"Okay, okay." I walk backward down the hall, keeping my eyes on her.

I reach behind me and pull my shirt over my head, dropping it to the floor before swiftly removing everything else.

Her eyes watch my every move, taking in the inked skin I reveal.

"Can I tempt you to join me?"

Her teeth sink into her bottom lip.

"Sorry, you're on your own this time." With a wink, she turns away and starts pulling things from one of the bags she carried in.

The temptation to walk back to her and demand she come with me is high, but after a few seconds of watching, I turn toward the bedroom and have a very quick, very cold shower.

"HOLY SHIT, DO I LIVE HERE?" I ask when I walk back into my living area.

Harlow has set up the table. It's covered in a cloth and has candles flickering in the center.

As I look around the rest of the room, I find candles on every surface.

She stands in the middle of everything she's done, looking unsure of herself.

"D-do you like it?"

I focus on her as she nervously plays with one of the curls around her shoulders.

I open my mouth to tell her yes, but I find something else coming out. "This place hasn't felt like a home since the day I picked up the keys. But suddenly, everything feels right."

"Yeah?" she asks, a wide smile spreading across her lips.

"It's incredible. Thank you."

Closing the space between us, I slide my hand into her hair and lower my lips to hers.

She just opens up for me when the buzzer I didn't know I had on the oven starts ringing and breaks our moment.

"I need to get our dinner," she mutters against my lips when I refuse to let her go.

"We don't need dinner. I can eat you instead." Her cheeks brighten with my words. I fucking love making her blush.

"As tempting as that is, I'm starved."

Releasing her, I watch as she effortlessly moves about in my kitchen.

"Here," she says, sliding a bottle of beer my way, proving that she knows I'm watching her.

"Do you realise that you're the first person to cook in this kitchen?"

"I'd hardly call reheating something I made earlier cooking."

"It's more than I've done."

"How long have you been here exactly?"

"About two and a half months."

"And you haven't cooked anything?"

"Guilty."

"How are you still alive?"

Walking over, I wrap my arms around her waist as she plates up the dinner. "I get by," I whisper in her ear.

She laughs, moving out of my hold and carrying our plates over to the makeshift table.

I watch her sitting opposite me as she takes a sip of her own drink before lifting her knife and fork to dig in.

"What are you waiting for? It's going to get cold."

"Thank you for this." Dropping a forkful of her food into my mouth, I can't help groaning in delight.

"It's nothing. I had fun making it all this afternoon. It's nice having someone beside Brooke to cook for."

I can't help but laugh at the mention of her best friend. "What?"

"Nothing, just thinking how different you two are."

Harlow shrugs. "I told you."

"How did you meet?" I ask, desperate to know more about her.

Her face drops immediately as she casts her eyes to the corner of the room.

"I-it's okay, you don't need to tell me."

"No, it's fine. It's just weird talking about my life back then." She thinks for a moment, chewing on a little more of her dinner. "I was fourteen, almost fifteen, when I moved into their house." My brows draw together, not putting two and two together straight away. "I'd been in some awful foster and group homes up until that point. Living through those after losing my family hadn't turned me into the nicest of teenagers. But Brooke's parents never once gave up on me, no matter what drama I brought their way. And Brooke and I struck up an unlikely friendship that's lasted us all this time."

"Oh, wow. I thought you were going to say you met at college or something."

"It wasn't quite that simple. Brooke has been through ...

a lot with me, and just like her parents, she stuck by my side the whole time. I owe her everything."

"Are you saying I need to be nicer to her?"

"Never. She's a pain in the ass and deserves your banter."

I laugh. "Good to know. So, you're still close to her parents then?"

"Yeah, quite close. My uncle died in service when I was almost eighteen and my aunt came back from where they were posted. I moved in with her. I couldn't pass up the chance to be with the only family I had left."

"Jesus, Harlow."

She shrugs like it's nothing. "It is what it is. If it weren't for Brooke and my aunt, I don't think I'd be here now."

My chin drops at her admission. "If it helps at all, I'm really fucking glad you are."

She looks up at me, her large, dark eyes staring into mine, making my heart beat a little faster in my chest. She might have been the last thing I expected—wanted—to find, but already, I can't imagine her not being in my life.

"So, what about you? What about your family?"

"My mum and sisters live in London," I say, rattling off the easy stuff without a second thought. "My sisters are both at university. Mum's just come back from Germany. She was living with my dad. But he ..." I trail off. There are only a couple of people who know about this, and those in this country who do thankfully didn't need me to tell them. They found out through the family gossip. "He was cheating on her. He left, and she was forced out of married quarters and sent home. Only, she didn't have a home because my dad was everything."

"Oh shit. Corey, I'm so sorry."

"We all thought it would be fine. Dad's been in the

army all his life and worked his way up the ranks; he should have had a decent amount of money behind him. Mum sure seemed to think he did. Turned out a younger woman wasn't the only thing he was hiding, because he'd lost everything gambling online.

"Thankfully, my sisters' tuition had already been paid. But Mum came back with nowhere to live, and nothing to her name."

"Fucking hell. What an asshole."

I nod, unable to do anything but agree. "We found my mum a flat, and my sisters moved in with her to save on their own rent. Then debt collector letters started appearing for credit cards and loans Dad had taken out in Mum's name." I blow out a breath as I remember the devastation on her face when she admitted just how many there were. "I came over here for a couple of weeks to get away. Things were already hard, and finding out all that about my parents didn't really help. I'd already left London. I was running a studio in Manchester, and then I found the studio here and things just started falling into place. My boss, Zach, is always looking to expand his empire, and when I sent him the details, he bought it without even visiting. He made me an offer I couldn't refuse, and here I am."

"You left your mum and sisters behind?" Guilt twists my stomach that they're in London, fighting daily. But my reality isn't much better.

"Yeah," I admit sadly. "I was already living miles away and unable to visit much. I earn more here, so although I'm in a different country, I'm able to help by sending more back to help dig my mum out of the debt she's drowning in."

"Corey," she says softly, her head tilting to the side. "You're sending everything back to them, aren't you?"

"Everything I can, yeah."

Putting her knife and fork down, she pushes from her chair and walks toward me. Seeing her intention, I push my own chair back and allow her the space she needs to drop onto my lap.

"Thank you," she says, placing her palm on my rough cheek and looking into my eyes.

I shake my head slightly. "Believe it or not, that's the least dramatic part of what I left behind." Her eyes widen at my admission, but she doesn't ask. I knew she wouldn't.

"You're pretty amazing. You know that?"

"Nah. I'm just trying to do right by my family while running from my nightmares."

She leans forward, resting her forehead against mine. "Your mum must be so proud of you."

Forcing her to look up, I find her eyes full of unshed tears. "Yours too," I whisper so quietly that I'm unsure if she hears me until a sob erupts from her throat.

"Shit. I'm sorry." She's up and off my lap before I have a chance to pull her back.

"Harlow, it's okay. You don't have to—"

"Just give me a minute." Before I know what's going on, she's disappeared toward the bathroom and left me alone with my thoughts.

She's the first person aside from Zach that I've properly explained any of that to. When I told Zach, I was in the middle of dealing with it all and trying to get Mum moved. But telling Harlow just then was so easy. I don't know if it's because the dust has settled and my life right now is somewhat stable, or if it's her. Part of me wants to tell her the rest, the things that keep me up at night, but I doubt those words will come as easily.

After only a few minutes, she returns and drops into her seat.

"So, I guess that helps to explain this place," she says, taking the heat off her.

"I haven't really had the time or energy to make this a home. I've lived and breathed the studio since I got here. I just turn up to sleep, really."

"It's a nice place. And I love that you can see the ocean."

"Definite perk," I agree, returning my focus to dinner.

20

HARLOW

Corey snores lightly behind me with his hand resting possessively on my hip, but my head is spinning, and I know I don't stand a chance of shutting off anytime soon.

Our conversation flicks in and out of my mind along with his reality. No wonder this place is what it is, and why he's behind on his rent. He's literally sending every penny he earns back to his mom. The second the words were out of his mouth, I regretted not following through with my intention of helping the other day. Out of everyone I've ever met, he deserves it.

My heart aches for this kind guy who's fighting daily for those he loves. I could see the guilt in his eyes when he talked about moving over here and leaving them behind. But he doesn't need to feel that. He's doing everything for them right now. He's about to be homeless, for fuck's sake, all because he's more concerned about them having a roof over their heads than he is his own.

Unable to lie here any longer, I slip from Corey's hold. His snoring doesn't falter as I pull one of the sheets from the bed and wrap it around myself.

The curtain blows from the door we left slightly open last night. I slip outside and take a deep breath of fresh air.

It's been a long time since I've been able to see the ocean from a bedroom window.

Suddenly, as I stand there, I'm a kid again.

The ocean was always my happy place, whether I was on the beach or just at my window. When things weren't going my way, when I was in trouble or when I was fighting with my sister, it gave me the escape I needed to be able to clear my head.

It took me a lot of years to go back to the beach and to be able to find the same peace as the waves crashed in.

I stand there for the longest time, just staring at the inky black ocean with the moon and stars reflecting in its enticing water.

I lose myself in memories from the past and thoughts of my future. It's weird; I've never really looked much further than the end of the week or the month, but suddenly, I have images of years down the line. All of which include Corey.

It seems he's managed to do things that others spent years attempting. He's scaled my walls and somehow managed to take up residence on the inside. And as scary as it is, I don't want him to leave.

The door opening behind me breaks the silence before Corey's arms slip around my waist and his chin rests on my shoulder.

"Hey. I thought you'd left again."

"I couldn't sleep."

Turning, he places a kiss on my neck. A shudder runs up my spine at the softness.

"I'm sorry."

"It's not your fault."

"Really? I got you talking earlier."

"Honestly, it's fine. I needed it. I needed to tell you."

"Yeah?" I can hear his delight in that one word. He knows how much it means for me to tell him about a life that I hold so close to my chest. He understands.

"My parents had this incredible house," I say quietly, his arms tightening around my middle. "I had this huge window seat in my bedroom that looked out over the ocean. It was so peaceful. I would sit there for hours, reading, doing homework, listening to music. It was my happy place.

"Then one day, it was all gone. They were all gone, and I was taken from the house to start a new, unwanted life."

Corey peppers kisses along the length of my shoulder as I speak, letting me know that he's here and listening. It means everything.

My heart clenches, but it's not just with sadness as I think about my family. For the first time ever, there's more. There's hope, joy, possibility. All because of this beautifully broken man behind me.

"It was my ninth birthday. I had friends coming around for a party that night. I'd told my mum that I'd wanted a birthday cake like my friend had a few weeks previously. She didn't take it seriously and instead made me one herself." My teeth grind as I remember how selfish I was as I looked at the cake she'd so lovingly made. I wince as I say the next few words. "I told her I didn't want it. That she had to go to the store and get me the other one. I'd told all my friends it was what I was having, and I couldn't be seen lying.

"Mom was angry. I remember seeing it in her eyes, but she never let on. She just listened to me, and after a few minutes she told me to go upstairs and sort myself out. I turned my music up loud and tried to calm down. I was a kid; to me, the wrong cake meant the party was ruined. My life was over.

"I had no idea how true that was until a few hours later."

"Harlow," Corey breathes, clearly assuming parts of what happened next.

"Mom called up the stairs that they were going out. It had already been arranged that they were picking up a couple of my friends for the sleepover. I was still sulking, so I refused to go. I had no idea, but they'd decided to stop by the store to get the right cake.

"Only, they never made it out of the mall, because some madman with a gun decided that that day, that hour, those few fucking minutes would be the perfect time to unleash hell on some unsuspecting, innocent people."

Corey gasps as I shudder out a breath, trying to keep myself together.

"They only went there because I was too fucking selfish to appreciate a handmade cake Mom had spent hours icing for me. I was a spoiled little brat who only cared what her friends thought." My voice cracks, and Corey turns me to face him, pulling me into his arms and holding me tight against his body.

My body trembles with the regret, guilt and grief that wash through it like a crashing wave.

I don't feel myself moving until I find myself wrapped in Corey's arms and back on his bed.

He holds me so tightly that it brings more tears to my eyes. It's just a hug. It's just his arms holding me to him. But it feels different from any I've had before.

Most were just full of sympathy. A few were empathetic. But without going through something similar, something so life changing, it's hard to really understand just how agonizing it is.

His lips press against the top of my head as I cling to him as if he'll single-handedly stop me from drowning.

Maybe he will.

Maybe that's why I fell into his lap a few weeks ago.

His kisses move down to my face before he finds my lips.

I don't react at first. I can't. I'm still too lost in the images of that day—some reality, but many I've made up over the years as I tried to piece together what really happened in that mall. I've seen enough mass shootings in the news that I've been able to build a pretty clear picture. I know where they were found. I know they had the cake.

I know it's all my fault.

Corey doesn't say anything, and for that I'm grateful.

So instead of telling me that he understands, that he can't imagine how hard it must be, he shows me.

He kisses across my jaw and down my neck. His tongue licks at the sensitive spot under my ear, and a moan falls from my lips.

Awkwardly, he manages to unwrap me from the sheet, and my skin burns when his hand lands on my waist.

My entire body heats as the pain of those memories begins to subside, the feeling of Corey's touch forcing me back to the here and now.

His lips brush across my breasts, my nipples puckering as he kisses around them. Teasing me. Taking me away from the pain.

"Oh God." His tongue flicks my nipple once, and a bolt of lust shoots down to my core. "More," I moan. I need more. I need everything. Everything he can offer me.

Slowly, he kisses down my stomach, his tongue dipping

into my navel before he blows a stream of air across my sensitive core.

"Oh God," I repeat, my hips lifting from the bed in need.

His tattooed fingers wrap around my thighs to hold me in place, and I can't take my eyes away from him.

He's so gentle with me as he parts my lips that it brings tears to my eyes. I watch as he stares at me for a beat, before the soft and gentle man between my legs vanishes and the one I'm much more used to appears.

He dives forward, his lips capturing my clit, and I scream as he sucks and flicks my little bundle of nerves with his tongue.

My hands thread into his hair and tug, attempting to get him even closer.

"Fuck, Corey. I need you." And I do, I need him so fucking badly. I need his hands on me, burning into my skin. I want his lips on mine. I need him stretching me open so that the only thing I can think about is him and what he does to me. "More," I cry. "More."

At my demand, he slides two fingers inside me. The sensation engulfs me, and it gives me exactly what I need. Everything in my head fades away, and the only thing I can think about is this very moment as he plays my body toward the ultimate pleasure.

He never lets up. His tongue licks, his teeth nip, and his fingers find that mind-spinning place inside me until my arms give up and I fall back on the bed, unable to continue watching what he's doing.

"Come," he rumbles against me as he ups the ante.

My body is a trembling mess by the time he pushes me off the ledge. And fuck, do I fucking fly.

My chest is heaving, my body covered in a sheen of sweat when he crawls back up my body.

He doesn't miss a beat. The second he's hovering over me, his hand slides over my collarbone and wraps possessively around my throat. Our eyes connect for the briefest moment before he captures my lips in a bruising kiss. Tasting myself on his tongue only spurs me on.

My legs wrap around his waist, and I shift myself until his cock is right where I want it.

His kiss doesn't falter as his hand begins trailing around my body, driving me crazy with need.

"Corey, please." I thrust my hips up, trying to gain some friction.

"Condom," he groans in my ear, reminding me that we weren't so careful last night.

"It's okay, we're safe right now."

"Harlow." His need and torment over doing the right thing are clear in his voice.

"I'm due in—"

Clearly unable to wait any longer and deciding that he trusts me, he surges forward and fills me in one move. My back arches, my pussy contracting around him as I adjust to the sudden invasion.

"Jesus, Harlow." It's only then that I realize he's stopped moving.

"Corey, are you—"

I don't get to ask before he moves once more. His tongue sweeps into my mouth and his cock thrusts deeper inside me. His hand lands on my hip with a bruising grip, but the bite of pain only adds to the pleasure, and I lose myself even deeper to this incredible man.

He kisses, bites, and sucks at every bit of skin he can find as the rhythm of his hips gets faster and faster until we're both forced to pull our lips away in favor of breathing as we race toward our climaxes.

"Oh God, Corey."

"Come, Harlow. Let me feel ... fuuuuuck." He doesn't even get the demand out and I detonate, my pussy pulling him in even deeper until he stills, groans, and releases everything he has inside me. His muscles pull tight, his ink flexing and stretching over the top in the most delicious way as he loses control.

He falls on top of me, and I wrap my arms around him and hold as tight as I can. I've used sex a lot to forget, to drown out the pain in my heart and the endless images in my head, but never has it been quite like that.

Brooke was right. Corey isn't like those of my past. He's so, so much more.

He wasn't chasing the thrill of the high. He wasn't just desperate for some action. That was about me. About helping me to forget, to push away my demons.

Finding his rough chin, I encourage his face from the crook of my neck. It takes him a few seconds to move, but when he does and our eyes connect, something in his makes my breath catch.

The blue is dark from pleasure, but there's more to it than that, and as much as it might scare me, excitement tingles beneath my skin about what it is we might have found here ... two lost souls desperate for something to cling on to as their lives spin out of control around them.

"Corey, I—"

He shakes his head, cutting off my words. "No. No more talking."

I nod, unable to agree verbally.

His lips find mine and we make out in his bed for hours. There's no more, just his incredible kiss and burning touch until we both pass out, wrapped in each other's arms.

WE'RE FINALLY awoken when my alarm starts blaring from wherever I abandoned my cell phone last night.

"No," Corey groans, pulling me back tighter into his body.

As my cell falls silent, the temptation to close my eyes once more and drift back off is strong, but I know I can't. Not only will it start up again momentarily, but I've got to go to work.

Why did I get a job again?

Spinning in his arms, I lay my palm against his rough cheek. His eyes remain shut, but his lips twitch with a smile.

"You stay there. Go back to sleep."

"I don't think so."

He rolls onto his back, pulling me with him so I have no choice but to straddle his waist. His cock is hard and ready beneath me, and a rush of heat heads south in my body.

Sadly, before I get a chance to do anything about it, my alarm starts up again.

"Fucking hell."

Corey rocks his hips into me.

"Either stop it and come back, or ignore it."

I look from him to where my purse sits on the chair at the other side of the room.

"Just give me a second."

I climb from his lap and walk over, His eyes burning into my back the entire time.

"I know you're staring."

"Good."

I laugh at him as I silence my cell. Spinning on the tips of my toes, I find Corey exactly how I left him—head on his pillow, his body fully exposed from where I threw the covers off, and his cock hard and resting well up onto his stomach.

"Now this is the kind of wake-up call I could really get used to," I confess.

"Me too." He winks and gestures for me to rejoin him, which I do almost instantly.

I take his hand in mine once I'm close enough to climb back on top of his body.

His eyes shutter closed when I take his solid length in my hand and prepare to sink down on him.

"Are you sure this is safe?" he asks right at the last minute.

"I'm sure, but I'll book a doctor's appointment later and get on some birth control."

"Good. I don't want anything between us again."

His lids flicker up, and the look in his eyes makes my breathing falter. He's serious. Deadly serious.

I have to bite down on the inside of my lips to stop me asking what this is and where we go from here.

It's not important right now. Just enjoy the ride.

I listen to that little voice in my head and take him inside me until I'm fully seated.

I stare into his emotion-filled dark eyes, and I know that the second I get to work this morning, I'm making that phone call. He deserves it.

21

———

COREY

"Can I drive you to work?" I ask when Harlow emerges from my bathroom, ready for a day at the office.

I run my eyes over her body-hugging black dress, and it just tells me what I already know. I'm falling—and fast.

The thought of ripping it from her body and dragging her back to bed is all-consuming, but I know I can't. She has a job, and so do I. We've got other people who depend on us for shit.

"I didn't think you had a car," she asks, slipping her feet into her shoes. They do incredible things for her calves, making me forget she just said anything. "Corey?"

"Shit, sorry. Just, you look ... Fuck. You look really fucking hot. So ... are there many guys in your office?" I ask teasingly, running my fingers through my hair.

She smirks, happy to play along

"A few. Most are quite young, too. And they all wear these suits." She bites down on her bottom lip, and I have to swallow a bubble of jealousy that makes itself known.

She leans over me, forcing me to rest back on my elbows.

"But I'm pretty sure none of them could make me scream like you did last night."

"Damn fucking straight."

"You've got nothing to worry about."

"Good to know. So, back to my original question."

"How are you going to drive me to work without a car?"

"I'm going to drive you in yours," I say with a shrug, like it's obvious.

Pushing from the bed, I tug on a pair of trousers followed by a clean T-shirt, and I'm ready to go.

"Is that it? Is that all you do in the mornings?"

"What? I had a shower and brushed my teeth, too."

"It should be illegal to look that good with that little effort."

"What should be illegal is any other man getting to see just how hot your arse is in this dress." I pull her to me and squeeze it hard.

"Ow," she complains.

"Nice try. We both know you loved it. Now, come on. We can pick up breakfast on the way."

She smiles at me before I turn and leave her in the bedroom.

If someone had told me that I'd wake up feeling this alive, this happy, after the heavy conversations that happened between us last night, I'd have said they were an idiot. But that's exactly how this morning feels, and I know Harlow is thinking the same. It's right there in her chestnut eyes.

She feels lighter, having told me everything she went though. I can see it's no longer resting heavy on her shoulders.

I'm sure, like me, there's more to her story. I doubt she

was taken in by Brooke's parents and suddenly had the perfect life.

"Let's go, then," I say when she joins me.

"Shit, I didn't tidy up," she mutters, looking around the living area and kitchen at the mess we made last night.

"There's always time for that later. Come on, we don't want you being late."

After texting Laura an order to go, we make a quick pit stop at her diner before heading farther into town. I follow the signs for the Crown Arena, and she points to her parking space once I'm there.

"What are you doing?" she asks when I kill the engine and go to get out with her.

"It's your car. I'm leaving it with you."

"But you work on the other side of town."

"It's fine. I'll grab an Uber."

"Take it."

"But—"

"No buts." She rests her hand on my thigh, and the heat burns through the fabric of my trousers. "If you're done in time, come and pick me up, or just message if you're not and I'll find another way home."

"No, I can't—"

"Corey," she snaps, effectively cutting off my argument. "Just do it."

"Okay," I mutter, knowing full well that I'll do whatever it takes to ensure my afternoon client is done in plenty of time to collect her. I refuse to take her car and force her to find another way home. Plus, if I'm honest, I don't want her going home. I want her with me.

A trickle of concern runs down my spine that I'm about to find myself evicted any day now, and that I won't have a home to take her back to, but I push it away, just like I've done for the past few weeks.

"You okay?" she asks, noticing the change in me.

"Yeah, just looking forward to picking you up later."

"Oh yeah? Got big plans, have you?"

"I might have." It's a lie; I haven't planned anything. But there's plenty of time to do so.

She smiles at me. It's so innocent yet full of passion. It totally disarms me.

Leaning over, I wrap my hand around the nape of her neck and pull her into me.

"Thank you for trusting me last night." My lips brush against hers as I say the words.

"You too." Her hand lands on my shoulder, and she tugs to close the last bit of space between us. I know she wants to kiss me, but equally I know she wants to end the conversation.

I heard the pain in every word she said last night. I know how hard it was for her to tell me.

Do I feel guilty for not returning the favour? Hell yeah. But equally, I'm not sure I'll ever be able to say the words. I've never explained it to anyone. The only people who know about it are those who were around at the time. Even all these years on, the pain is just too much. Merely thinking about it shreds me.

"I finish at five. But no pressure. If you can't make it back, just give me the heads up, yeah?"

"I'll be here."

"Okay. See you then."

She hesitates to get out of the car. It's not until I laugh at her for hovering that she finally pushes the door open and walks towards the imposing building. I watch her every movement, my eyes locked on her arse as it sways.

Before she disappears through the main doors, she turns and gives me a smile and wave. I return the gesture before reversing her car from the space.

Suddenly thoughts of tomorrow aren't so scary.

Making the most of having a vehicle, I run a few errands and do a little grocery shopping before making the trip I'm dreading ... to my letting agent.

I pull up out the front of their shop and kill the engine. I've been here countless times, trying to buy myself some more time. They were lenient to start with, but I know this is it. That final eviction notice is more than enough evidence. It doesn't stop me blowing out a large breath and pushing the car door open.

Before, I might have been okay with living in my room at the studio. But it's not just me now. I need to think of Harlow. My priorities are suddenly a little different.

I want to be the man she deserves if we're going to be continuing with whatever this is that I refuse to label. I want to be someone she can be proud of. I want to have a place where she can stay the night and enjoy spending time.

"Mr. Edwards, how lovely to see you," Chris, the guy who's been dealing with me announces as I walk towards his desk. "What can I help you with?"

I take a seat when he gestures for me to do so.

"I need to come up with a plan. I can't lose the flat. Not now. I've got a little money from last month. It's not the whole amount, but—"

Chris's brows draw together in confusion as he looks at his computer. "Your account has already been settled."

"I'm sorry, what?" I lean towards him, thinking I misheard.

He clicks about on his computer for a few seconds before nodding.

"Full payment plus six months of advanced rent was made this morning. Look." He spins the computer screen to show me.

I stare at the four little letters in red, and confusion washes through me.

Paid.

"But how? I don't have that kind of money. If I did, I'd have sorted this out weeks ago."

"I don't know. There's no name attached."

I sit back in the chair and let his words register in my brain.

My account's been paid.

But no one knew about this.

No one would...

Unless they've seen the letter.

22

HARLOW

The second I get in the building, I pull my cell out and find the number for the letting agent. I have no doubts this time as I connect the call and put my cell to my ear.

It rings a couple of times before someone answers. My heart hammers in my chest, but I know I'm doing the right thing.

"Hi, I'd like to make a payment on an account," I say to the cheery woman on the other end.

"Okay, great. Do you have any of the account details?"

"Um, no. I have the address of the apartment in question, if that helps."

"Sure."

Between us, we eventually figure it out, although she's very professional and doesn't divulge any of Corey's information. By the time I hang up, all I know is how much in rent arrears he was. No longer. I've secured him a home and hopefully taken a weight off his mind for a while.

Something inside me aches to do more, to turn that empty and cold apartment into a home, but I know I might have already overstepped. He could either be really grateful for this, or really furious. Only time will tell, but I fear doing any more will definitely push him into the latter category. I might not know him all that well yet, but I know he won't take too kindly to charity—not that that's what this is. I'm just helping a friend in need. He's more than welcome to pay me back if he feels the need.

Feeling better about myself and my good deed for the day, I walk through to my office with a smile playing on my lips. It doesn't go unnoticed by my colleagues.

After dropping my purse at my desk, I head for a coffee.

"Good morning," Reese sings from where she's waiting for the machine.

"Morning."

She narrows her eyes at me suspiciously. "There's something different about you."

I'm not naive enough to think that Brooke hasn't already filled her in.

"Oh yeah? How so?"

"There's a twinkle in your eye. He's doing good things for you."

I bark a laugh. "It could certainly be described that way."

"From what I've heard, that would be putting it lightly."

"Fucking Brooke," I mutter, much to her amusement. "Is there anything she hasn't told you?"

"Only the things you haven't told her." She winks at me as she takes her now full mug from the machine.

"She's in so much trouble when she finds a serious guy. I'm going to shout all the details from the rooftops."

"Aw, she's just happy for you. And maybe just a tad jealous."

"Just a tad. She'd had Corey locked and loaded, as far as she was concerned."

"It's going to take someone very special to put up with her brand of crazy."

I snort. "You said it."

We switch places so I can make my morning coffee.

"So, is it serious enough for him to attend your masquerade ball?"

"I don't know. I haven't invited him yet, if that's what you're getting at."

"You should. Fletch and Milo will be there, so he'll have people to talk to."

"I'll see. I'm not sure getting dressed up in a tux and making small talk is really his thing."

"You think it's Fletch's?" she laughs.

I shrug, because I know from first-hand experience just how easy he makes all the schmoozing look. "He's a natural."

"Years of practice. Invite him," she says before moving toward the door as our boss, the team owner's wife, pokes her head in.

"You ready, Reese?" she asks softly.

"On my way. Give us an hour and then come join us to go through the final details?" she directs at me.

"Sure thing."

I make my coffee and head for my desk to get all of those details together.

I've been working on this almost since my first day. It's like my baby, and I'm terrified that I've missed something or that something is going to go horribly wrong at the last minute.

I've got a couple of incredible celebrity guest speakers—Fletcher Ferguson included. I've managed to sell tables to some insanely wealthy and influential people, all of whom I hope will be more than generous on the night as they bid on the vast range of donated items. They range from a case of champagne to a two-night stay in a private château in the Loire Valley in France.

I shake my hands out as nerves hit me. I've never organized something so big before, and although I'm confident that I've covered all angles and thought of all the potential downfalls, my fear is still there, niggling that it's not going to be successful.

By the time my hour comes to an end, I've got everything ready to go. I'm over-prepared, I know I am, but my need to prove myself and this event gets the better of me.

With my clipboard under my arm, I make myself a fresh coffee and head for the conference room.

I knock before Mags calls for me to join them.

Pushing the door open, I'm relieved to find it's just her and Reese waiting for me. It's what I was expecting, but there was a part of me that was worried I'd have more eyes on me.

"Come and grab a seat, Harlow," Mags says softly as Reese smiles at me.

In previous years, she's organized this event. But this year, she's handed it over to me so she could work on other things. I'm certainly feeling the pressure of stepping into her shoes and raising the funds we need to help support the ice hockey players of the future and our local community.

"Right, hit us with the details."

I talk through my schedule for the night, how I've arranged the rooms we've hired, and the costs versus my projected profit based on the rough figures each auction lot should bring in.

"Harlow, this is incredible," Mags says, pride oozing from her kind face. While her husband might be the big boss around here, Mags loves getting involved where she can, and especially with any kind of event we're running. The woman lives to get dressed up and socialize.

"T-Thank you."

"It looks like you've got it all covered. But if you need anything, please don't hesitate to call me," Reese says encouragingly.

"I will, thank you so much. I think—" My words are cut off as the conference room door behind me flies open.

The tension in the room changes instantly, and a shiver of fear runs down my spine, but I have no idea why.

Reese's eyes widen in shock for a beat before her chin drops.

Poor Mags just looks confused.

"I'm so sorry, he just stormed past me," Sharon, our receptionist rushes out as I shift in my chair.

I have no idea who I'm expecting to find behind me, although that shiver of awareness should give me a clue.

Spinning on my seat, I turn to look.

My eyes lock on to a very familiar face, but I've never seen this expression before. The anger laced through every inch of him has dread sitting in the pit of my stomach. His brows are pulled tight, his lips are pressed into a thin line, and his shoulders are bunched with tension.

"Corey, what's—" I jump from my seat, desperate to know what's going on.

Reese and Mags are already both on their feet, waiting to discover what's about to happen and if they need to get security up here—assuming they're not already on their way.

"Please." His voice is hard and cold. "Please tell me you didn't. Tell me it wasn't you."

"What ... I don't...." My mind spins, failing to connect the dots for a few moments.

Then it hits me.

His rent.

He knows.

I swallow nervously, and it's enough for him to know that I'm guilty.

"I'm not a fucking charity case, Harlow. You had no right to go behind my back like that. No fucking right, let alone snooping to find out in the first place."

"I wasn't snooping, I—"

"I don't care. It was out of order. You had no right," he repeats again, his body almost vibrating with anger. His hands lift to his hair as he tugs, trying to get himself together.

"Sir, I think you need to leave," Mags says calmly as Reese comes to stand at my side in support.

"I'm going," he spits before turning to the door.

I race forward, afraid of what this might mean for us.

"You can pay me back. I just needed to help. You've been through so—"

"No," he bellows, making me take a step back. "I'll figure out a way to get it back to you. But we are done here." He storms through the door and down the corridor. I'm powerless but to watch him leave.

Inside I scream for him to come back, for him to hear me out, but none of the words pass my lips.

"Oh my God," I sob, stumbling back until Reese manages to get me on a chair.

I knew there was a possibility that he'd be angry, but I never expected...

Mags places a fresh glass of water in front of me before Reese drops down beside me.

"He'll be okay. Just let him cool off, then he'll listen."

"You think?" I ask through tear-filled eyes.

She chews on her bottom lip for a second. "Sure." She sounds about as uncertain as I feel, and it doesn't ease the dread filling me.

"I was just trying to do something nice. To help him out. I knew I should have told him, but—" My voice cracks, and I stop.

"I know. And when he calms down, he'll see that." I can see the question in her eyes, but we're not close enough for her to feel like she's able to pry.

"His arrears and six months' rent."

"Jesus, Harlow. Are you some kind of secret millionaire or something?"

I shrug, my eyes drifting to Mags because she knows the truth. But she doesn't say a word. "Or something. I've got inheritance," is all I give as a reason. It's not a lie. It's just the kind of inheritance that keeps on giving.

Reaching out a shaky hand, I take a sip of the cool water and try to get myself under control. Everything was going too well. Everything was too perfect. This was always going to happen. I was just too blissfully unaware as I enjoyed the perks of finally having a man who understood me.

"Just give him some time. If I've learned anything from Fletch, it's that men are almost as complicated as women; they just don't like to show it. Let him cool down and then, when he least expects it, prove to him just how much he needs you. Rock his world the way it needs rocking and prove your place beside him."

"Wise words, right there," Mags agrees with a soft smile playing on her lips.

I nod at her, in awe that she manages to look at her man

every day and not be a total fumbling idiot like I am every time I'm so much as in the same room as him.

"I don't know much about him, but Corey seems like a good man. Milo sure has good things to say, but he's also alluded to a dark past. Just be gentle with him. He'll figure things out."

"I hope you're right," I mutter.

"I know you've got Brooke, but if you need anything, even just a chat, I'm here." I offer her a weak smile so she knows I hear. "And," she says, pulling my clipboard closer, "this is really incredible. It's going to be a huge success, Harlow. Focus on this while he—"

"I'm so sorry." Sandra comes rushing back in, looking panicked. "Harlow, there's a call on line one for you. It's urgent."

I stare at her and my body turns cold. I recognize that grief-stricken look on her face. I know it too well.

I race to the phone, but I already know the words I'm about to hear. My hand trembles as I lift it to my ear.

Even as I wait for a voice, my body begins to shut down. This kind of stuff is easier to deal with when you're numb.

"Hello." My voice is hollow when it comes out.

"Is that Harlow Winters?"

"Speaking."

"I've got you down as Mrs. Winslow's emergency contact. She's currently being admitted to—"

I don't even wait for her to say the hospital name; I know where she is. "I'm coming. Tell her I'm coming right now."

I slam the phone down and race from the room.

"Harlow, wait," Reese calls.

"It's my aunt. She's in hospital."

"Shit. Let me drive you. You can't—"

"Whatever, but I'm going right now."

"Okay, I'm coming."

I don't see the hallway before me; I just take off—until I come to an abrupt stop as I crash into something. Some*one*. Warm hands grip my upper arms to steady me, and when I look up, I find those mesmerizing green eyes staring down at me.

"Harlow, are you okay?" Fletch asks, concern lacing his voice. "I just saw Corey and—"

"Ah, perfect timing. We need to get Harlow to the hospital, now," Reese announces.

"Shit, are you okay?" He looks me over like there might be something wrong with me.

"Her aunt's been taken in." They share a look that makes me wonder how much they really know about my life before Fletch jumps into action.

"Okay, let's go. You ready for a fast ride?" he asks me. On any other day, I'd blush like a tomato, but today I barely register his words as I follow him with Reese by my side to the exit.

I'm on autopilot as I climb into the back of the black Range Rover I'm directed to. Both Fletch and Reese talk to me. I hear the sound of their words, but I don't register any of them. The only time I speak is to give directions, but it soon becomes apparent that Fletch knows exactly where he's going, so I fall silent as I watch the world outside pass in a blur.

It feels like only minutes later, Fletch is pulling up in front of the hospital so I can climb out.

"I'll park and meet you inside."

"No, no. You two can go. I'll be fine."

Totally ignoring my words, Reese pushes the door open and steps out beside me. "I'll message you where we are."

Fletch nods before she closes the door and links her arm through mine.

I walk into that hospital not knowing if my aunt is dead or alive. She's here, under this roof, with terminal cancer. Nothing good is coming out of this, but just how bad is it?

Seeing as I cut the woman off on the phone before I had a chance to find out where she is, we have to stop by reception. But in only moments, Reese has me in the elevator and we're riding to the fourth floor.

"You don't have to do this."

"I know, but I want to."

"Hi, I'm here for Mrs. Winslow," I say to the nurse who's sitting behind the desk when we walk into the ward.

"Perfect timing. The doctor is with her now. I'm assuming you're ..." She looks down at her computer. "Harlow?"

"Yes."

"Please follow me."

"I'll wait here," Reese says, pointing to a couple of chairs.

"You can go, it's okay."

"I'll call Brooke."

"Thank you," I mouth as I rush behind the nurse to find out what's going on.

It's not the first time I've seen my aunt hooked up to machines in a hospital bed, but unlike previously, this time I have no idea if she'll get through it.

"Your aunt had a severe seizure. She was very lucky that it happened while she was in the garden and her neighbor saw her."

Guilt slams into me. I should have been there. I should have been keeping an eye on her, but I was enjoying myself with Corey.

"She was unconscious when the paramedics got to her. There are no guarantees with anything here, Ms …"

"Harlow."

"Harlow," the doctor nods. "But with your aunt's medical history and the progression of her disease, I would be surprised if she recovers from this. It's still early days, but the signs aren't positive, I'm afraid. I'm so sorry."

A sob rumbles up my throat as I stare at her looking old, weak, and tiny in the hospital bed.

"C-can I sit with her?"

"Of course. Take all the time you need. Call if you need anything."

He points to a red button that I glance at, and after a few seconds, he completes the notes he was writing when I entered and leaves me to it.

Blowing out a shaky breath, I pull the empty chair closer to my aunt's side. I find her hand resting on top of the stark white sheet and take it in mine. It's cold and, I swear, thinner than the last time I held it.

"I'm so sorry," I whisper around the ball of emotion clogging my throat.

I'd told her time and time again that I'd move in. That I'd keep an eye on her and make sure she had everything she needed. But she always refused. And I let her. I should have pushed it further. I should have been there. It shouldn't have been down to the neighbors to rescue her.

What if she weren't in the garden?

A sob hits me at the thought. If I forgot to ring and check on her at lunch and then got distracted by Corey after work, I might not have touched base with her today … and she'd have been…

I lose my fight with my tears and drop my forehead to her shoulder as I cry.

I knew this day was coming. I thought I'd somewhat prepared myself for it. But I didn't realize that nothing could possibly compare to this agonizing moment. She's all the family I've got left, and there is literally nothing I can do to save her right now. No amount of money in the world would be able to keep her here with me.

It would be selfish to even try.

She's made her wishes very clear from the first time she was diagnosed. When her time came, she wanted to go with dignity. I agreed—what else could I do? But I never could have imagined back then what this moment would feel like, knowing that she's slipping away from me.

The minutes pass with the beeping of the machines around me and my aunt's shallowing breaths.

I forget about everything else, about Corey's anger, about work and the ball, and just focus on this moment, hoping like hell that she knows that I'm here, that I'm supporting her in the only way I can.

Nurses come and go, checking her vitals, but none of them give me any kind of indication that things are improving. With each visit, any hope I had that the doctor might have been wrong starts to dwindle until all that's left is despair.

"Harlow." The sound of my name barely registers, and it's not until I'm physically pulled from the chair and into my best friend's arms that I realize I'm no longer alone. "I'm sorry it took me so long to get here," she whispers into my ear, and she holds me.

"She's ... she's going, B."

"I know, honey. I know."

When we part, Brooke's cheeks are almost as tear-stained as mine.

She takes my face in her hands and stares into my eyes. "It's going to be okay."

I nod at her. I know she's not trying to tell me that my aunt will be okay, no one can do that, but she's telling me that I'm strong enough, that I can do this and survive.

Brooke drags over the other chair in the room so she can sit beside me.

"Here, it's got all the extras. Thought you could probably use them." She hands me a Starbucks cup that I didn't even realize she'd brought in with her.

"Thank you," I mutter, popping the top off and looking down at the cream and marshmallows hiding beneath.

We sit in silence while we sip on our drinks, lost in our thoughts.

"Don't you think the smell in this place is stronger than ever?" I ask Brooke when the silence and the incessant beeping becomes too much to bear.

"Uh ... smells like normal hospital to me. Sterile and cold." *And like* death. I nod. I've probably just been surrounded by it for too long. Although I have no idea how long I've actually been here.

"Have they said anything about timings or ..." Brooke trails off. She wants to ask the question about as much as I want to hear the answer.

"Nope. All they've said is that they don't think she'll wake up. But it's all guesswork, really."

"Would you like me to get you anything? Call anyone ... Corey perhaps?"

"No. Definitely not."

Her brows rise. "But—"

"I fucked it up."

"*You* fucked it up? Wow, I wasn't expecting it to happen

that way around." She says it as a joke, and on any other day I might be amused by it, but not today.

"I tried to help, and he's taken it the wrong way. He turned up at work earlier, pissed off."

"What did you do?"

I blow out a breath, not really wanting to tell Brooke his secrets, but I know that I'm not going to get out of it.

"He's been struggling money-wise. He's got family issues, and he's supporting them instead of looking after himself."

"Oh God, Harlow. What did you do?" she asks again, knowing me well enough to know my penchant for helping everyone I can.

"I paid his overdue rent ..."

"Harlow."

"And another six months'."

"Jesus. You didn't tell him either, did you?"

I shake my head. "He stormed into our meeting, shouting about not being a charity case."

"Fucking hell. You should have told him. Or at least offered."

"He wouldn't have accepted it. He was going to be evicted. I had to do something."

"I get it. I do. But—"

"He doesn't," I finish for her. "I told him about my family. About how they ..." I hiccup, unable to say the words while surrounded by too much death already.

"Really?" Pride lights up her features.

"It felt good, actually. I felt lighter. He was incredible. He ..." I trail off, thinking about just how sweet and gentle he was. How he gave me exactly what I needed in that moment. "I don't want it to be over," I admit. "I think ... I think I'm falling for him."

"You think?" she asks with a quirked brow.

"Oh, shush. Do you have to look so smug?"

"I'm just glad you're the one with the man problems for once."

"Great, thanks," I mutter, making her chuckle.

"He'll come around. It was probably just a shock. It's not the kind of surprise that most people can afford to do for the guy they're dating.

"Give it a few days and he'll be begging for you to come back. You mark my words. That man is obsessed with you."

"We'll see," I whisper. "He's not exactly my top priority right now." I look at my aunt, who's still lying there in the same condition as when I raced through the door earlier.

Something tells me I'm in this for the long haul.

23

HARLOW

I take up residence in the uncomfortable chair by my aunt's beside for four days. Four long days full of endless nurses and doctor's visits. Of sympathetic looks from Brooke and Reese when they turn up with decent coffee and try to convince me to leave.

The doctor said I could stay as long as I liked, and I'm taking him up on the offer. I wasn't there for her when she needed me most; there's no way in hell I'm leaving her now. I'd never forgive myself.

"Any change?" Brooke asks when she stops off on her way to work.

"They think we're at the end. Vitals are dropping."

"Shit."

"It's okay. It's what she would want," I say, trying to hold my voice steady. Nothing about this is okay, but at least she's not suffering. It could have been much worse.

"I just stopped in to bring you this." She hands over a bag and a coffee. "I know you won't eat otherwise. I need to do a few things after work, but I'll be back later, okay?"

"Sure, thank you. How many shots of coffee are in

this?" I ask when the strong scent hits my nose. My stomach turns over at the smell, reminding me that I can't remember the last time I ate.

"It's just a standard cappuccino." She narrows her eyes at me. "Are you feeling okay?"

I can't help but think it's a stupid question. I haven't left this room in four days. I've been sleeping in a chair and only nibbled on some of the food she's turned up with. I'm only wearing different clothes from when I arrived because she brought them for me.

"No, I'm really fucking not." My voice cracks with emotion and exhaustion.

Unfazed by my outburst, Brooke reaches over and takes my hand, squeezing in support.

"You really need to come home to sleep."

I glance over my shoulder at my aunt. "I will ... soon."

Brooke nods and continues to hold my hand. "I'll be back later, okay?" She squeezes again before dropping a kiss to my cheek. "Call me if you need anything."

"Thank you," I whisper as she walks away.

Sitting back in the chair that has become my home, I take a sip of coffee. The warmth is soothing, but much like the smell, I don't get the joy I usually do when the taste hits me.

Fucking hell, I need some sleep.

Nibbling at the pastry, I watch my aunt, wondering if today is going to be the day I'm forced to walk out of here and leave her behind.

For her sake, I hope it is. Guilt swamps me at having such thoughts, but I know it's what she wants, and I need to think about her right now, not me. She always told me that when the time came, she didn't want it to drag on. I remember her telling me horror stories from the TV or newspapers where people ended up in hospitals and care homes for months as the disease slowly ate away at their bodies. I shudder at the thought.

As hard as it is to accept her wishes, to allow her the peace she craves. I know she's right. I'd want the exact same thing.

I curl back up in the only position I've found that's vaguely comfortable, and, with the beeping of the machine in my ears, I drift off to sleep.

It's fitful and full of nightmares involving losing my aunt and Corey simultaneously.

I can see myself curled up in this chair as a team of nurses and doctors come racing in for my aunt, who's still lying lifeless on the bed.

They do all the checks I'm now used to them doing, but the atmosphere surrounding them is different. The looks on their faces are different.

My heart starts to race, knowing what they're telling me without needing words. This is it. This is the end.

I wake with a start, my heart still trying to pound out of my chest.

It was just a dream.

Just a dream.

Until I open my eyes and find the exact image that was just in my head, only now it's before me as two nurses and a doctor stand beside my aunt.

My heart plummets.

"No," I cry. "No, please."

I scramble from the chair and over to the bed. I take her hand in mine. It's cold, but then it has been since I first arrived here.

"We're so sorry, Harlow. She's at peace now."

"No," I cry, dropping my head as realization hits me.

I've been sitting here religiously so that she wasn't alone, and I was asleep when she needed me the most. A sob rumbles up my throat as I run my eyes over her. She looks so peaceful. As if she's just drifted off to sleep.

My eyes burn as tears fight to be set free.

Everything around me begins to blur, and my legs start to feel a little funny.

One of the nurses must notice that I'm not doing so well because she races around the bed just in time to catch me when my knees buckle.

"Whoa," she says softly. "I've got you."

She lowers me back to my chair as I struggle to pull the air I need into my lungs.

"Try to control your breathing, honey. In. Out. In. Out." I focus on her words, and after a few seconds, things start to come back to me. The room stops spinning.

"Is-is she really gone?"

"I'm so sorry. Is there anyone we can call for you? Your friend, maybe?"

I shake my head. I need a little time alone to try to process this. Brooke will be back later. Nothing will have changed by then. A miracle isn't likely to happen.

The nurse allows me to stay with my aunt to attempt to say my goodbyes. I have no idea how long they give me; my grasp on reality is long gone. All I know is that when she comes back and softly tells me that they need to do their jobs, it's not at all long enough.

Although, I'm not sure any amount of time ever will be.

Reluctantly, I tidy up the few bits I have scattered around the room before standing beside my aunt and doing one of the hardest things I've ever done in my life.

I never got the chance to do this with my parents. The social workers decided I was too young to be able to deal with it, so I never got a final goodbye. I was left with the memory of refusing to acknowledge them as they walked out of the house to collect my friends and that stupid birthday cake.

Placing my hand on her cheek, I look down at her peaceful face.

"Sleep t-tight." My voice cracks, and a sob erupts from my throat.

I back out of the room, not wanting to leave her. Tears streak down my cheeks, but no noise comes from me. I'm too numb.

That all changes when I look up and find Brooke and Reese standing off to the side, waiting for me.

I wail and they both run at me, thankfully catching me before I hit the floor.

"She's gone," I cry as they both hold me.

"We know. We're so sorry."

We stand there locked in our embrace for the longest time, but eventually, Reese pulls away.

"We should get you home."

I nod, unable to do anything else. Just moving my legs in the direction of the exit is hard enough.

The journey home is a blur. I feel nothing. Everything is numb.

I'm ushered toward the couch and drop into the corner when encouraged to do so. Brooke pulls the blanket from the back and throws it over my legs.

"I'm going to make you a coffee," she says softly. "Would you like anything to eat?"

I shake my head. I don't have the stomach for it.

She nods and backs out of the room.

Their whispered voices float through the air, but I don't

know what they're saying as I stare at the blank TV in front of me.

It's like life is going on around me while someone's hit my pause button.

I'm exhausted, but if I close my eyes, her gaunt face is all I see. If I keep them open, then I'm reminded of what's happened.

There's no relief.

None at all.

After a few minutes or what could have been hours, Brooke and Reese join me once more.

"Here you go. I know you said you didn't want it, but I made you a sandwich. You really should try to eat something."

I nod.

"Just relax. Don't worry about what comes next. We've got everything under control."

I nod again.

A concerned look passes between them, but they don't say anything. They just sit with me in silence. It's all I need.

At some point, Reese gives me a hug and says she'll come back tomorrow. Brooke orders takeout from our favorite restaurant, and I poke it around the plate for a while before giving up and curling back up under the blanket.

I end up passing out with my head in Brooke's lap as she gently plays with my hair like my mom used to when I was a kid.

The next thing I know, it's dark and Brooke is telling me that we should go to bed. I allow her to drag me from the couch and up the stairs. She pulls the sheets back and tucks me in.

"You want me to stay?" she whispers when I reach for her hand.

"Please," I whisper, and she immediately climbs into bed behind me.

"Everything will be okay, Harlow. I promise."

I want to shout. I want to scream. How can anything be okay? Everyone has left me.

Everyone.

I DRIFT OFF A FEW TIMES, but when Brooke stirs a few hours after the sun rises, I'm staring at the wall in a daze.

"Harlow," she whispers.

"Yeah?"

"How are you doing?"

I roll onto my back so I can stare at the ceiling for a change of scenery. My stomach rolls.

"Fuck," I bark, jumping from the bed and racing toward my bathroom to throw up.

"Jesus, are you okay?" Brooke asks from the doorway when I've finished and slumped back against the wall.

"Yeah." Pushing my sweat-damp hair from my face, I risk a look up at her.

Her brows are pulled with concern.

"You need to look after yourself," she chastises. "Take a shower. I'll make you some breakfast. Which you *will* eat," she adds in a stern voice.

"Fine." I roll my eyes at her, but even doing that takes more effort than I've got right now. What I really want to do is crawl back into bed.

"Thirty minutes max, or I'm coming back to get you," she warns before leaving me alone on the bathroom floor.

I love her to death, but right now, I wish she'd allow me to wallow in peace. I know she's just doing what she thinks is best for me, but the thought of showering and attempting to be normal just seems wrong.

"DON'T YOU FEEL BETTER NOW?" Brooke asks when I join her in the kitchen wearing a clean hoodie and yoga pants, and still with wet hair.

"No, not really," I mutter.

I take a seat as she reaches into the cupboard for my mug and places it under the coffee machine.

"You want a strong one?"

"Please."

I really fucking need a strong one. My eyes are swollen from the crying and burning from the lack of sleep, and my body feels like I'm trudging through mud just walking.

Only, when she places the steaming mug in front of me and the scent of the coffee beans hits my nose, I dart for the sink.

"Okay, that's it. I'm not ignoring it this time."

"What?" I mutter, reaching for a glass so I can rinse my mouth.

"Is there any chance you could be pregnant?"

My eyebrows almost hit my hairline. "What?"

"Is there any chance—"

"I heard you. I'm not fucking deaf."

"Sorry," she mutters. "Well, is there?"

"No, I'm due on ... wait, what day is it?"

"Saturday."

"Um ..." I say, stalling for time as I try to get my brain to function, to work this out.

"Harlow?"

"I was due on ... Tuesday." *Fuck.* I'm never late. *Never.* "It's probably just the stress of this week," I say, attempting to push the idea aside, but I can tell by the look on Brooke's face that she's not going to forget about this.

"Put some shoes on. We're going to the store."

"I'm sure it's fine. Just give it a day or two."

"So you'll be a week late? No. Get your shoes."

"Really?"

"Yes. Unless you just so happen to have a test in your bedroom."

"Of course I don't. Before C-Corey," I stumble over his name, not wanting to allow thoughts of him and how we left things to enter my head, "I hadn't had sex in forever. There was no way in hell I'd have been pregnant unless the myth about sitting on the same chair as a guy is actually true."

"You used protection, right?" I can tell from the firm set of her lips that she's about to give me a lecture if I say no.

"Of course." *I think.* I know we went without this past weekend, but I was due on my period, and it was as safe as it could be.

But that first night...

There were condoms. I remember watching him rolling them on. Hell, I remember doing it myself. I also remember standing on one as I made my escape. But did we use one every time? I don't know. There was too much Macallan to remember it all clearly.

"Really?" She juts her hip out.

Brooke might be reckless with some things, but she's

always safe where sex is concerned, or at least she claims to be. As far as I know, she hasn't even had a scare, so she must practice what she preaches.

"I guess we're about to find out."

Thankfully, Brooke allows me to stay in her car while she runs into the store to get what we need.

When she emerges, it's with the test, as promised, but also a huge bar of chocolate, the biggest tub of ice cream she could find, and a bottle of wine—although that one might be just for her.

It's not until we pull up back outside the house and my eyes land on my car parked in its spot outside that I remember he was the last one to use it.

"H-Has he been here?"

"I assume so. I didn't actually see him. I found your keys under the doormat."

"He borrowed it on Monday and was meant to pick me up again after work," I say sadly.

"Have you heard from him?"

"I haven't looked at my cell since Monday morning. It's probably dead in my purse."

"So he might have been ringing all this time?"

"I highly doubt it." My voice is cold and empty. Exactly how I feel right now.

"Come on then. Let's see what this says."

"Do we have to?"

"You'd rather not know?"

"I think I might, yeah."

"You can't live like that. Knowledge is power." Brooke climbs out of the car, but I don't move. Not for a long few seconds, anyway.

With a deep sigh, I push the door open and follow my

best friend into our house and up to my bathroom. No time like the present, I guess.

"How long do we have to wait?" I ask, sitting down on the end of my bed with the stick in my hand.

"It says three minutes."

"Great," I mutter, already feeling like it's been a year.

"It's been two," Brooke says, looking at her watch. "You wanna look now, or—"

"Wait until three. We'll know for sure then."

Silence falls around us, and I can almost imagine the ticking of the clock as it counts down.

"Okay. Three minutes. You can look now."

"I don't think I can," I admit, my hand beginning to tremble.

"Shall I...?" She steps forward and holds her hand out. But as much as turning the stick over might terrify me, allowing her to see it first is worse.

"No."

My stomach turns. My hands shake and my mouth goes dry.

I drag in a long, slow breath and close my eyes.

When I pull them open again, I've spun the stick, and the result is staring right back at me.

Fuck.

The trembling of my hands gets more violent as the room starts spinning.

"Well?" Brooke asks, getting impatient.

"F-four weeks."

"You're pregnant?"

I swallow, trying to force the lump down that's blocking my airway. "It would seem so."

Closing the space between us, she drops down beside me.

My eyes are still locked on the confirmation as she wraps her arm around my shoulder and pulls me into her body.

"Are you okay?" she asks after I don't respond. "I kind of expected you to react."

She's right. I'm not crying, screaming, or even feeling a sliver of happiness.

"I ... um ... I'm not sure I can deal with this right now."

"Okaaay."

"I'm just gonna ..." I stand, placing the test on the dresser before slipping my shoes off and crawling into bed.

"Harlow, you need to eat something."

"I'm not hungry."

"But—" I cut her with a look that stops any argument falling from her lips. "Okay. I'll ... um ..." She starts backing out of the room, and I allow her to go.

I need to be alone.

I need ... I've no idea what I need.

After a few minutes, Brooke heads downstairs, but it's not long before I hear the hushed sound of her voice as she talks to someone. A little bit of panic erupts that she might be talking to Corey, but I know she'd never do that to me.

I lie there curled up in a ball as I run through all the things I need to do. I've got a funeral and a wake to plan. I need to make arrangements with the funeral directors, choose flowers, songs, readings...

I must drift off to sleep, because when I wake again, the sun is setting outside, casting an orange glow around the room.

Sitting up, I look at my clock, and my eyes widen. I knew I was tired, but Christ.

My stomach grumbles, and I pull my aching body to sit on the edge of the bed.

When was the last time I ate?

I shake my head, because everything is hazy. I don't even know what day it is.

Looking around my room for signs, my eyes land on the white plastic stick on the dresser, and everything comes crashing down.

I'm pregnant.

The sound of the doorbell drags me from my nightmare, and my heart rate picks up. I really, really don't want to see anyone. But after only a few seconds and a couple of muffled words from Brooke, the door is closed and everything falls silent.

Risking a look out of the window, I breathe a sigh of relief when I watch a delivery man head back to his van.

After visiting the bathroom to freshen up, I drag in some courage and head downstairs.

As I descend, the scent of flowers hits me.

"Jesus," I mutter when I come to a stop in the living room doorway. Every surface is covered in flowers. No wonder the scent almost knocked me on my ass.

"You're awake. How are you feeling?" Brooke asks after placing the newest addition to my floral collection on the sideboard.

"I've been better. Where the hell are all these from?"

Flowers of all colors, size and design cover the room. They're pretty, sure. But it's a little over the top.

"Everyone. I haven't opened any of the cards. Reese brought these. The bigger one's from everyone in your office, and those are from her and Fletch. These sunflowers are from Mom and Dad—they hoped they'd make you smile. I don't know for sure about the others. I thought you'd want to open them."

I nod, feeling totally out of my depth and overwhelmed

that people took time out of their lives to do this. I know I'm surrounded by kind people, but I really didn't expect it.

My stomach grumbles once again, so loudly that Brooke doesn't miss it.

"What do you want? I'll cook or order anything."

"Chinese," I say without a second thought. "And cheesecake."

"You got it." She pulls her cell from her back pocket and starts tapping away. "Is there anything else you need while I'm at it?"

"No, I don't think so."

Ignoring her, I take a step into the room and run my fingertip over the soft, bright yellow petals of the sunflowers. They really are beautiful. I pluck the card from the center and flip it over.

> *All our love and thoughts,*
> *We're here for whatever you need.*
> *Sarah and Neil*
> *Xxx*

My heart aches, reading their words.

I move to the next ones and find similar messages from Mags, Reese, my aunt's best friend, some others from work, and even some of the players. But it's the final bouquet that makes me pause. I have no idea why—there's nothing that really makes it stand out against the others. Just a feeling. A premonition.

My hand shakes as I reach for the card and pull it from its little envelope.

I'm sorry for your loss.
Yours.
C x

I gasp, my eyes burning with tears as I stare at his handwriting and the small sketch of a dandelion in the corner of the card. It's the same as my tattoo.

24

———

COREY

Fletch tried to stop me as I marched toward him in my need to escape that building and her. But nothing was going to.

A red haze had descended, and I couldn't see my way through it, let alone figure out a way to banish it.

My heart raced, and my hands trembled with my need to break something, hurt someone.

And all for what?

Because she tried to help me.

I threw her car keys at the receptionist as I left and took off on foot. Driving over here surrounded by her scent was bad enough. I couldn't bear it again.

I walked for hours, trying to regulate my breathing and talk myself down. I shouldn't have gone marching in there like that. I should have waited until later, and we could have talked it out in private. But I was just too fucking angry.

I ended up on the beach, where I sat and watched the waves crash onto the shore, trying to figure out where I—we —go. All the while, Oz was forced to cancel my appointments when I didn't show my face at the studio.

I should have swallowed my pride and picked her up

from work as planned and allowed her to explain. But my fear of her looking at me like a charity case was too much to bear. I told myself that nothing had changed, but it didn't matter.

All these questions spun around in my head. Where did she get that kind of money from? How the hell am I going to pay her back?

But none of them were important enough to get me moving.

The time for her to finish work came and went, and I still sat on the sand in an angry daze.

When I did move, it was only because the tide was coming in and I had little choice.

I stopped at a store on the way back to my flat and found myself a bottle of whisky—not Macallan; there's no way I could stomach that—and I spent the rest of the night drinking myself into oblivion.

Aside from turning up to the shop still smelling of the previous night's alcohol, that's pretty much how I spend the next four days: losing myself in work or whisky. I'm not sure what else to do to numb the pain of walking away from her. When I told her that being with her makes me feel free in a way I'd never experienced before, I don't think I had totally appreciated just how true that was. But without her, I'm drowning.

My alcohol-induced nightmares are worse than ever, and each time I wake from one, my chest heaving and covered in a sheen of sweat, she's the first thing I look for. But all that stares back at me is an empty bed.

I spend the week almost like I'm back in England and fighting to get through each day. I thought I'd left this feeling of loneliness and desperation behind; turns out it was just in wait, ready to knock me back down to Earth once again.

I guess that's what happens when you try to outrun your demons. They find you eventually.

By Friday, I'm exhausted. My sleep is almost as bad as it's ever been, and my hangovers are starting to roll into one giant one. I've no idea where one day ends and another begins.

Work is the only time the voices in my head lessen. I need to go to her. We need to talk. But I'm no good to anyone like this.

I'm a fucking mess, and I won't allow her to try to bring me back to life. I need to figure out a way to do that for myself. I refuse to be that dependent on her, or anyone.

It's almost the end of the day, and I'm already dreading having to go home and be alone and for the walls to close in on me once again. A commotion out in the studio reception has me pausing as I tidy everything away for the night, but I don't bother to go and look. It's probably just Oz and JJ causing a scene once again.

I'm not expecting a knock at my door, but when it comes, I call out for whomever it is to enter.

Assuming it's one of the guys who knows better than to just storm in with the mood I've been in this week, I continue with what I'm doing. Only, when a throat clears behind me, I'm forced to look over my shoulder to see who's there.

"F-Fletch? How's it going?" I guess that explains the excitement on the other side of the door.

"I'm good, man."

"I thought you'd want Snake if you were after some more ink."

"I'm not. I'm here for you."

"Okay. Well, get up on the chair then," I say, ready to halt my tidying up if he needs me to do something.

"Nah, not like that. We need to talk."

"Ah," I say, realisation hitting me. "Reese sent you?"

He shrugs and looks a little guilty. "Yes and no. There's a bar down the street. Shall we?"

"Sure." Abandoning my studio as it is, I follow him out.

He says his goodbyes to Snake and JJ, who looks up at him as if she's imagining climbing him like a tree, and we head across the street.

"So, to what do I owe this pleasure?" I ask when he places two glasses and a bottle of scotch in the center of the table we've taken over.

"How are you doing?" Memories of our rooftop chat come back to me.

"Yeah, you know," I say, not really explaining anything.

He blows out a breath as he swirls his glass and watches the amber liquid race around. "Harlow's aunt died."

My heart drops. Losing another family member is the last thing she needs.

"I know this probably isn't what you want to hear, and it isn't really my place to be telling you this, but ... Reese can be persuasive when she wants to be. Harlow isn't in a good place, man. I think she might need you."

"She barely knows me," I mutter, downing my drink in one in the hope of dulling the ache those words cause in my chest.

"She knows you enough to help you out when you need it." He quirks an eyebrow and I groan, hating that he knows what she did. "I know you're scared. I understand that this is bigger than just taking a chance on a girl. But you're going to need to make a decision. Is she worth it? And if you decide she is, you need to show her. Be there for her when she needs you so that she can do the same in return when the time comes."

I nod, unable to find the words.

Fletch gives me a moment, his attention drifting to the other side of the bar.

I want to be there for her,. I want to be the man she deserves. But can I put my issues aside for long enough to be that?

The TV behind my head changes, and it has Fletch looking up. I glance over my shoulder to see what's got his attention and find a news report on the upcoming season.

"You all ready for it?" I ask, happy to divert the conversation away from me.

"Ready as I can be. You planning on watching some games?"

"Yeah, definitely." I managed to get to the last few games of the season after I moved. Milo dragged me out after to celebrate their wins. I can't lie; I'm looking forward to the season starting again and having something other than work to focus on.

His face flashes on the screen, and he sinks down in his chair a little, pulling his hat lower in the hope that no one notices him.

"You can go, if you like. You don't need to babysit me."

"What? Don't be stupid. I'm not passing up a night of freedom. Actually ..." He pulls his phone out and taps away for a few seconds. "Reinforcements will be here momentarily."

"Reinforcements?"

"Yep, not that they'll be any better with advice than I am."

Not ten minutes later is there a commotion at the

entrance, and when I look over, I spot two familiar faces heading our way.

"Linc, Handsy. You know Corey, right?"

"Sure do." They nod before joining us.

Two more glasses appear before us, and they both take the drink Fletch offers them.

Linc swallows it down before leaning forward on his elbows, his eyes locked on mine. "So, Corey, what has us here at a bar drinking top-shelf whiskey tonight?"

"He just needed a night away from reality," Fletch says coyly, refilling my glass.

"That we can do," Handsy agrees before swallowing his drink.

Harlow aside, the night turns out to be one of the best I've had since moving here. I've hung out occasionally with the guys after a win, but they're usually too distracted. But spending time with Fletch, Linc and Handsy is just easy, relaxed. We shoot the shit, give each other shit, and just ... hang.

By the time I'm back in my flat later that night with my head spinning once again, I feel lighter for the first time since walking out of that letting agent office at the beginning of the week.

Once I'm in bed, I pull my phone from my pocket and bring up an app that allows me to send her flowers. When it prompts me to upload my own message for the card, I scramble out of bed to find a pen and piece of paper. The second I write her name, I know what to add.

The need to be with her supporting her right now burns through me as I redraw a part of the tattoo she allowed me to ink on her.

I'm still angry that she went ahead and bailed me out like she did, but I'm not angry enough to ignore the fact that she's going through a hard time. Plus, the gesture will make me feel that little bit better about the fact that I should probably do as Fletch suggested and push my pride aside and go and see her myself.

I tell myself that I will, but then I end up convincing myself that she's probably surrounded by family right now who are supporting her through this. After the way I treated her, the last thing she needs is to see me.

25

HARLOW

"You should call him," Brooke says as we continue staring down at the card.

"N-No, I can't. He clearly knows what's going on," I wave the card in front of her as evidence. "Yet he decided to send these instead of come himself." I fight to keep my voice strong, but the sympathy in Brooke's eyes tells me that I don't do a very good job.

"He doesn't know everything, though. Does he?"

"He couldn't cope with me giving him a few thousand dollars. You really think he's going to take well to me following that up with a baby?"

"He's got a right to know."

"I know. I just ... I just need to get my head around it before I attempt to figure out how I'm going to tell him."

She wraps her arm around my shoulder. "Do what feels right. I'll support you all the way."

"Thank you," I mutter into her shoulder when she pulls me in for a hug.

"I don't know if you wanted me to or not, but I called the funeral directors when you were asleep just to get things moving." I nod, thankful that she's made that first step for me, because it was one of the things I was dreading the most. "Did you know your aunt had already planned and paid for her funeral?"

"What?"

"Apparently, it's all done. You just need to confirm a date. The rest has been taken care of."

I stare at her, totally taken aback—but then, this is my aunt we're talking about. I'm not sure why I'm so surprised.

"I should have seen this coming," I mutter, falling onto the couch and pulling my knees up so I can wrap my arms around them.

"I guess so. She just wanted to make all of this as easy on you as possible."

"Did they give you a date?"

"They said they could do Wednesday. I've held it for you, but you need to ring and confirm."

A sob rips up my throat.

"Shit, what's wrong? It doesn't have to be Wednesday if you don't want."

"It's-it's not that. I just ..." I steel myself to continue. "I have no idea if I'm relieved or disappointed."

"Why would you be disappointed?"

"It would have given me something to think about," I admit.

"I think you've got enough on your plate right now, don't you?"

"But what am I meant to do between now and then?"

"Sleep. Book a doctor's appointment, maybe. Talk to Corey," she suggests, making my stomach somersault.

How the hell am I meant to even broach the subject of my pregnancy with him?

"Everything will be fine," Brooke says with a smile on her face and an optimism that I don't feel.

Our Chinese arrives, and I eat some of it before I make my excuses and head up to bed.

I love Brooke, and I know she's just trying to make all of this easier, but I need to be alone.

It's late, or at least I think it is, seeing as my room is in darkness, when the doorbell rings again.

Praying it's just another flower delivery, I roll over and curl myself up in a ball.

Voices filter up to me. I know who it is immediately. I'd recognize his deep rumble anywhere, but I make no effort to move.

I'm mentally drained and physically exhausted. I don't have it in me to deal with what he'll want to talk about ... what I need to tell him.

Light footsteps climb the stairs, and I breathe a sigh of relief that Brooke hasn't just sent him up.

She cracks my door open. It squeaks slightly like it usually does, but I don't move. I don't so much as flinch as I attempt to make it look like I'm sleeping.

After a few seconds, she backs out of the room and descends the stairs once again. Knowing she's telling him that I'm sleeping guts me. Tears burn my eyes, and my body trembles with my sobs.

This is too much. It's all just too much.

OTHER THAN HAVING no choice but to speak to the funeral directors and the venue for the wake, the next three days all blur into one. I sleep, I cry, I throw up, I eat, and mostly I throw up again. Every day the doorbell rings, and every day I hide in my room. Whether it be Corey's daily visit that Brooke insists on telling me about the second she's closed the door behind him, or her parents or Reese, I refuse to talk to any of them.

I just want to be in my own little bubble where I can pretend things are all still normal.

The funeral is this afternoon, so whether I like it or not, I'm going to have to leave this room and face the world so I can say goodbye to someone else who shouldn't have left me so soon.

"Good morning," Brooke sings, marching into my room and dragging the curtains open. They haven't been like that in a while, and the sun from the outside world burns my eyes.

"Hey, stop that," I complain.

"Harlow," she sighs. "I've let you hide and wallow. Today it stops. Today you reenter the world again. People want to see you. They need to see with their own eyes that you're okay."

Guilt twists my insides that I'm making people worry about me.

"Do you think he's going to be there?" Having to face him while trying to deal with the service is my biggest fear right now. I'm not sure I need my two disastrous worlds blending together into one. Each alone is hard enough to deal with; I don't need them joining forces.

"I don't know. He didn't say."

"He didn't say? B, he's been here every day. How hasn't that come up?"

She shrugs. "We just didn't talk about it."

"So what did you talk about?" Not all of his visits have been quick ones with him staying on the other side of the door. I know she's invited him in, hoping I'd come down and face my issues.

"You," she admits, hesitantly. "He's worried about you. So am I. So is everyone. I know this is hard right now, and the added stress of ..." She nods toward my stomach like I need the reminder. "But you really should talk to him. Hear him out."

"One thing at a time. Did I smell toast?"

"You did. Here." She passes me the tray she'd abandoned on the dresser.

Sitting myself up, I accept it and immediately shove a piece of buttered toast in my mouth in the hope that it'll help keep any sickness at bay.

Brooke watches me for a beat before turning to my closet.

"Have you decided what you're wearing today?"

"Nope. Probably the first thing I find."

"Don't be like that. Your aunt specifically said she wanted everyone in bright colors. I know it's hard, but she wants you to celebrate her today. And to be honest, she was kinda epic, so I think she deserves you to pull out all the stops."

I roll my eyes. My aunt organizing her own funeral might have been a surprise, but her desire to ditch the black for today had been in the plans for a long time.

"What about this?"

I risk a glance up. "No."

"What? Why? It's so pretty."

I sigh. "Just no."

She huffs and puts it back in before rummaging around again.

"B, it's okay. I can find something."

"Okay," she says, holding her hands up and backing

away from my closet. "You've got two hours until the cars will be here. If you need anything, call me."

"I will," I promise before watching her back out of the room.

I'm not ready for today. Not that I think I ever could be.

I move on autopilot as I get myself in the shower and begin getting ready. I try to keep my imagination in check to stop it wandering to my family's funeral all those years ago. That day, I prayed I'd never have to say goodbye to anyone ever again. But here we are.

I blow-dry my hair, leaving it curly as I know my aunt liked it, and apply some light makeup. In reality, I'm going to wash it all away with my tears in the coming hours.

Standing at my closet like Brooke did not so long ago, I run my eyes over everything, trying to find the right dress. Nothing feels quite right. Add that to the fact that I feel totally bloated and sick right now, and nothing really appeals.

In the end, I pull out a long, flowing, floral maxi dress that's covered in big, bright flowers and team it with a pink cardigan.

I glance at myself in the mirror, and a small smile turns up the corners of my lips. She'd approve of this. I turn to the side and run my hand over my stomach. Despite the fact that I feel more bloated than I ever have in my life, it's not at all noticeable.

Digging deep for some strength, I abandon my sanctuary in search of Brooke.

The smell of her coffee filling the kitchen makes my stomach turn over, but thankfully, I manage to keep the toast down for now.

She turns to me, her eyes softening as she takes in my outfit. "You look lovely."

"You too."

"There's a stack of unopened cards on the coffee table, if you'd like to look through them."

"Uh ... no, I think today is already going to be hard enough."

She nods. "You need anything before we go? More food? Drink?"

"I'm good, thanks. I just need ... I just need to do this—say goodbye—and then I can focus on the future." My hand presses against my stomach, a move that Brooke doesn't miss.

She opens her mouth to say something, but I cut her off.

"I know. I'll talk to him soon. I promise."

Our journey to the church is in silence. Brooke holds my hand the entire way and never once lets go.

My best friend might be all kinds of crazy at times, but I'd never swap her. She's ... incredible. I never would have got through any of this without her. She's like my guardian angel.

"Thank you," I whisper, turning to her.

"What for?"

"This." I nod to our joined hands. "Everything. I just need you to know that I really appreciate it."

"I know you do, sweetie. I also know that you'd do the exact same thing for me."

I smile at her. I'd do anything for her.

The second we're out of the car, I'm pulled into her parents' arms. Sarah sobs as she holds me while her dad is more stoic, like always, when he wraps an arm around my shoulder.

They both speak to me, but aside from the standard "we're sorry for your loss," I don't hear a word of it.

I'm too numb.

Reese runs over the second she sees me and wraps her arms around my shoulders, holding me tightly. When she pulls back, her eyes are filled with tears.

"You've got this, Harlow." She reaches down and squeezes my hand as Fletch joins us.

I glance around the people loitering outside the church and find all their eyes on him. For once, I'm glad of his presence, even if I'm about to do something stupid, because it means no one is looking at me, waiting for me to break.

"Harlow, we're so sorry for your loss."

"Thank you. And thank you for being here. All of you," I say, glancing at where the rest of the team are huddled together. "I really appreciate it, and not just because everyone is staring at you and not me right now."

He chuckles. "I do aim to please." He winks, and my face flushes beet red while Reese slaps his shoulder.

"I can't take you anywhere."

Grateful that I was able to stay solidly on both feet and not accidently grope him this time, I make my excuses and wander over to see the vicar so he can talk through proceedings.

My aunt wasn't an overly religious person, but this church was where her parents got married and the only place she wanted to say her own vows.

With Brooke on one side of me and her mom the other, they hold my hands to try to keep me steady through the service.

It's beautiful, it really is. I never would have done such a good job if I'd had to plan it all over the past few days.

All too soon, we're forced to say our final goodbyes and are walking away from the committal.

My legs move, but I don't register that I'm going anywhere. The previous numbness has turned into total emptiness. All I want to do is go running back to my bedroom to hide.

Aside from the Vipers family, there aren't all that many people here. My aunt kept her circle quite small, but even still, it's too many to deal with. Some of their interest in the celebrities in our midst has waned, and I'm feeling more eyes burning into me. Each pair is full of sympathy. I have no doubt they know my story if they knew my aunt.

"I'm proud of you," Brooke whispers, coming back to join me. She's hardly left my side, for which I'm grateful.

"He didn't come." I don't mean for the words to come out loud, and I gasp when I realize that they do.

She reaches up and wipes a tear from my cheek. I didn't even know it had fallen, it's such a common feeling these days.

"Look up, H," Brooke says quietly. She stands aside, and I gasp.

Right at the other side of the church, shadowed by overhanging trees, is a bench.

"Oh my God."

As if he knows I'm staring at him, his head lifts from where it was hanging between his shoulders, his elbows on his knees, and our eyes connect.

Something crackles between us. Something I remember all too well even from that very first night.

He's here. He came. For me.

"What do you want to do? We really need to be moving toward the wake."

I'm silent for a beat, my connection with Corey as strong as ever, before I say the words that gut me. All I want to do is run into his arms, feel his strength wrap around me, and hear promises that he's never going to let go.

But I can't. That can't happen until we've talked, and

that can't happen until I've done this for my aunt. She deserves my full attention. Well, as much as I'm capable of right now.

"One thing at a time," I say, repeating my previous words.

"Okay. So, we go?"

"Yes."

I hold his stare for one final second before breaking it and turning away from him.

A sob rumbles up my throat, but I catch it before it escapes. Everything feels wrong about walking away, but it's all I can do right now.

"Everything okay?" I ask Brooke as she drops her cell back into her purse as the car pulls away.

"Yep. I'm good. You don't need to be worrying about me."

She takes my hand once again, and I blow out a breath.

Did I just make a mistake?

I fucking hate funerals. After the last one I attended, I told myself I wouldn't go to another until it was for, God forbid, my mum or sisters. Everyone else, I'll mourn from a distance, because even just sitting outside of one brings back haunting memories that I don't need.

Yet outside of a funeral is exactly where I find myself.

It's been over a week now since my last regrettable encounter with Harlow, and I'm fucking dying. My anger over what she did has somewhat diminished as my desperation has taken over.

Fletch's words from the other night are on repeat in my mind. I knew he was right the moment he said them. It's the reason I've been standing on the wrong side of her front door for the past four days.

I need to see her. I need to hold her. Tell her that I'm here for anything she needs right now. But Brooke successfully kept me away. Only once did she allow me inside, and that was only because I turned up at the same time as a flower delivery.

Knowing that she's lost someone important to her put

the issue with my flat and the money into perspective. Money doesn't matter, not in the grand scheme of things. But family, people you love? They are everything. I also can't ignore what an incredible thing she's done for me. She's lifted the weight that was pressing down on me, allowing me to both support my family and live a life here.

She doesn't see me before the service starts, as per my intention. I need to be here for her, but equally, I don't want to be a distraction. There's time for us after.

I'll be waiting.

I'll do whatever it takes, because while I might have tried to turn a blind eye to what was developing between us while we were spending time together, it was impossible to ignore when it was gone.

I've missed a lot of things in my life. My family when I was on tour. My boys after the accident. My mum and sisters now. English chocolate. Fry-ups. But none of it compares to the massive hole she left when I ruined what we had. It was like a dark crater I was teetering on the edge of.

I'd been in that dark, lonely place before. It was not somewhere I was going to fall willingly this time.

I had to fight.

So, I'm here.

Waiting. Giving us a chance. Because, hell, we both deserve it. We've only skimmed the surface of my issues, and I fear the same can be said for Harlow. But together, we just make sense. We see the darkness within each other's souls, and we understand it. We accept it. We embrace it. And fuck, I need that back.

My heart is damn near beating out of my chest when people start emerging from around the back of the church. My palms begin to sweat as I wait to see her once again.

I was here when she first arrived. Although she looked exhausted, devastated about all of this, she was also just as beautiful as she was the first night I laid eyes on her. My need for her has only grown stronger as our time together has gone on.

I don't miss her looking around as people try to engage her in conversation.

Part of me wants to run when our eyes lock, but my muscles turn to stone as we stare at each other.

My fists clench.

Fuck, I need her.

I'm just about to push from the bench and walk over to take her in my arms when she turns away from me, dismissing me without a second thought.

Pain sears through my chest. I know she has no idea how hard just being here is for me, she has no reason to, but still, fuck. It hurts.

I lift my hand to rub at the ache in my chest, hoping that it will abate, but it never does.

My phone vibrating in my pocket distracts me, and I pull it out.

A little hope creeps in.

Brook: Self-preservation. Be at the house later. She's ready.

Fucking hell. I hope she's right.

I DON'T KNOW what I'm meant to do to waste the day, but an hour or so after Harlow walked away from me, I find myself standing at my aunt and uncle's front door. The camper that I have such fond memories of is sitting in the driveway, and I can't help but remember that night.

My chest aches as it hits home just how much I've missed her.

Somehow, in only a short amount of time, she's managed to find a place in my heart that I wasn't even aware existed.

I ring the bell and wait.

"Corey!" my aunt announces in surprise when she pulls the door open to greet me. "Shouldn't you be at work?" she asks before realising what she's just said and corrects herself. "Not that I don't want you here, of course. Come in, come in."

The scent of her home baking fills the house, and my stomach grumbles loudly.

"Perfect timing. I've just pulled fresh sausage rolls out of the oven."

I want to tell her that food isn't what I came for, but the second my eyes land on the golden, crisp pastry sitting on the counter, I can't.

"Would you like a coffee, too?"

"If you don't mind."

"Of course I don't mind, silly. Take a seat." She rattles around, sorting everything out. "I've got a cake in the oven, too. It'll be ready in a few minutes."

"Sounds fantastic. Thank you so much."

She brings everything over and takes a seat opposite me.

"So, to what do I owe this pleasure?"

I shrug, wondering exactly what to tell her. "I ... um ... I'm having a rough day."

"Is everyone okay?"

"Yeah, yeah, everyone is fine. I ... I met someone."

"The girl Milo mentioned when you were here last?"

"Yeah. Harlow." I can't stop my lips curling at the mention of her name, and if the delight that appears on my aunt's face says anything, she didn't miss it.

"Okay, so what's happened?"

"I fu—I screwed it up."

She reaches over and squeezes my hand that's resting on the table. "I'm sure that's not true, Corey."

"She did something really nice for me, and I freaked out. Now she's lost someone close to her, and she isn't letting me anywhere near her to support her and ..."

"You're in love with her?"

"Um ..." My heart pounds and my head spins, but I know that I need to stop running from this.

"Yeah. I think I might be heading in that direction."

"Oh, Corey," she sighs. "Relationships are hard. Especially the beginning. Trying to figure out who each other is, all their little quirks ..." She smiles fondly as she reminisces. "But if you think she's worth it, then you've got to fight."

"I know," I mutter, ashamed that I haven't fought harder for her.

"So, why are you here?"

"It was the funeral today. I sat outside the church so I could be there for her. Milo and the guys went to support her as well. But I couldn't." She nods in understanding. "I'm planning on going to see her once she's home. I just needed ... I don't know. But being at that funeral ... it's the first one since ..." My words falter, and my aunt reaches for my hand once again.

"Does she know?" I shake my head. "If you think she's the one, then you owe it to her to tell her everything."

"I know," I whisper. "It's just finding the words. She's

been through so much herself, and I'd hate to burden her with more of my baggage."

"If she feels the same, then your past won't feel like baggage. It will help her get to know you, know what's in there." She nods down to my heart.

"I didn't think there was anything in there until I met her."

"Sometimes all it takes is the right person. Some just have the ability to see inside us and help take the weight of the things that press down on us."

I stare at my aunt, wondering for the first time what her story might be. She shakes her head, clearly sensing where my thoughts are.

"You need to go to her tonight and tell her, show her how you feel. And when she's strong enough, you need to tell her everything."

The buzzer on the oven beeps, and she jumps up. "My cake!"

We chat about much more mundane things until my uncle comes home, and I end up eating with them.

"I should probably head out," I say after being forced to stay where I am and not help with the cleaning up.

"Would you like to borrow the camper?"

"That would be fantastic. Are you sure?"

"Of course. Keep it for the weekend, if you like. Make use of it."

Walking over, I pull my aunt into my arms. "Thank you," I whisper in her hair.

"You're welcome. If you ever need anything, you know where I am. Your mother would never forgive me if I weren't here for you."

As always at the mention of my family, guilt twists my gut. I probably should have called my mum for advice, but the thought of putting more on her plate puts me off, so when we do talk, I skim the surface of my issues.

After she hands me the key to the camper and I get my uncle's speech once again about looking after his baby, I climb inside and head towards the place I want to be more than anything but am equally terrified of.

I sit out on the street outside Harlow's for long minutes. I've had a message from Brooke to say that they're home, but nothing more.

After giving myself a pep talk, I climb from the car before collecting the doughnuts I stopped to pick up on the way over. I wanted to buy more flowers, but after seeing her living room the other day, I already know she's got enough of those.

With the box in hand, I make my way over. I don't get a chance to knock on the front door, because it's pulled open before I even come to a stop.

"I didn't think you were going to come in." I look back at the camper, my cheeks heating.

"Sorry, I ... uh ... had a call?" I don't mean it to come out as a question, but it does nonetheless. She quirks an eyebrow at me, clearly not believing a word.

"Come in. Harlow's asleep on the sofa. She's not in a good place. I hope that seeing you will help. She keeps telling me she doesn't want to, but I know her better than she realizes I do." The box of doughnuts is lifted from my hand, and I can't help wondering if I'm going to see them again with the way she's staring down at them.

"If I didn't freak out, then none of this would have happened."

Brooke reaches out, and I still when her hand lands on my forearm. She stares up at me, and I'm unable to react.

I'm too desperate for the insight that I sense is on the tip of her tongue.

"My best friend is complicated, but her heart is always in the right place. She keeps a lot of stuff about her life hidden, although I think really she's just trying to hide it from herself. All of it reminds her too much of her parents. But there would have been no ulterior motive behind what she did. She genuinely just wants to help."

I nod at her, because although I lost my shit when I found out about the money, I knew deep down that there wasn't anything malicious about it. Harlow doesn't have a malicious bone in her body.

"I'll make myself scarce, but holler if you need me."

"Thank you, Brooke. I really appreciate it."

She nods before heading up the stairs, taking the doughnuts with her.

She didn't give me a great impression when I first met her, but I fear I might have Brooke all wrong. Maybe her friendship with Harlow's makes more sense than first appeared.

Rolling my shoulders back, I walk through into their living room.

I scan the mass of flowers and sympathy cards covering every surface before I find her curled up on the end of the sofa.

Dropping to my haunches in front of her, I allow myself a couple of seconds to take her in. Her red hair hangs in curls around her shoulders, and her makeup is smudged around her eyes from where she's been crying today, but her complexion is paler than I remember, the circles under her eyes darker.

My heart aches for what she's been going through for

the past week or so, and I kick myself for not being more forceful and making her see me so I could look after her.

She shifts in her sleep, and I can't help wondering if she's uncomfortable with her head at such a weird angle.

Making a snap decision, I stand and slide my arms under her slight body. It takes hardly any effort to lift her. The second she's against my chest, she nuzzles her cheek against me and moans lightly.

Does she know I'm here? That she's in my arms?

"Corey," she mumbles. Every muscle in my body freezes, but when I look down, I find her eyes are still closed with sleep.

As smoothly as I can, I walk us up the stairs and to her bedroom. I manage to pull her sheets back before lowering her to the bed.

She immediately curls onto her side and stays asleep.

Unable to keep the distance between us now that I've touched her, I toe my shoes off and pull my hoodie from my body before crawling in behind her.

I close the space between us until her back is pressed up against my front, and I wrap my arm around her waist. After a few seconds, her hand finds mine and she tangles our fingers together.

"Harlow?" I whisper, thinking she might be awake, but I get no reply.

With her in my arms once again, I soon drift off into a peaceful sleep alongside her.

HARLOW

When I wake, I feel better than I have in days—until I try to stretch my legs out and find that I can't. Something, or someone, is in the way.

Brooke never cuddl ... *fuck*.

Cracking one eye open, I risk a look at the arm that's wrapped tightly around my waist.

It's definitely too hairy and tattooed to belong to Brooke.

"Morning," he murmurs in his deep, husky voice, and I tense.

"C-Corey, what are you doing?"

"Well, I was sleeping, until you turned into stone beneath me. Relax," he encourages, pulling me deeper into his body.

I allow it, but only because it feels too damn good after so long. I've craved this feeling. The contentment, the feeling of safety that comes only when I'm in his arms.

"W-why are you here?"

"Because you need me, and because we need to talk."

"I never said I needed—"

"Shh." His lips press to my bare shoulder, and I

shudder. It's such a simple move, but I feel it all the way down to my toes. "I'm so sorry for freaking out. I was blindsided by it, and my anger took over."

"I was just trying to help," I whisper back.

"I know. I know I should have been thanking you, not shouting at you. I just ... I'm not used to anyone helping me out, and I didn't know how to deal with it."

"I should have talked to you about it."

"Yes." His lips press against my heated skin once again. "You." Kiss. "Should." Kiss. "Have."

My heart begins to race as heat floods my core. It's a welcome relief from the sickness I seem to get every morning right now. That thought has a lead weight settling in my belly.

He's right. We have a lot to talk about.

As much as I want to do this with the barrier that's between us right now, my need to look into his eyes has me flipping over in his arms.

"Hey," he whispers, his blue eyes twinkling with delight and naughty thoughts.

"Hey." Everything inside me relaxes, just knowing that he's here. Everything that I've been through in the past week or so feels that much easier to bear.

"I'm so sorry about your aunt, Harlow."

I nod, a huge lump forming once again in my throat. Will losing her ever get easier, or will I forever picture her lying in that hospital bed in her final minutes?

"I've been here almost every day trying to see you, trying to tell you how sorry I am. I should have pushed harder. I'm sorry."

"N-no, it's okay. I didn't want ... I couldn't ..." I sigh, not able to find the right words to express how I've felt the past few days.

"It's okay. I get it."

Knowing he's lost people he cared about, I tell myself that he really does. He must, or he'd still be angry at me. I shut him out, ignored him, yet here he is, with his arm wrapped around me and looking into my eyes, just like I remember.

I close my eyes for a beat as I prepare the words I need to say to him.

"My family." He nods to tell me he's listening. "My dad ... he owned vineyards. A lot of them, actually. He'd taken a step back from running the business when my sister and I were babies. He said it took too much of his time, and we were more important. So, he brought in a team to manage the business, and he just oversaw it.

"When they died, all that fell to me. It was put into trust until I was twenty-one, thankfully, but then everything was mine."

"Fucking hell," he mutters, his eyes not leaving mine for even a second.

"I don't want anything to do with it. I can't. It reminds me too much of them, of everything I've lost. But that doesn't stop the money coming in. I don't need it. I certainly don't earn it. But it's mine, nonetheless.

"I donate a lot of it, and until my current job, I've only taken voluntary positions. But I couldn't turn down the chance combining my two passions. To give talented kids a chance achieve their dreams."

"You do more than they're aware of, don't you?" he asks, narrowing his eyes at me.

"I might, yeah." I think of my wages every month being wired straight back into the foundation, and the prizes I've organized for the ball. "Fuck. The gala."

"It's okay, Reese has it under control," he soothes,

cupping my cheek in his hand and brushing his thumb over my skin.

"I need to call her, make sure everything is okay."

"Everything *is* okay. Just chill."

I nod at him, although I do anything but relax, and I have no doubt he can sense it.

"Just focus on you. Everything else is totally under control."

He leans forward, his lips gently brushing mine.

"For now, just let me look after you. Let me do what I've been desperate to do, to make up for screwing this up."

"Corey, I—"

"No, Harlow. It's my turn. I'm so fucking sorry. I was an idiot. But I need you. I need you so fucking much." He leans over me, pressing me into the mattress as his lips capture mine.

I want to hesitate, morning breath and all that, but the second his tongue teases to get inside, my lips part, allowing him in.

His hand squeezes my hip before running up my body until he's palming my breast. It's only then that I realize I'm still wearing yesterday's dress.

He kisses me so deeply, so passionately that it brings tears to my eyes.

"Oh God, Corey," I moan when he leaves my lips in favor of my neck.

"I've got you, baby."

He pulls the straps from my shoulder before sitting at my legs and pulling the fabric of my dress down my body.

"Fuck, you're so beautiful," he mutters, taking in my nude strapless bra and matching panties. "I've missed you so fucking much."

I want to return the sentiment, but I can't. I'm too lost.

His lips land on my collarbone, and he licks and nips his way down to the swell of my breasts.

"Please," I moan, arching my back so he can release them.

They're swollen, tender, extra sensitive and so desperate for his touch.

He follows my demand and slips his hand behind my back so he can unhook the fabric. In seconds it's free of my body, and I sigh.

"I-I need you." I arch again, offering myself up to him.

"My little goddess," he murmurs before reaching behind him, pulling his T-shirt off, and diving for my breasts.

"Oh God, oh God," I chant as he takes a nipple in his mouth and sucks until I almost combust beneath him. So fucking sensitive. "Keep going." My fingers thread in his hair to hold him in place. I'm so close already. His scent, his touch, his tongue as he flicks it over my tight bud builds me higher and higher.

He switches sides, his eyes meeting mine as he does so.

"More, Corey. I need more."

He nods, sucking the other side deep into his mouth. I cry out, but it's nothing compared to when his fingers slip inside my panties and he finds my already swollen clit.

"Oh God, yes. Yes," I cry as he teases me to perfection.

His mouth continues as his fingers push inside me. I writhe as my release gets within touching distance.

"Corey, Corey. Fuck, I need ... I need. Fuuuuuck." He bites down on one of my nipples, and I lose all control.

"You need what, Lo?"

I nod, my breathing too erratic to even think about forming words as my body floats back down to Earth.

Settling himself between my legs, he pops the button on

his pants and pushes them and his boxers down his thighs, too impatient to remove them completely.

He palms his hard cock a few times. The sight has me burning up. There's something so hot about a guy shamelessly taking the pleasure he needs.

"I need …"

"I've got you. I know exactly what you need."

Taking the lace of my panties in his hand, he tugs until they rip.

"Corey," I gasp, more turned on than I want to admit by the caveman move.

Hooking one hand behind my knee, he pushes my thigh up to my stomach before teasing the head of his cock around my clit.

My hips grind, needing more, desperate to feel him pushing inside me and stretching me. And in only seconds, he gives me my wish.

"Yes, yes, yes," I cry as he fills me to the hilt in one swift move.

Folding over my body, he drops his face into the crook of my neck.

"Fuck," he groans. "Fuck, I've missed this. Missed you. Fuck. I'm so sorry. Fuck."

My hands trail down his back until I grip onto his ass, encouraging him to move more than the slow thrusts he's doing right now.

After kissing down my neck, he pulls back and stares at me.

"Harlow," he breathes. "Fuck."

In that moment, I feel everything he's not saying out loud but is as clear as day in his eyes.

"I know, Corey. I know."

"Jesus, fuck."

His hand once again finds the back of my knee while the other grips my hip before he really starts to move.

His pace increases with each thrust, and all too soon I'm racing toward another mind-blowing release. Corey has always dragged the best out of me, but with our time apart, they're even more powerful.

He lowers his thumb to my clit, and I detonate.

"Corey," I cry, breaking the silence, I'm sure letting Brooke know exactly what's going down in here.

Seconds after my orgasm crashes into me, he stills and roars his own release.

The moment my orgasm starts to subside, my stomach turns over.

Oh no. No, no, no.

Scrambling to get up, I fly toward the bathroom and get to the toilet just in time.

I'm not aware of what he's doing as I heave into the bowl until his fingers brush my back as he gathers my hair for me.

Once I'm happy I've finished, I wipe my mouth with some tissue and sit back.

"Are you okay?" he asks, concern knitting his brows.

"Um ..."

His eyes burn into me as I stand and make use of the mouthwash sitting next to the basin.

"There's something else I need to tell you."

His eyes are wide, fear evident within them, but there's no hiding now. "I'm pregnant, Corey."

"No. No, no, no." His hands lift to his hair, and he tugs so hard I think it's going to come out. "No. No," he repeats, looking around the room with a horrified expression on his face that I'm sure I'll remember until my dying day. Not once does he meet my eyes. "Fuck," he barks before storming from the room and, soon after, the house.

I sag back against the counter, my head spinning. Did that really just happen?

How did we go from orgasmic bliss to him running like his ass was on fire in a matter of seconds?

Footsteps race toward me, and when I look up, I find Brooke holding a towel out for me. I'd totally forgotten that I was standing here naked.

"What the hell happened?"

"I told him."

"Fuck."

She gathers me up in her arms, but I don't cry. I'm pretty sure I've run out of tears.

HARLOW

"He's not coming back, is he?" Brooke asks from her end of the couch.

It's been hours since I told Corey ran from the house. To begin with, I thought that maybe he just needed a breather and he'd be back. He'd just told me how much he'd missed me, how much he needed me, and yet he's vanished.

"Doesn't look that way, does it?"

"Why do you sound so ... okay?"

I can't help but laugh at her. Okay? She thinks I'm okay? Clearly, I'm a better actress than I ever gave myself credit for.

"Okay, now you're just freaking me out," she mutters.

"Nothing about my life is okay right now, B. But if I don't laugh, I'll cry, and if I do that there's a chance I'll never stop."

Her face falls, and I hate it. I hate being on the receiving end of her pity.

"Stop, or I'll go back to hiding in my room. I need you to be ... normal, if that's at all possible."

She sticks her tongue out at me. "I need a drink. You want one—fuck."

"A glass of water would be great, thanks."

"I'm sorry," she whispers with a wince as she leaves the room.

Lifting my cell from the cushion beside me, I check it for the millionth time, but he hasn't been in touch. Fuck knows where he's gone—half his clothes are still upstairs in my room. The only thing that disappeared with him was his shoes.

I want to call again. Send a text, even. But what's the point? I'm not lowering myself to begging. If he cares about me like he claims to, if he has any interest in this baby, then he'll come back. It's whether or not I let him in that he should be worried about.

We spend the night lounging on the couch with pizza and ice cream, and Brooke does her best to try to distract me from my disastrous life. But the ball of dread which seems to have taken up residence in my stomach, and the flowers and cards that cover every surface, are an unwelcome reminder of what I'm dealing with right now.

"Why's my life so dramatic, B? Why can't it be more like yours?"

"I wish I had the answer. At some point the tables will turn, I'm sure. You'll run off into the sunset while I'm left here with some big drama that threatens to drag me under."

"I wouldn't leave you—you know that."

"Maybe not, but you'll have your baby, and Corey, hopefully. You deserve that sunset."

I smile at her because while I can't really argue, there's no way I'm leaving her. She's my sister. We might not always live in the same house, but we'll always be connected.

"We'll see. Knowing my luck, the bailiffs will turn up telling me something's gone very wrong, and I'll go from being a millionaire to poor and a single mom in a matter of minutes."

"That's not going to happen."

"Nor should getting pregnant the first time I had sex after forever, but it did."

"You can't blame anyone but yourself for that one."

"Fair point. I was drunk and Corey was ..."

"Hot?"

"Yeah, that."

I sigh, wishing that I'd gone about this morning differently.

"Did you at least explain about the money?"

"I did."

Silence settles around us as we both stare at whatever it is on the TV.

"You should know, that was really fucking hot, listening to you both this morning."

"Stop talking. Stop it right now."

"What? I can't help it. All the moaning, groaning, crying out his name."

"Jesus. I need to buy you your own house."

She laughs, reaching for her wine.

"What are you going to do?" She looks down at my belly.

"I have no idea."

"You could move back home, bring your baby up in a place you love. Give him or her the memories you have and create some new ones."

I sigh, thinking of my childhood home that's been sitting empty since the day I was picked up and taken away.

It's mine now, just like everything else my parents

owned. I never had it in me to sell it. I always had the idea that when I had a family that I could make it my home, like Brooke just described, but I'm not sure I want to now that the time is approaching. Not that it's anything like I imagined. I thought I'd be happily married and having a planned child, not a drunken accident—albeit a fun one.

The time drags on, but still, there's no word from him.

It's almost two hours later when the doorbell rings.

"Oh my God, is it him?" I ask Brooke who's staring at me with wide eyes.

"Because I can see through walls," she mutters. "Go and find out."

I stop in front of the mirror in the hallway, smooth my hair down, and wipe under my eyes. I look like hell, but I haven't exactly got the time to fix it.

Lifting my hand, I open the door.

My shoulders slump in disappointment the second I see who's on the other side.

"Do you get the feeling she was expecting it to be someone else?" Fletch quips.

"I'm so sorry. It's just ... it's complicated."

"That man of yours still not pulled his head out of his ass?"

"Can we come in?" Reese asks, ignoring her other half.

"Of course." I push the door wider and stand back.

Reese walks past and straight into the living room, Fletch following.

"He'll figure his shit out. It just takes some of us longer than others," Fletch assures me.

"Thanks," I mutter, although I'm beginning to wonder if it might all just be too much for him.

"I'm so sorry to barge in on you like this. I just had a

couple of questions about tomorrow night, if you don't mind," Reese says when I join them all in the living room.

"No, of course not. I'm so sorry I left everything to you."

"It's nothing. You'd done a fantastic job. There are only a couple of things left to finalize."

Reese pulls her iPad out from her purse and powers it up. I sit down beside her so we can go through whatever it is.

"Do you want drinks?" Brooke asks, jumping up and making herself useful.

DIVING INTO WORK was exactly what I needed. For the first time in almost two weeks, I was able to think about something other than my grief or my pregnancy. It was a welcome relief.

"What are you doing?" Brooke asks in shock after doing a double take when I join her in the kitchen the next afternoon. "I mean ... you look incredible, but—"

"I'm going to the ball," I announce.

"Um ... okay. Reese said you didn't need to though, right?"

"I think I need it. I put so much work into this. I want to see it all come together. See all my hours pay off."

"Okay, yeah. That sounds like a good idea. Give me thirty minutes and I'll come with you."

I lift a brow. "You can be ready for a gala in thirty minutes?"

"Okay, forty ... forty-five tops."

"I'm going to go now—I want to check all the details, make sure everything is as it should be. You've got a ticket, so just turn up tonight as a guest and find me once you're inside. You'd be bored."

"You're right. I could never look good enough for all your wealthy and famous guests in only forty-five minutes."

"Brooke, you're gorgeous just as you are. Any guy would be lucky to have you."

Her eyes widen.

"You just haven't found the right one yet."

Thankfully, my cell alerts me that my car is outside before Brooke can cause me any harm.

Lifting up the front of my full-length, navy evening dress, I make my way toward the front door.

It feels weird, taking a step outside, but at the same time it feels good. I inhale a deep lungful of fresh air and take a moment to center myself. This is what my aunt would want: for me to see this event through and to hold my head high and continue with my life.

I rub my hand over my belly. She'd have loved to meet this one. But clearly it wasn't meant to be. Much like Corey and I might not be. Only time will tell.

But I can do this.

As I take one step after another, my confidence grows, and a little happiness begins to creep its way in.

My knee bounces on the ride to the venue, nerves fluttering in my belly. But all of that is washed away when I step inside and see my plans in real life.

The rooms look exactly like I'd pictured in my mind, and I can't help but gasp as I walk into the main room to find the tables laid up as I imagined with the black, white and silver centerpieces looking incredible and drawing everyone's eyes to the floor-to-ceiling windows on the other side of the room that showcase the ocean beyond. Reese did an incredible job bringing this to life.

"Is it as you hoped it would be?" the woman herself asks, appearing around a corner, looking like a total knock-out in a floor-length red dress.

"And then some. It's incredible."

"I'm glad you approve."

"I can't thank you enough for all this."

"You're more than welcome."

I look behind her, waiting for Fletch to emerge and knock me on my ass. "Fletch not with you?"

"He's coming later. He had an errand to run last-minute. Come on, we need to make sure the kitchen's on schedule."

With everything running like clockwork, Reese, Mags and I make our way to the entrance to greet our guests as they arrive.

Their limos and expensive cars file around the entrance before the couple of paparazzi snap photos of them.

Reese is cool as a cucumber as she greets everyone enthusiastically, no matter if they're lifelong Vipers season ticket holders, or A-list celebrities we've managed to entice to spend the night parting with their well hard-earned cash. I feel like a hot mess who needs to go and compose herself by the time the stream of people lessens and we're able to move from the entrance.

"That guest list. You did good, girl."

"Your boyfriend and the team sure helped. Did you notice how many are women?"

Reese shakes her head, a knowing smile on her face. "I'll allow them to look—for the cause, you know. But there's only one bed he'll be in tonight." She winks, and I laugh—until my own reality chooses that moment to slam into me. I'll be going home and climbing into an empty and cold bed.

Reese must see my mood change, because she reaches

out to touch my arm. "Still no word?" Brooke couldn't keep her mouth shut yesterday as she explained that Corey was once again MIA. I was just grateful she managed to keep the reason for it under wraps. For now, at least.

"Nothing."

"Everything's going to be okay. I've got a good feeling."

"I'm glad one of us does. Come on, we've got rich people to schmooze."

Reese links her arm through mine, and we make our way to the grand room where everyone is loitering with glasses of champagne and scotch to start their evening.

I do a lap of the guests and get pulled into a couple of conversations about how incredible this event is, helping stoke my confidence a little before Reese catches up with me once more.

"You ready?"

I glance at the little stage set up off to one side of the room, and my stomach drops.

I've never been any good at public speaking, and I'm not sure right now will be any different. But this is my baby, and I refuse to send her up there to start proceedings because I'm too chickenshit.

"Yes," I say, blowing out a calming breath. "I've got this."

Opening my purse, I pull out the notes I wrote weeks ago. I've memorized the words, but having the piece of paper in my hand helps to ground me slightly.

As I climb up on stage, I think of my aunt. She should have been here tonight, and I know that she would have been cheering me on right now, probably already on her third glass of champagne and working the room, trying to talk to every person here.

A pang of pain shoots through me, but when I look up

from the makeshift stage, my eyes lock with Brooke's, her parents standing to the side of her with smiles on their faces.

"You got this," she mouths in support, and I nod back at her.

Stepping up to the microphone, I tap the top, and a fuzzy noise erupts from the speakers around the room.

"G-Good evening. Firstly, I'd like to thank you for agreeing to spend your evening with us as we raise vital funds for the LA Vipers Foundation ..." The more I say, the more I relax, and I soon find my grip on the paper in my hand lessening as I get into my flow, talking about all the things we're doing to support the young athletes in our community.

I've just about finished explaining how this evening's silent auction will work when the door at the opposite side of the room opens.

I don't think anything of it, assuming it'll be a member of the hotel staff tasked with helping us tonight, but when Fletch steps into the room looking like sin in his tux, my words falter.

Things are only made worse when he's followed by none other than Corey, who's also dressed perfectly for the evening.

Holy shit.

I'm pretty sure I don't say that out loud, but I can't be sure.

His eyes hold mine as I finish what I was saying. I have no idea if it comes out making any sense—I'm too lost in the intensity in his eyes to focus on the words. I just have to hope that I've rehearsed it enough times that muscle memory takes over.

I thank everyone and step down from the stage as a round of applause sounds out. I'm not entirely sure my speech deserves it, but I appreciate the gesture as I make my way toward the back of the room.

People must see the determination on my face, because a couple move out of my way so that I have a clear path to Corey.

I come to a stop right in front of him. My heart pounds in my chest, and my hands tremble. I have no idea if I'm angry at him for taking off like he did, or just relieved to see him.

My emotions war as he stares into my eyes. The rest of the room fades to nothing as I wait to hear what he's got to say for himself.

Fletch squeezes his shoulder before stepping away from us and disappearing from my vision.

"Can we talk?"

29

COREY

"Now? You want to talk now?" she snaps.

"Um ... yeah," I say, knowing that if she makes me wait, I'll probably chicken out of having the conversation I really don't want to.

"I'm working, Corey," she fumes.

"I know. I know, I just ... I need to explain."

She turns to look over her shoulder. Everyone is busy chatting, enjoying the drinks being passed around, and a few are heading towards the other room where I assume the silent auction is.

"This is incredible, by the way. You should be proud of yourself."

"Reese had to finish it," she mutters. After a few seconds, she turns to me. "This had better be good."

Reaching out, I take her hand in mine and pull her back to the door I entered through only minutes ago.

That last person I was expecting to find at the other end of my buzzer earlier tonight was Fletch, holding a suit bag.

He'd been sent on a mission by Reese, and as much as I

wanted to ignore him and continue hiding like the little bitch I was becoming, I couldn't.

Safe to say his argument was convincing, because I'm now standing here in a bloody tux, about to rip open my chest and bleed out for the woman I've realized owns my heart.

"Where the hell are we going? Out there would have been just fine." She points out toward the hotel reception we just walked through as the lift doors close behind me.

"I'm not doing this in public, Harlow."

She opens her mouth to argue, but when her eyes land on my face, she closes it again.

"W-What's wrong?"

"I'm ... I'm terrified, okay? There are things I need to explain to you. Things I haven't told another living soul, and ..."

"It's okay," she says, placing her warm hand on my forearm and squeezing gently.

"It's not. I need you to understand. I need you to know everything."

"Okay." She swallows nervously as the lift dings to announce our arrival.

Pulling the card out that Fletch handed me, I look for a room number, only instead I find a name.

That fucker gave me the key to a suite.

Glancing up at the signs, I turn left.

Harlow follows me to the first door, and, after tapping the card, I push it open.

"A little presumptuous, don't you think?" she asks, looking around at the vast space.

"I didn't have anything to do with it. Fletch gave me the key, told me it was mine for the night to do with as I wish."

"So he's the reason you're here right now then."

"Partly," I say, stepping toward her. "He gave me a push. But the real reason I'm here is for you."

"Okay, so …"

Blowing out a shaky breath, I find the minibar and locate a bottle of scotch. Grabbing two glasses, I lower them to the coffee table.

"Drink?" I ask, looking up at Harlow.

Her lips press into a thin line. "I can't drink, Corey."

"Oh, fuck. Yeah. Sorry. Do you mind if I...?"

"Knock yourself out."

Relief floods me that I'm going to be able to take the edge off the conversation that's about to happen.

I pour myself a glass and down the lot in one before repeating the action with a second.

"Come and sit down, please?" I can't cope with her hovering nervously as if she's about to bolt.

She hesitates but eventually joins me on the other end of the sofa.

"Losing my boys and the drama with my family weren't the only reasons I needed to escape my old life." I pause, preparing to lay it all out for her. "Carla and I had been friends all our lives. Our fathers served together, and we ended up in the same boarding school while our parents were elsewhere.

"We both partied pretty hard in our younger years, along with everyone else around us. Most of us were army brats with parents all around the world. We thought we were invincible.

"I was never interested in Carla in that way—she was just my friend. But one night we got really drunk and ended up kissing. One thing led to another, and ..."

"You got her pregnant?" Harlow guesses.

Unable to hold her eyes, I stare down at my hands. "We

were only fifteen. We were so young and naive. She stayed in school as long as she could before she left and had our daughter." Harlow gasps, but I don't focus on her. I can't, or I'll stop and never get the words out.

"I enlisted the second I finished school. I didn't have any choice, thanks to my father, but I promised her that I'd support her in any way I could. I had a responsibility to our daughter, and I fully intended on being there for her, although we both agreed nothing would happen between the two of us.

"I joined the army, and she stayed home to bring up ... our baby," I say, unable to even mention her name. "I'd see them both as often as I could, but I got swallowed up into squaddie life, and ... I was young," I sigh, regretting not being a better father. A better friend.

"Things were ... fine. L-Layla was growing up faster than I'd ever thought possible. She started school, all that stuff. I missed most of it because I was away, and I hated having to see it all in photographs.

"When I was discharged, I told myself that it was my chance to make things right. To be the father she needed and deserved.

"I hadn't seen either of them for quite some time, and when I got back from rehab, I barely recognized Carla. She was a mess. I'd been sending them money every month, but I had no idea it was all going directly to her dealer. I had no clue that she'd spiraled out of control.

"Anyway, once I got myself sorted and Zach gave me a chance at the studio, I swore to myself that I'd get a place of my own and go for custody. I might not have had a clue about how to bring up a child, but I was damn sure I could do a hell of a better job than Carla."

My eyes remain on my hands as I fiddle with my fingers, attempting to stop them trembling.

I pause, taking a moment before I continue.

"I started proceedings with a lawyer, and they agreed that I'd have a solid chance of winning. Only, we never got that far." My voice cracks, and Harlow slides across the sofa until she's holding my hands and her huge, dark eyes are staring into mine.

"A couple of nights before the court case, I was trying to sleep when I got a call. There had been a fire at Carla's flat and ... I could tell by the voice on the other end of the phone that it was bad.

"I raced over there." I pause as the images of that fateful night fill my mind. Harlow squeezes my hands and slides even closer. I desperately want to look at her again, but I fear that if I do, I'll break down and put off saying any more.

"Flames billowed from the windows; smoke poured into the night sky. It was terrifying. The firemen did everything they could, but the blaze was too hot for them to get into the flat.

"By the time they got inside, it was too l-late. She was only eight. She had her whole life ahead of her."

"Oh my God." Her voice is full of emotion as she crawls onto my lap and wraps her arms around my shoulders.

"It had barely been a year since I lost my boys, and then that happened." My body trembles as I'm taken back to that night. I was useless, utterly useless. After all my military training, when it mattered, all I could do was stand there and watch my world burn.

Lacing my arms around her waist, I hold her to me, and I will the images to subside. I know it's wishful thinking—they're always there, just waiting to pop up, usually in my sleep, and threaten to break me all over again.

"I'm so sorry, Corey. I'm so sorry," she whispers softly in my ear before she presses her lips to my neck and starts gently kissing me.

Once I'm feeling a little more in control of myself. I wrap my hands around her forearms and push her back so I can look at her.

She has black makeup streaked down her face where she's been crying with me.

She reaches out and brushes her thumbs over my cheeks, clearing away my own tears.

"I'm so sorry," she says again.

"Harlow, I'm ... I'm terrified. I can't go through that again. I can't lose ..."

"Shh," she soothes, still holding my face. "That was a terrible, terrible accident. The chances of it—"

"I can't lose you, Harlow." I drop my hand to her smooth belly. "I can't lose either of you."

A sob rips up Harlow's throat before she falls onto my chest and cries.

Rubbing my hands up and down her back, I sit in silence, my own thoughts running rampant around my head as she gets herself together.

"I didn't think you wanted us," she admits into the crook of my neck.

"I'm so fucking sorry. This was my issue; it had nothing to do with you. I want you more than anything."

We sit locked in our embrace for the longest time, just soaking up strength from each other and making silent promises that we're both too scared to say out loud.

"Harlow?" I whisper after long minutes.

She pulls her head from my shoulder and looks at me through tear-filled eyes. The emotion staring back at me guts me to my core.

"I ... fuck."

"It's okay," she says, lifting her palm to rest on my cheek. "I know. I'm scared too."

"When did you find out?"

"The day after my aunt died. I was sick, couldn't stand the smell of coffee. Brooke made me take a test."

"So when do you think we ..."

"That first night."

I can't help but laugh.

"What's so funny?"

"I already thought that night was life changing. Apparently, I was right."

"You're a nightmare," she jokes, slapping my chest lightly before she falls silent.

"What's wrong?"

She's off my lap before I have a chance to stop her. I miss her contact immediately as she begins pacing back and forth in front of me.

"Before you, I hadn't been with anyone for ... years."

"Harlow, I'm not suggesting it isn't mine or anything," I say, sitting forward, wondering where she's going with this.

"Oh, I know. I just ... I need to explain why, and why going with you that night was so huge for me."

"Okay," I say, sitting back and continuing to watch her move back and forth.

"I was a nightmare teenager. From about the age of twelve, I was smoking and drinking. Anything to make me forget my life.

"I'd had the most perfect childhood. My parents were incredible and gave me everything I could have wanted. And then it was all gone. Ripped out from under my feet in the blink of an eye, and suddenly I had no one.

"No one cared. No one wanted me." Her voice cracks, and all I want to do is pull her back into my arms.

"I used alcohol, drugs, and ... sex to make myself feel better. I was a mess, and I hate looking back to that time in my life. I'm ashamed."

Pushing from the sofa, I stand in front of her to stop her from pacing.

"Hey," I say, reaching out and taking her cheeks in my hands. I clear the fresh tears away with my thumbs before kissing the tip of her nose. "If you're telling me this because you think it's going to turn me off, then you need to think again. Nothing could do that. I want you, Harlow. Just the way you are, with your kind heart, supportive nature, and fucked-up past."

A smile curls at her lips. "Yeah?"

"Baby, we've all done things we regret. You were just a child, unable to handle the life you'd been dealt. No one could criticise you for that."

"But the things I did ..." Her lip curls in disgust.

"It doesn't matter. You can give me all the details one day if it makes you feel better. But seriously, you're the one I want. Dark past and all."

"Really?" she breathes, as if she can't believe it.

"What do I need to do to make you believe I'm serious? Get down on one—"

"No, no," she says with wide, panic-filled eyes as she reaches out to grasp my upper arm in case I'm going to do as I just threatened.

"It's okay, it was a joke. Although I'm glad to know how you feel about that."

"Everything is just too much right now." She drops her hand to her belly, just one bit of evidence for how her life is at the moment.

"I know, baby. It will get better, I promise. And one day, I will ask you that question."

She bites into her bottom lip as she thinks and fights a small smile. She isn't as opposed to the idea as she previously made out.

"How about for now, we clean up and head back down?" I wipe at the stray makeup under her eyes. I hate to suggest it; what I really want to do is the exact opposite and dirty her up a little more. But I know how much this event means to her. I remember the sparkle she got in her eyes when she started telling me about it on the beach that night.

"Sounds good. I hope people are enjoying themselves."

"I have no doubt. It looked incredible."

"I just want to make a difference, you know?"

Wrapping my arms around her waist, I walk us toward the bathroom. "You do, Harlow. Every single day."

30

HARLOW

I'm not convinced I'm emotionally stable enough after all those confessions as we walk into the grand hall, hand in hand.

"See, everyone is having a great time," Corey whispers in my ear as I take in the guests, all laughing and joking around their tables as they wait for their dinner to be served. "So, show me everything."

"Okay, well, there's not all that much to see."

I take the lead and weave through the tables and guests. A few say hello, but thankfully no one stops me to chat. I did the best job I could with the little equipment I had to fix my face, but I'm sure it's still obvious that I had a breakdown not so long ago. I considered calling Brooke up to help, but the thought of having to explain it all over again put me off.

My heart is still breaking for the man standing behind me, for everything he's had to endure. Losing a child is one of the worst things that can happen to anyone, and in those circumstances ... I shudder at the thought. No wonder he freaked out, and I've no doubt that at some point in the future he'll do it again. You just can't experience that kind of loss and trauma and expect everything to be fine when memories of the past start popping up, and I'm sure my pregnancy and our baby will do just that. No matter how much he wants us, it's always going to be a reminder of what could have been with his daughter.

"And here are the auction lots," I announce as we walk into the connecting room.

I watch him as he looks at everything we have to offer.

"Harlow?" he asks, pulling me back into his chest and wrapping an arm around my waist. I sigh at the contact.

"Yeah," I breathe. As much as I want to be here right now to see everything I've worked so hard on, I can't help craving to be back in that suite upstairs with him.

"How many of these did you donate yourself?" he whispers.

I stiffen at the question. "Umm ..."

"Harlow?"

"A few."

He chuckles behind me. "Just a few?"

"Okay, quite a lot." I shrug. "Just helping the cause."

He spins me in his arms and takes my chin in his hands. "God, I love you." My eyes widen and my heart pounds in my chest, but I don't get a chance to say anything because his lips land on mine for the sweetest kiss of my life.

"Ah, good," a familiar voice says behind me. "You two have made up."

"Brooke," Corey greets when he lets me up for air.

"Oh my God, your chateau. I love this place," Brooke coos as she looks at the photograph. "We should really go back there again one day. Oh no, you should take Corey. It's so romantic."

I bristle at her words, wishing she'd keep her voice down.

"Oh yeah?" Corey asks, pulling my ass back until his hard cock presses against it and his lips brush across my neck.

"Oh, you could take her to London, show her where you're from, and you could travel Europe." She gets this far-off, dreamy look in her eyes.

"Sounds incredible, B. But there's just this little issue of us having jobs and lives, and a baby on the way."

"Ugh, a girl can dream." She waves it off. "Seriously, though. I'm glad you made up. Although, rumor has it that you've got a key to one of the best suites in this hotel, so I have no clue why the two of you are down here." She wiggles her eyebrows at us.

"She kinda has a point. If we were alone right now, I could peel this dress from your body and do all kinds of wicked things to you," Corey murmurs in my ear. It sends a violent shiver racing down my spine.

"I have no idea what you're whispering right now," Brooke admits. "But fuck, it's turning me on."

"And it's time for you to walk away," I quip, much to Corey's amusement.

"Aw, let her have her fun. She's only jealous. No one's going to make her scream tonight like I will you."

"Oh my God, stop it. Both of you."

"Christ, I need a man—and fast. Laters." Brooke stalks from the room, a woman on a mission.

Corey chuckles behind me, the sound making my insides clench with desire.

"Well...?"

"Well what, baby?"

"What are you waiting for? That suite is ours, right?"

"Just waiting for you to say the words." He takes my hand and we're out of there in a flash.

———

"GOOD MORNING," Reese sings when we finally make it out of the suite the next morning and down to the great hall to help clear up. "It was such an incredible night, Harlow. It's almost a shame you missed so much of it." She winks, and I silently groan.

Our absence was noticed, then.

"Yeah ... sorry about that."

"No need. Everything ran like clockwork. I'm just glad to see that smile on your face once again."

I glance up at Corey, my cheeks heating.

He stands beside me, smiling, his eyes darkening as he recalls all the ways he made me smile last night. I gently slap his chest.

"What?" he asks innocently.

"Nightmare," I mutter.

"So, do we have a final figure yet?"

"No, but from what we worked out quickly last night, it was a huge success. Some of the bids were insane."

"Tell me you didn't ..." Corey whispers in my ear, but I brush him off, much to his amusement.

"What needs doing?"

"Just tidying up and taking all this stuff out to the vans. My henchmen have already taken the first boxes."

"Henchm— oh," I say when Fletch comes walking back in the room, the rest of the team obediently trailing behind him. They're looking much more relaxed in casual clothes compared to Corey, who's back in his tux, albeit halfheartedly, much to my disappointment.

I, on the other hand, managed to lose my dress thanks to my best friend supplying me with a spare set of clothes that she had sent to the hotel.

"Morning, I trust you two had a good night," Fletch rasps, a smirk firmly planted on his lips.

"Fucking hell," I mutter, embarrassment racing through me.

"Things are good, if that's what you mean," Corey says, stepping up to him and clapping his hand against Fletch's shoulder. "Thanks, man. I owe you one," he whispers, but I catch it.

"For someone who claims not to do romance, Fletch is sure good at fixing people up," Reese says, an amused smile on her face.

"Sometimes a few words is all it takes."

"You two are good together. I hope this is the end of the bumps in the road for you."

I can't help but laugh. "Me too," I say, thinking about the bump we're soon going to be dealing with.

"SO, WHERE TO?" Corey asks as a car pulls up to take us away a couple of hours later. We ended up getting everything sorted and packed into the vans before we all sat down to have breakfast. I'd already thrown up the room service we'd ordered last night, and I was starved once again. It was nice. Normal, even. And I didn't even embarrass myself in front of Fletch, so I take that as a win. Although, it may have something to do with the fact that I'm much less interested in him and far more captivated by the man who was sitting at my side and insisting on some kind of contact with me at all times. I sure wasn't complaining.

The guys all happily chatted away about the upcoming season, and I allowed myself to get carried away with the excitement. It's been too long since I've seen them all on the ice.

"I really need to go home. But do you mind if we take a detour first? There's somewhere I'd like to go."

"For you, Harlow? Anywhere."

I nod and rattle off the new address to the driver.

As we head through town, my heart starts to beat faster, and my hands begin to tremble with anticipation.

"Are you okay?"

"I'm sorry. I'm just a little nervous."

"Why? Where are you taking me?" His brows pull together in mock concern.

"Nowhere weird. Just somewhere I haven't been for a really long time."

"Okaaay."

Sitting back, I watch the busy city disappear and the countryside become vaster as we race toward our destination.

As we approach the gates, I fight to keep my breathing steady. I don't want to freak out before we even get there.

"Whoa, what is this place?" Corey asks as we make our way up the long driveway before the house comes into view.

The second I see it, all my panic and anxiety vanishes.

I'm home.

A smile curls at my lips as I picture myself and my sister playing out on the grass. My mom sitting in her chair on the deck, reading her book, while my dad crashes about in his shed.

Emotion clogs my throat, but it's not the devastating grief I was expecting to feel. It's happiness. Contentment.

"This is my home. It's where I grew up, before ..."

"Harlow, it's ... incredible."

"Do you want to see inside?"

"Of course. If you do."

"I think it's time." My fingers wrap around the handle, and I go to push the door open.

"Wait, you haven't been back here?"

"Not since I was taken away."

"Wow. Okay."

We climb out of the car, and, feeling confident, I tell the driver he can leave.

Corey wraps his arm around my shoulder and pulls me into his side.

"I know you said you had money, but I think I might have underestimated the amount."

I chuckle at him, not wanting to go into specifics. "My dad, grandfather and my great-grandfather did a fantastic job with the business."

"So I see."

He releases me so I can pull the key from my purse. It's always been with my other house keys, just in case the mood ever struck me and I found myself here. Much like today.

I sill with my fingers wrapped around the doorknob.

"You don't have to do this," Corey says softly.

"I really do."

I push the door open wide to reveal an entryway I remember as if I were only here yesterday.

"Wow. It's ... perfect," Corey breathes as I step inside.

"Someone comes regularly to keep on top of things."

"You've kept it going all this time?" he asks in disbelief

as he follows me down to my favorite room in the house: the kitchen.

He looks around with wide eyes, taking everything in.

"I always planned to come back one day. To make this my home. To allow my kids to grow up with the same incredible memories I have."

Dragging his eyes away from his surroundings, he turns to me.

"What are you saying, Harlow?" He closes the space between us, his hands resting on my hips as he waits for my answer.

"I'm suggesting that we make this place our home. Our family home." Taking one of his hands, I slip it around to my belly.

He shakes his head as if he can't believe it.

"You want us to live together ... here?"

"I do. We can't stay at mine; it comes with Brooke," I laugh. "And your place is nice, but it's an apartment, and don't you think our little one deserves this?" I say, gesturing to the floor-to-ceiling windows at the other end of the kitchen that looks out over the land and ocean beyond.

"Do you know that I think?"

I shake my head shyly, not able to get a read on his expression.

"I think you are the most incredible woman I've ever met, and I think you're going to be an amazing mom."

"Yeah?" I can't help the wide smile that spreads across my lips at the prospect.

"Yeah. You know what else?"

I shake my head.

"I meant what I said last night. I love you, Harlow. The good, the bad, the ugly ... and everything in between."

A sob erupts at his words, that he's accepting those parts of me that I struggle to accept myself most days.

"Corey," I sob. "I love you, too."

He takes me in his arms and kisses me until we're both breathless.

"I guess you'd better show me around the rest of our home, then."

"You're really okay with this?"

"Baby, I'd be okay anywhere. As long as you're there."

My heart soars at his words, but one look in his eyes and I know he means it.

Some missing part of me fell into place that night he caught me, and I'm not sure it's a piece I could ever live without again.

Without knowing it, he's given me the strength to really embrace who I am, who I was. And he's allowed me to finally get over my fears and, for once, to look to the future and be excited for what's to come.

EPILOGUE

Harlow

Three months later...

"Are you nervous?" I ask Corey, whose fingers are incessantly fiddling with the underground ticket in his hands.

"Um ..."

"Why? I've spoken to your mom countless times on the phone."

"I know that. I've just ... I've never brought a girl home before."

Lacing my fingers through his, I rest my head on his shoulder. "You're cute."

"I'm anything but cute, Harlow."

I shrug, my own butterflies fluttering around in my belly. I'd be lying if I said I was calm about this. Corey's mom is the sweetest, but knowing I'm about to meet her in person does have nerves racing through me. He might have never brought a girl home before, but I've never done the whole meet-the-parents thing either—and not just because I don't have any.

The past three months have been nothing short of amazing. As we both came to terms with the fact that we'd be parents in the not-so-distant future, we set to work on getting the house ready.

I moved in with Corey, seeing as it was all paid for, while we made plans and set decorators to work. I might have wanted our baby to grow up in that house, but I wasn't overly fond of some of the wallpaper Mom chose all those years ago. Letting go was hard, but I knew it was time to start a new chapter. That house holds so many memories for me; how it's decorated doesn't change any of that, and I wanted it to reflect us as a couple, as a new family, not my old one.

We officially moved in two weeks ago. It was a bit of a shock to the system after living in Corey's small apartment, but we soon found our feet. We've turned one of the bedrooms into a den for him to work in when he's not at the studio; it's his man cave for when things get too much. He keeps warning me that at some point he's probably going to freak out, but so far, he's been nothing short of incredible. We've both started therapy, just to help us work through our thoughts and fears, and so far, it's working well for both of us.

He came with me to my first doctor and midwife appointment, and he held my hand tightly as we went to our first scan and got our first glimpse at our baby. The look of awe in his eyes as he stared at the screen is something I'll never forget. He never got to do any of this when Carla was pregnant. He might not have said much more about what happened since the night at the hotel, but he's mentioned his old friend a few times. I see the pain in his features as he does, and I know it's not because he doesn't want to tell me about his daughter, more that the pain is still just too raw to find the words. I get it, and I'll give him all the time he needs.

His mother, though ... she was less patient, and the second we confessed that we were officially together, she demanded we visit.

To her disappointment, we didn't jump straight on a plane. We both had busy schedules, plus I was still spending my mornings throwing up, and the prospect of doing so in the air didn't appeal. We agreed to wait until we'd had our first scan, and then we'd visit and give them our news in person.

It's only Brooke, Reese and Fletch who know thus far. It was important to both of us that his family were the next to find out that there was going to be a new arrival.

"It's this stop," Corey says, looking out at the underground sign.

I allow him to pull me from the seat and off the train.

It took quite a bit of convincing, because he is a man of pride and stubborn as hell, but eventually he conceded and allowed me to help out his family.

I invested in a nice house in a decent part of the city, and his mom and sisters moved in soon after. I knew it was the right decision, because the tension that had been pulling at his shoulders since the first night I met him began to loosen.

Without the stress of his family to worry about, Corey is like a new man. He gives me his incredible smile so much more often. It's amazing to see. And although I still miss my family with every day that passes, I'm grateful that they were able to help him and those he loves. It means everything to me to make their lives so much easier after they've been thrown into chaos.

"Fucking hell," Corey mutters the second we emerge from the underground station.

I'm about to ask what's wrong when a loud squeal hits my ears and three familiar women come racing at us.

They engulf us in a group hug as laughter rumbles up my throat.

It's one hell of a welcome.

"I thought you were waiting at home?" Corey asks his emotional mom when she eventually pulls away from holding him tight.

"We couldn't wait any longer." She turns her eyes from her son to me. "Harlow," she breathes, holding her arms out for me.

I immediately step into them and follow her lead. I've been hugged by Brooke's mom countless times in the past, but there's something about this one that reminds me of my own mom.

"Oh sweetie," Helen breathes when she pulls back and finds my cheeks wet with tears. Lifting her hands, she wipes them away.

I sniffle. "It's so good to finally meet you in person."

"You too. It's been a long time coming."

"As fun as this is, I didn't intend to spend the day on the path catching up. Shall we?" Corey says, pointing down the street with amusement dancing in his eyes. He might be acting cooler about this right now, but I see the emotion he's trying hard to cover at seeing his family again.

"We thought we could go for breakfast—if you're not too tired, that is."

"Fry-up?" Corey asks.

"Whatever you want."

"Lead the way."

Helen chuckles as Sadie and Natalie flank Corey's sides, taking an arm each. Love and adoration for their big brother oozes from both of them.

"They've really missed him," Helen muses, coming to stand beside me as we head down the street.

"He misses you all terribly."

"I know. It was the right thing for him to do, though. I know he's felt guilty about leaving us, but he needed the new start. He needed to find you."

Emotion clogs my throat once again. Damn pregnancy hormones.

"It's so good to be here. I've always wanted to visit."

"Well, we can do all the sights. It's been years since I did any of the tourist things."

"Sounds perfect."

We turn into an English-looking pub and find an empty table.

"So, what's good here?"

"Leave it with me, baby." Corey winks and I push the menu away, trusting him wholeheartedly. He's made me a few full English breakfasts since living together, but each time he tells me that it's not quite the real thing.

He orders for us all, and we sit chatting about everything we've been up to before Corey places his hand on my thigh.

Racing to pull our scan photo from my purse, I hand it to him under the table.

"We've actually got something to tell you," Corey says, causing all conversation to immediately halt. Helen's eyes sparkle as they drop to my ring finger. She quickly covers her disappointment when she finds it bare.

"Well, go on. Don't keep us waiting."

A wide smile splits Corey's face a beat before he reveals our secret by sliding the picture toward her. He's been excited to tell his mom that she's going to have a second chance at being a grandmother. She hardly spent any time with Layla, seeing as she was almost always abroad with his dad.

"Oh my God," Helen cries, her hand flying up to cover her mouth. "Really?" Tears fill her eyes, as do mine at her happiness.

"Really. Sixteen weeks in."

She quickly takes the scan and stares down at our little fuzzy baby.

Helen jumps up as if her chair just bit her ass and lunges for me. I manage to stand just in time for her to pull me into her arms.

"Thank you, Harlow. Thank you so much," she whispers in a shaky voice. "You've brought him back to life."

ONCE I'VE EATEN the biggest English breakfast I've ever seen in my life, we head back to their house so that I can have a nap.

Corey has agreed to go out with his friends tonight. Now he's got over his apprehension of me meeting his family, he wants to introduce me to everyone.

"Are you nearly ready? The Uber will be here in two minutes," he calls as he walks through to the guest room at his mom's house. "Whoa," he says, stopping in the doorway, his eyes locked on my chest. "Second thoughts, we'll just get a hotel for the night."

"So yeah, my dress doesn't really fit anymore," I sulk.

It's one of my favorites, but seeing as my breasts have practically quadrupled in size in the past few weeks, it's almost obscene.

"It looks fucking perfect to me."

"You say that now; wait until you're introducing me to your friends."

He pales slightly. "Yeah, we're definitely going to a hotel."

Swatting his hand away, I step into my shoes and grab my shawl in the hope it might cover my cleavage. "Come on, they'll be waiting."

"They can wait until another night," he sulks but reluctantly follows me from the room and down the stairs.

"Harlow, you look gorgeous," Helen gushes when she comes to say goodbye.

"Thank you."

"Careful with this one, Corey. Someone might want to steal her."

"She won't be leaving my sight," he mutters, making us both laugh.

"Have a great night."

She waves us off, and we find the Uber waiting for us.

Corey confirms our destination and the car sets off, giving me my first glimpse of London by night. I keep my nose practically against the window the entire time, taking everything in, much to Corey's amusement.

"You adding more to that must-see list you're hiding in your purse?"

I turn to look at him. "I'm not hiding it, I was just planning out loud."

"Right. You weren't that loud about it, because I had no idea."

"Well, you do now. The most important thing is

spending time with your family and friends, but if we get time, I'd like to see a few places."

"Your wish is my command, baby."

I smile at him before turning back to the window.

I've always wanted to travel. We used to go to at least two different holiday locations each year when I was a kid, but with everything that happened, I never really got to do it recently. It's something I hope we can rectify in the coming years.

"We're here," Corey announces as the car comes to a stop outside a bar called The Pear Tree.

We thank the driver and climb out.

"Come here," he says, pulling me into his side. "Look down there. You see that pink sign?" I nod. "That's the original Rebel Ink. Where it all started. I'll take you there another day. For now, you get to meet the guys who make it what it is."

He holds the door open for me, and I step through. Everything seems calm, normal, until he follows me inside. Then an eruption of noise comes from the corner of the bar and four tattooed guys come running at us.

I stand aside with a huge smile on my face as the four of them greet Corey as if they never thought they'd see him again.

"You'll get used to them eventually," a soft voice comes from beside me. Pulling my eyes away from the bromance unfurling before me, I find the kind eyes of a woman with pink hair. "Hey, I'm Tabitha. Although everyone calls me Biff. You must be Harlow. I've heard so much about you."

"Really?" I ask, baffled about how that can be.

"Yep. You've really stolen that guy's heart, it seems."

I look over to where he's laughing and joking with his friends, and my heart damn near explodes in my chest with everything I feel for him. Seeing him back here with the people that mean the world to him is everything to me.

"The same can be said for me."

I look back to find her staring at me with a wide smile on her face.

"Let's introduce you to this lot."

"Hey, Kitten. Who's your new friend?" the blond guy asks with a wink at me. He knows full well who I am—as do I, as I watch him sweep Biff into his arms. She's not the only one who's had a full rundown as to who everyone is. "Hey, I'm Zach," he says. I expect him to hold his hand out, but much to my surprise, he releases his girl and pulls me into a huge bear hug.

"Um ... hey," I say with a laugh.

"Get your hands off my girl, motherfucker," Corey barks.

"S'all good, man. Just thanking her for looking after our boy." Zach winks at Corey, but it doesn't help relax him at all.

"So, you've met my overly-handsy boss. This is Titch, Spike, and the old one is D."

"Fuck you, man," D grunts, much to everyone's amusement.

"This is Danni, Titch's wife. Kaz, Spike's girl, and Piper, D's ol' lady."

After a round of hellos and hugs, we all head over to the table they vacated when we arrived.

"Right, drinks," Zach says, rubbing his hands together. "Pint?" he asks Corey. "Wine, cocktail...?" he says, turning to me.

"Um ... just an orange juice, please."

Everyone's silent for a beat. As far as I know, they have no idea about the baby, but it seems that's all about to end.

"Hell, yes. She's pregnant." Another round of excitement ensues, and I can't help but sit here and laugh as they all give us their congratulations.

I love LA. It's my home, and it's where all the memories of my family are, but after even being here for just a few hours, I already know that I could make this place home. From the second I stepped off the plane, I was just relaxed. I'm not sure if it's just the company and I'd feel that way wherever I am in the world, as long as Corey is by my side, or if it's the place.

I turn to look at him as he laughs with his friends. He must feel my stare, because he turns his eyes on me.

"Everything okay?"

"Yeah," I say with a smile. "Everything is perfect."

I have no idea if he'd ever want to move back, but I decide there and then that if he ever brought it up, there's no way I'd stop him. I think we could be really happy here.

OUR TWO WEEKS in Corey's home city pass in the blink of an eye. We spend time with his family every day and meet up with his Rebel Ink family more often than not. I get a tour of the studio, which looks freakishly like the one I'm used to in LA. I even spend a day with Biff and her best friend Danni while the guys hang out. It's incredible, but it reminds me of just how much I miss my own best friend. We've hardly been separated since I arrived at her home all those years ago. Whenever we've been on vacation, we've been together, so being so many miles apart is weird. We've spoken every day, but it's not the same.

Tonight, Corey told me that he's taking me out. And that's all I know. It's our last night in London, so I hope he's got something good planned. I've still got a few things on my to-see list that we're yet to tick off.

He's told me to wear something comfortable, so I pull on a pair of leggings and an oversized T-shirt. I might have the smallest of small bumps, but I'm already struggling with proper pants.

After slipping my feet into a pair of sneakers, I go in search of my man.

I find him sitting in the living room with his mom and sisters.

"Here she is," Helen announces, smiling at me as I join them.

"You ready to go?" Corey asks.

"Sure am."

"We'll see you before you go tomorrow, right?" Sadie asks.

"Of course. Our flight isn't until five. We've got almost the whole day."

"Good. I'm not bored of you yet."

"Nice," Corey jokes as he takes my hand.

"Have a great night," Helen calls as he leads me out of the house.

Unbeknownst to me, there's an Uber waiting outside. I climb in, sit back, and wait to see where we're headed for the night.

"Are you looking forward to going home?" Corey asks me.

"Yes and no. I'm going to really miss your family, but I can't wait to see Brooke and tell her everything. What about you? Ready to get back to the sun, ocean and sand?"

"Yeah. I love it here, but there's too much pain."

"You think you could ever move back?"

He shrugs. "I don't know. I think we both know better

than anyone that you can't predict the future. I'll just take things one day at a time."

"That sounds perfect. I just want you to know that, if you wanted to, it wouldn't be out of the question for me."

He stares at me for a beat. His eyes are so intense that it makes my heart race. "Fucking hell, Harlow."

"What?" I ask.

Reaching out, he wraps his hand around the back of my neck. "How the fuck was I so lucky to find you?" He doesn't give me a chance to respond, because his lips brush mine before his tongue slips between them.

I moan into his kiss, sliding my hand up his torso. I've always wanted him, but with the added hormones racing around my body, one touch from him and it makes me damn near desperate. I can't wait to get back to our large, empty house so we can make up for having to be so quiet and restrained while under his mother's roof.

The car comes to a stop, and sadly, we have to break apart.

"Where are we?"

"On the west bank. I thought we could have a nighttime trip on the London Eye. It was on your list, right?"

I can't help my lips twitching in excitement. "Yes. I can't wait."

"Come on then." We walk along the river, chatting about our time here and the things we want to do when we get home.

It turns out that Corey has booked us our own pod, so I get to enjoy the sights of London by night without the distraction of anyone else.

In no time, we're stepping inside and moving our way around.

"This is amazing," I say in total awe, my nose almost

pressed against the glass as I stare out at the incredible city beyond.

"I'm glad you like it."

The view is out of this world when we get to the top, and my eyes hungrily flit around, trying to take it all in.

"Harlow?" Corey asks from somewhere behind me.

"Yeah, what's—oh my God," I gasp when I find him down on one knee behind me.

"Harlow Winters, by some miracle, you've brought me back to life. You've shown me that the world still has color in it. And you've shown me that it's possible to bounce back from the darkest of times. I don't want to spend another day without you by my side. Will you do me the honor of agreeing to be my wife?"

"Oh my God, Corey." My eyes fill with tears and my hand trembles in front of my mouth as I try to cover that it's gaping open in shock.

He reaches into his jacket pocket and pulls out a small black box. The world around me blurs as I watch him flip it open.

"Oh my God," I repeat. "You're serious."

"Deadly. Now, will you marry me?"

"Yes. Corey. Yes."

He holds his hand out for me, and I reach for it. I blink, and he's got the ring in his hand and is sliding it up my finger. It stops at my second knuckle.

"Fuck," Corey barks, looking up at me with a horrified expression on his face. "I had Brooke give me the size. Shit."

"It's okay," I say with a laugh. "If I weren't pregnant, I'm sure it would fit perfectly fine."

Disappointment fills his eyes, but all I feel is excitement.

I drop to my knees with him and lift my other hand to his cheek.

"I love you so much, Corey. The ring is perfect."

"Yeah?" he asks, the twinkle returning to his eyes.

I lift my hand, the princess-cut diamond sparkling before me. It's simple; it's classic. It's utterly perfect.

He's perfect.

"I love you so much, Harlow. Both of you," he says, dropping his hand to my belly. "I want everything with you."

"I love you, too," I sob as he crashes our lips together to seal the deal.

And just like that, two broken souls become one.

Want more? Get a Catch You Bonus scene just for subscribing to my newsletter!

Catch You is a standalone within the Rebel Ink series. If you loved Corey then you'll love the rest of my dirty-talking British bad boys.

Start the series with Corey's boss Zach in Hate You now!

Psst... want more Corey & Harlow? You can read this short, and more, over in my Happily Ever After Book Club on Patreon.

Become a member now.

CATCH YOU

BREAKING THE PUCKING RULES
SNEAK PEEK

Chapter 1
Casey

The second Dad's name pops up on my screen, I can predict what's coming.

"Hey, kiddo. I'm really sorry, but I need a raincheck on breakfast."

A sad smile pulls at my lips. I got too used to our Wednesday morning breakfast dates during the off season.

That's all over now.

He hesitates then adds sheepishly, "Any chance you could do me a favor, though?"

"You got it," I say.

"I left my bible on the kitchen counter..." he trails off.

A laugh spills free.

"Would you like a coffee as well?"

"You're too good to me."

"Someone's got to be," I tease.

"Love you, Care Bear."

The call cuts and I take the final turn toward the house I grew up in.

Killing the engine in the driveway, I waste no time in climbing out and finding my key.

The second I open the door, familiarity rushes over me. The scent of happiness and safety fills my nose.

I love this place. Always have, always will. I have so many fantastic memories here—my father being the main one.

As I step into the kitchen, I find the room in its usual state of chaos, and I can't help but smile. Dad isn't the cleanest or most organized of people, unless it comes to work.

Collecting a stray glass and mug, I dump them in the sink, doing my bit to help.

I'm twenty-three. I shouldn't care that he's busy and blown off our date. But the sad truth of it is that it's the only date of any kind I've had in...longer than I want to admit.

A loud sigh passes my lips.

Glancing around the room, I quickly locate what I came here for.

It's not a real bible. My father doesn't have a single religious bone in his body, unless you count his lifetime commitment to hockey. I'm pretty sure he's prayed to that puck a few times over the years.

His bible is his life. His calendar, his playbook...his everything.

He starts a new one immediately after the end of each season and begins filling it with notes for the next one.

By the time the season is upon us, it always looks like it does now: bursting at the seams, full of scraps of paper with plays scribbled on them, notes about players, and phone numbers. Women's phone numbers.

I shake my head.

Dad is a good-looking man. After years of playing hockey, his body is still something to be proud of. And as the single head coach for the LA Vipers, he is hot property with all the desperate women in a fifty-mile radius.

He's not interested, though.

He's too focused on his job, on his team, and on me.

Don't get me wrong, when I was a teenager, I loved that I didn't have to share him with anything but hockey. But now that I'm older, I do wish he could find someone to enjoy life with.

I lift the bible from the counter and tuck it under my arm before heading back to my car, placing it safely on the passenger's seat.

***

Walking through the arena is almost as familiar as walking into Dad's house.

It's my second home.

Some of my earliest memories are from here, watching Dad utterly destroying his opponents on the ice.

I loved it just as much then as I do now. Hockey isn't just a game. It's a lifestyle. One I can't imagine not living.

Sucking in a deep breath, I walk toward the rink where I have no doubt I'll find the man I'm looking for.

The scraping of skates on ice and men shouting get steadily louder, and my speed increases.

If I could, I'd spend all my days sitting in the stands watching them train. Watching Dad boss them around.

The second I turn the corner, my eyes fall on the rink, and without meaning to, they search out number fifty-five. It's been the same since he was traded here last season.

Kodie Rivers is a hockey god.

Always has been and always will be.

I'm honored to get the chance to watch him in action.

The truth is, I've been watching him for years. Since he first took to the ice in college.

Even in high school, he was the best, and that allowed him to have his pick of colleges. And things have only gotten better since.

Especially for me.

When it was announced that he was coming to LA, I thought all my Christmases had come at once.

There's just one tiny issue...

I'm the coach's daughter.

It doesn't matter how much I might obsess over a player; it's never going to happen.

They wouldn't risk losing the respect of my father. A night with me isn't worth it.

I get it. I do. And before Kodie joined the Vipers, it never really bothered me.

I saw them all as adopted uncles, big brothers, and friends.

But now...

I used to have photos of him stuck inside my high school textbooks. I'd have had them on my bedroom wall if I didn't think my dad would lose his shit over it.

I've followed Kodie's career, his life, ever since he first stole my attention all those years ago.

And now that he's here, I'm no less intrigued by him. If anything, I'd say my slight obsession is worse.

Managing to rip my eyes away from his form speeding across the ice, I spot Dad.

Determined to look like a woman in control of her life, I

hold my head high, clutch his bible tighter to my chest and keep walking.

He's just a hockey player. Just a man.

No big deal.

But it is a big deal. He's Kodie fucking Rivers.

Gritting my teeth, I do my best to stuff down the excitable hormonal teenage girl who seems to pop up every time I'm anywhere near him and focus on the task at hand.

Noticing movement in his direction, Dad looks up. The second he discovers it's me, his entire face lights up.

"Care Bear," he mouths, making my cheeks burn red.

I'm not sure I'll ever truly feel like an adult when I'm in my father's company. Somehow, no matter how old I am or what I've managed to achieve, I still feel like a little girl.

I continue around the rink, and I've almost reached him when two players slam into the plexiglass beside me. A startled shriek rips from my lips as I twist around to see who it is.

My breath catches, my heart racing even faster when I lock onto a pair of mesmerizing dark brown eyes that I'd know anywhere.

I try to swallow, but my mouth has gone completely dry.

Never before have I been this girl. I've been surrounded by hot hockey boys all my life. Sure, I've crushed on a few, but none of them have caused the kind of reaction that Kodie Rivers does.

It should be illegal.

As much as I'd love for him to look excited to see me, the only expression on his face is one of irritation. I guess that's understandable when you've just been body checked by a teammate.

I have no idea if he recognizes me—I pray that he does, but I can understand that I'm probably not as big a part of his life as he is mine. He gives me a curt nod of acknowledgement, and that alone is enough to cause a riot of butterflies in my stomach.

Get a fucking grip, Casey.

I force myself to look away and at the much more amused-looking man behind him.

Lincoln Storm.

Now, if there was a player who would probably throw caution to the wind and be willing to hook up with the coach's daughter, it would be Linc.

He's been a Viper since his rookie year. He's a great player...in both senses of the word. He works hard and he plays harder.

The opposite of Kodie, who lives a much quieter life.

Linc smirks at me in accomplishment, and a beat before he releases Kodie, he winks. That should be the move to give me butterflies, but nope. There are none for him.

A deep growl fills the air as a shadow falls over me.

"Eyes off my daughter, Storm." The warning in Dad's voice makes my stomach knot. I risk glancing over and find Dad glaring daggers at one of his best players. "Drop and give me fifty," he commands.

Knowing he's fucked up, Linc instantly pushes back and drops to his hands on the ice.

Dad watches him for a few seconds, but once he's happy he's driven off any potential suitors, he turns to me with a soft smile playing on his lips.

"You're an angel," he says, his voice suddenly softer and calmer.

"It's not like it's out of my way," I tease, looking up at him and smiling.

Sure, he has a few more wrinkles and a couple of gray

hairs at his temples these days, but James Watson is still a very good-looking man. I can't blame women for acting the way they do around him.

"Even still. Appreciate it, kiddo."

Linc finishes his punishment and he and Kodie take off across the ice again to join the rest of the team, who are watching with amused expressions.

After taking his bible and coffee, Dad promises to make up for missing breakfast by taking me out to dinner instead.

Not wanting to take up any more of his time, I stretch up on my toes to give him a kiss on the cheek and wish him a good day, and then I walk away from the rink without looking back.

The second I pull my car door open, something flutters into the footwell. It must have fallen out of Dad's bible.

With a frown, I reach over and retrieve an envelope. I'm about to turn back and take it to Dad when the messy, unfamiliar writing across the front steals my attention.

Coach Watson, I know you don't want to go, but here is your ticket. Please don't waste it.

It's signed by the team owner.

My heart rate begins to increase as I predict what's hiding inside.

Climbing into my car, I look around the lot nervously. It's deserted, but it doesn't stop me from slumping lower in my seat as I tuck my finger under the unsealed flap. My hand shakes as I pull out the single ticket inside.

My stomach twists with anticipation.

For years, the LA Vipers' fundraising department has

organized a masquerade ball in the weeks leading up to the preseason.

Getting your hands on a ticket is like finding unicorn shit.

Every single year, my dad is given one. And every single year, he donates to the cause but refuses to attend, saying that it's not his thing.

I've begged for his ticket every year since I was seventeen, to no avail.

It's not that he's trying to keep me away from hockey. That would be really hard, considering I also work for the franchise. But it would be safe to say that he likes to keep me at arm's length from the team.

That wouldn't have been the case if I were a boy. Hanging out with all the hot hockey players would have been a requirement. I'm not sure it's fair that just because I was born with a vagina, I'm barely allowed to hang out with them.

It was fine when I was little. I was welcomed in as if I were one of their own kids. But as I hit my teen years, as I grew boobs, Dad started limiting my visits.

The team has changed a lot since then. There are only a handful of veterans now who remember me as a kid. I guess that's the issue.

I clutch the slip of paper tighter, feeling like the kid holding the golden ticket.

I shouldn't.

Dad will kill me if he finds out I've taken it.

He'll know, a little voice screams, but one look at the arena and I swallow it down.

Dad won't know. Every year that ticket goes in the trash.

It's a masquerade ball...what if no one finds out?

If I can secure a good enough mask and dye my hair, then no one has to know. Not Dad, not Gary, our GM, or any of the players.

For one night, I'll just be a woman at a party.

A party that a certain number fifty-five will be attending...

For more of Casey and Kodie's story, keep reading
Breaking the Pucking Rules

WOULD YOU LIKE A FREE BOOK?

Get your free copy of All In On You, the prequel to my steamy contemporary romance series, Rebel Ink Subscribe to my newsletter for your free copy!

ABOUT THE AUTHOR

Tracy Lorraine is a *USA Today* and *Wall Street Journal* bestselling new adult and contemporary romance author. Tracy has recently turned thirty and lives in a cute Cotswold village in England with her husband, baby girl and lovable but slightly crazy dog. Having always been a bookaholic with her head stuck in her Kindle, Tracy decided to try her hand at a story idea she dreamt up and hasn't looked back since.

Be the first to find out about new releases and offers. Sign up to my newsletter here.

If you want to know what I'm up to and see teasers and snippets of what I'm working on, then you need to be in my Facebook group. Join Tracy's Angels here.

Keep up to date with Tracy's books at
www.tracylorraine.com

<u>Defy You</u> #3

<u>Play You</u> #4

Catch You

<u>Rosewood High Series</u>

<u>Thorn</u> #1

<u>Paine</u> #2

<u>Savage</u> #3

<u>Fierce</u> #4

<u>Hunter</u> #5

Faze (#6 Prequel)

<u>Fury</u> #6

<u>Legend</u> #7

<u>Maddison Kings University Series</u>

<u>TMYM: Prequel</u>

<u>TRYS</u> #1

<u>TDYW</u> #2

<u>TBYS</u> #3

<u>TVYC</u> #4

<u>TDYD</u> #5

<u>TDYR</u> #6

<u>TRYD</u> #7

<u>Knight's Ridge Empire Series</u>

<u>Wicked Summer Knight</u>: Prequel (Stella & Seb)

<u>Wicked Knight</u> #1 (Stella & Seb)

<u>Wicked Princess</u> #2 (Stella & Seb)

<u>Harrow Creek Hawks Series</u>

Merciless #1

Relentless #2

Lawless #3

Fearless #4

<u>Callahan Billionaires</u>

By His Vow #1

By His Rule #2

By His Play #3

<u>Seattle Saints</u>

Broken Saint #1

<u>LA Vipers</u>

Breaking the Pucking Rules

<u>Never Forget Series</u>

<u>Never Forget Him</u> #1

<u>Never Forget Us</u> #2

<u>Everywhere & Nowhere</u> #3

<u>Chasing Series</u>

<u>Chasing Logan</u>

<u>Standalones</u>

Naughty & Nice